Megan Clawson was bo[...] Lincolnshire. In 2018, she [...] English with Film at King's C[...]ge London. The daughter of a Beefeater, Megan lived inside the Tower of London with her dad and little dog, Ethel, for many years. The experience of living inside the real-life palace and fortress and falling for her own royal guard still inspires much of her writing. Working as an English tutor and TV and film extra alongside her writing, she is always at her happiest when living a life that feels like fiction. *Falling Hard for the Royal Guard* was her debut novel, published in 2023.

Also by Megan Clawson:

Falling Hard for the Royal Guard
Love at First Knight

KILTED LOVERS

MEGAN CLAWSON

avon.

Published by AVON
A division of HarperCollins*Publishers* Ltd
1 London Bridge Street
London SE1 9GF

www.harpercollins.co.uk

HarperCollins*Publishers*
Macken House, 39/40 Mayor Street Upper
Dublin 1, D01 C9W8, Ireland

A Paperback Original 2025
1
First published in Great Britain by HarperCollins*Publishers* 2025

A catalogue record for this book is available from the British Library.

ISBN: 978-0-00-872708-6

This novel is entirely a work of fiction. The names, characters and incidents
portrayed in it are the work of the author's imagination. Any resemblance to
actual persons, living or dead, events or localities is entirely coincidental.

Set in Sabon LT Std by HarperCollins*Publishers* India

Printed and bound in Great Britain by Clays Ltd, Elcograf S.p.A.

MIX
Paper | Supporting
responsible forestry
FSC™ C007454
FSC
www.fsc.org

This book contains FSC™ certified paper and other controlled
sources to ensure responsible forest management.

For more information visit: www.harpercollins.co.uk/green

For all of us who were told that
true love only exists in fairy tales
and 'silly little romance books' . . .

That was just an excuse for them to do the bare minimum.

Dump the pillock.

Chapter 1

Finding true love when you have a noble title is as much of a myth as fairy godmothers, talking candelabras, and magic mirrors. My mother's hand was won by a duke, and my grandfather found his own princess, but a peerage alone is not enough to make a fairy tale.

Cinderella would have certainly been a far less romantic fable had Prince Charming given his eponymous princess a spreadsheet of when and where she was allowed to hold his hand. No one would have stuck around for the ending of *Beauty and the Beast* had the household decided to remain forever cursed, to watch the castle crumble, rather than allow a commoner to marry into the family. *Snow White* would have never been granted her happily ever after had the press caught wind of her living arrangements and decided that she was too much of a hussy to deserve the hand of their precious prince.

I call it our family curse. Perhaps it's reparations for history, or as payment for believing ourselves to be second only to God, but we are destined to be eternally unhappy in love. What is the point in crowns and castles, if at the end of all your days you are perpetually alone?

No one will bother to write the love story of Lady Alice Walpole. Even I cannot find the romance in my present situation: draped over the lap of the heir to the Fortnum and Mason fortune, trying to sound interested as he talks about how much he detests tea for the fifth time this hour.

'It, well, it just hurts, doesn't it? It's so . . . hot—'

'Music!' I cut him off and get to my feet before he can utter another mind-numbing syllable. 'This sad party is lacking in many things (*most notably in the quality of company*),' I announce, adding the parenthesis in a murmur, 'but it is music that I believe I am most desirous of. Don't you agree, Barty?' Tea-boy makes a series of posh vocalisations in a bumbling attempt to concur.

In the drawing room of Barty's grandparents' Kensington town house, the new-adults of the British elites have gathered to sip martinis from crystal glasses and chase them down with cheap cigarettes. Quite the juxtaposition, but they always like to pretend they're down to earth when they're trundling down to the local off-licence after one whiff of imported vodka.

'Yes, some *fucking* music, please!' A rasping voice speaks up from behind the haze of the room: Kitty Harley-King, daughter of a billionaire. Her 'thing' is that she swears like a sailor, but with about as much conviction as a priest repeating the words of a sinner back to him during confession. The heiress's education cost her parents close to

2

two and half million at a boarding school in Luxembourg and somehow the only skill sets she acquired were how to pick out the most expensive wine from smell alone, and how to curse her mother in every way possible whilst spending her billions liberally. But she's harmless, and the most tolerable of the bunch.

Kitty glides across the room as though propelled by her boyfriend's cigar smoke pluming under the folds of her dress. Dancing between the furniture as if she has already conjured the cadences of a song in her mind, her bare feet slap the marble floor before she stretches out a finger to finally hit play. A record spins on a rusting gramophone but the drum and bass music that is emitted from it is crystal clear.

'Oh, what an absolute tune!' Hugo Maddocks, the queen's godson, takes another drag from his cigarette and rests his head against the arm of the chaise longue in the way that one would as one listens to Bach or a particularly moving Chopin, as opposed to Chase and Status.

It's ironic really. They strive so hard to create an illusion of class and history, but it's all just powered by a mistreated iPhone connected via an AUX cable.

I say 'they', but I suppose it is really 'we'. Just like them, I am here, in this room, of my own volition, trying to scrape together just enough serotonin from socialisation and a little tipple so that I don't lose my mind. Not one of them knows when my birthday is. Or any of my middle names. All they know is that my father is the largest landowner in the country, after the king, and that's all that matters.

'Don't we have anything we can dance to?' I attempt

to elevate my voice over the music that thumps around the high ceilings. Barty only squints at me, as though it will help him hear me better. Kitty is already dancing, or convulsing. Either way, she doesn't take any notice. 'Hugo? Anything with a bit more melody?' Without acknowledging me, he slides his sunglasses over his eyes and swigs from his glass.

I don't bother attempting to ask Felix, Kitty's Danish royalty boyfriend. He snores softly from the sofa and his still-lit cigar burns at the rug. The rest of the bodies in the room seem to continue their conversations as though their voices are in any way audible over the throbbing bass. I don't suppose they have even noticed; listening isn't really anyone's strong suit here. We have very little to impress each other with. If they actually want to be listened to, they go down to the UCL student union and tell the students that their father's accounting firms are offering internships. It usually gives them the required amount of attention for an evening.

'Why do we never do anything fun?' I cut the music and every eye in the room falls on me in a scowl.

'Speak for yourself – I had a line off some army major's sword last Sunday,' a voice I can't decipher shouts from a shadowy corner.

'When did we stop hosting balls? And when did we start wearing dinner jackets to sit on ugly patterned sofas whilst we— Is that a . . . vape, Barty? Oh, for heaven's sake!' My 'date' chokes on his cloud of sweet-scented vapour.

'It's watermelon candyfloss . . .' Barty sheepishly looks around the room. 'Cigarettes do awful things for my asthma.' He punctuates his sentence with another cough and all I can do is stare in disbelief.

'Keep your bonnet on, Jane Eyre. The gentry no longer sit about in fine houses and drink tea. We have far better things to be doing,' Hugo croons.

'First things first, I'm pretty sure you mean Jane *Austen*. And secondly, if you took off those pompous sunglasses for half a second, you'd realise that is exactly what we're doing!' I fling out a hand to point at one of Kitty's boarding school friends who sits at a table, cup of tea in one hand and the snout of her snorting pug resting on the other.

Hugo raises the lenses and follows my directions, and, after a short glance, shrugs as if to say: 'I suppose you're right.' Though he would never say anything of the sort out loud.

'I am so bloody bored!' I huff like a disgruntled toddler and fall back into the seat beside Barty, the tulle of my dress bunching around me in an itchy blanket of rainbow.

'Perhaps I've come to the wrong place; I was told there was to be a party here.' In all my moaning, I hadn't noticed that a tall gentleman, whose face I haven't had the pleasure of seeing before, had slid through the door behind me. 'I realise now I must have stumbled upon a morgue.' Like a candle in a crypt, his smile seems to make the whole room glow a little brighter, feel a little warmer.

'Atticus, my good man! How the devil are you?' Hugo shows more gusto than I have seen from him all evening as he leaps up to take Atticus by the hand. 'You shall have to excuse little Alice, the poor dear; she won't stop dreaming about balls. And not the fun kind, mind you!' I blush from my seat but still can't draw my eyes away from the stranger, at least not until his dark pair find them and he makes me tremble with another disarming smile.

'Hughie, Hughie, Hughie, perhaps if you made fewer jokes like that, you might actually see the appeal in culture.' It's Hugo's turn to blush as Atticus moves to fix his full attention on me. '*Little Alice*, I think a ball sounds like a rather fantastic idea.' With a wink so subtle that I have to ask myself if it's a figment of my imagination, he runs a wide hand through his blond hair before being chaperoned away to the bar by another of his friends.

'Kitty,' I whisper loudly to the woman now draped across the rug, flapping her arms and legs as though making a snow angel in the tufts.

She replies with an airy 'mmhmm'.

'Who was that? That just came in?'

Sitting upright with a jolt, she scans her eyes about the room.

'Hugo?' Kitty giggles to herself before flopping back down again. 'You are silly, Alice. He's been here the whole time.'

'Atticus, Kitty. I meant Atticus.'

'Oh, well why didn't you say!' I roll my eyes but don't interrupt her in case she goes off on a tangent about Portuguese fruit or something. 'That handsome pint of wine is Atticus Beaumont. New money. I'm not too sure in what kind of business but it seems to be good enough for half of the heiresses in London. He is rather sought after, but impossible to pin down.'

Atticus's arrival has seemingly breathed a bit of life back

into the room. He circles about the disengaged groups, chatting away like the previously absent host catching up with his guests. So preoccupied with observing the stranger, I don't notice Barty sliding closer to me until he intertwines his fingers with mine and awkwardly bends my wrist in a strange attempt to kiss my fingertips.

'My grandparents have a jacuzzi bath on the third floor. It's very . . . steamy.' Barty grins at me after he squeaks out the last word with a heavy breath.

'It helps your asthma I suppose? You should probably head up now – you're sounding a little wheezy.' I stare straight ahead, unable to look at what I assume is his 'sexy face' without the threat of uncontrollable laughter overpowering me.

After clearing his throat, he continues sharper now, if not a little more flustered: 'I mean, would you – do you fancy – perhaps joining me?'

A laugh bursts from me before I can attempt to hold it in. 'You're inviting me to join you in your *grandparents'* jacuzzi?' It's hardly inviting me to his library with a rolling ladder, or scouring the country to return my glass slipper now, is it?

'I was about to come over and properly introduce myself, but I think I may have chosen a rather inconvenient time.' Atticus's amused tone interrupts us before Barty can stumble over another word, and I have to fight the urge to throw my arms around his neck and have him whisk me away like Rapunzel from her tower.

'I should like to argue, Atticus, that you might just be my fairy godmother.' An amused glint flashes across his eyes and he follows my every move as I shuffle to the edge of my seat to stare up at him.

'I would have preferred handsome knight in shining armour but in that case, my lady, you shall go to the ball.' He offers me his hand and I oblige him, grateful to have any excuse to get away from Barty, especially a handsome one.

'I suppose I should introduce myself, seeing as you have just saved me.' I laugh as we reach the bar, trying to calm the erratic beat of my heart and pretend for a moment that I am not sweating profusely under the stare of an attractive man. Atticus still clutches my hand in his as he pours me a drink with the other.

'No need. Everyone knows of the famous Lady Alice Walpole, the face of modern royalty. The Party Princess. The Heartbreaker.' He pushes aside a fair curl that had fallen across my face and hands me my drink.

I can't bring myself to say anything in reply. I feel detached from myself as my reputation is laid bare before me by a man who was a stranger only ten minutes ago. The national newspapers have hardly been kind in their representation, though that is a surprise to no one. After I was spotted having dinner with two men in a week, a few of the tabloids decided I had fallen from grace and gone from being the 'nation's sweetheart' to a 'serial dater'. Apparently, they were expecting me to just pop out with a husband without even giving me a chance to kiss a few frogs first.

One thing the fairy tales always get wrong is that your soulmate is the first handsome man you clap eyes on. If that were the case, I'd be stuck with Charles Devereux, the son of a family friend who was the love of my life at age six but once he had spent a few halves at Eton, developed an unfortunate habit of staring at my breasts with a smile that I can only compare to that of a serial killer. His hairline began receding as soon as he hit puberty, so I believe that was his karma.

If Prince Charming can scour the whole kingdom to find his princess, why can't I go on two dates in one week without being branded a man-eater?

I take a swig of the drink Atticus had poured for me, and the burning sensation fights off the numbness that has grown within me. Recollecting my composure, I give him a broad, almost-honest smile.

'Would you care to dance?' Atticus slides the glass out of my hand and places it gently on the side before taking my hand and leading me back across the room.

'What, here? They are all so miserable, I can hardly imagine that we'll be able to convince them to do anything aside from drink and smoke.' Looking about the room, I see that no one is taking any notice of us. Like spirits, we glide through the room unseen and I feel as though to hold hands with Atticus Beaumont is to be transported to another dimension. A dimension where one's heart beats irregularly, and one allows one's judgement to slip in favour of a little excitement.

'Absolutely not. I would say there is not a soul in that room worthy of seeing you dance, my lady. We must go somewhere where you have a true, worthy audience.' He pushes open the mahogany door and pulls us both through into the shadowy corridor.

'And who might that be?' The rational part of my brain attempts to remind me that I am disappearing into the night with a man whose name I only just learnt. And yet, my romantic heart soars as we seem to float down the spiral staircase.

Atticus pushes open the front door. The June breeze licks at my bare arms, and prickling goose bumps soon follow the early summer breath. 'Why, the stars of course.'

Instinctively I look up. The splattering of stars is hidden beneath a blanket of smog, unable to outshine the orange fluorescence of the street lamps. This is London after all. The sentiment was there, and it is perhaps the most romantic thing someone has ever said to me – though that isn't hard considering just half an hour ago I was being propositioned to try out someone's granny's bath.

I dance better without an audience anyway.

Beneath a street lamp in a Kensington alleyway, Atticus takes me by the waist and the heat of his body soon overtakes me until I no longer feel the cold of the night.

'May I be honest with you, Lady Alice?' Atticus speaks deeply, lowering his head so he is within a breath's distance.

'Just Alice, please,' I whisper, my heartbeat thumping in my ears.

'I could never do you the dishonour. Your title is your crowning glory and I have never seen one so deserving of the distinction.' He stares so intently into my eyes that I feel almost naked stood before him. 'I came here only with the wish of being your next object. To have my heart broken by you would be my greatest privilege.'

'I'm sorry?' I manage to splutter.

'I apologise for being so forward, but I came tonight with my only intention being to see you, and only you. I have admired you from afar and if you will have me, I wish to continue to love you closely this time.' I look for any hint of a smirk on his face, any sign that this may be some elaborate joke. Scanning the streets, I look for any long lenses poking out from between bins, or any journalists crouched behind any concealed corners. There are none. His face is sincere as he blinks at me expectantly.

'But—but we've only just met,' I whisper.

'Do you not believe in love at first sight?' He leans in and presses his lips to my cheek, lingering for a moment before pulling away.

Flustered, I reply, 'Yes, yes I suppose I do.'

Not *all* of the fairy tales can be wrong, can they?

Chapter 2

One Month Later

Stumbling through the front door, I shush Atticus with a giggle as his drunken limbs pinball between the furniture. With another fit of giggles, I trip over the rug and topple into the suit of armour displayed in the entryway.

The bodiless sentry drops his sword with a clatter and it's Atticus's turn to press a finger to his grinning lips. Picking up the blunt weapon, I try to prop it back against the armoured thigh but give up after it slips for a fourth time and, instead, I balance it against his codpiece.

'Sorry, sir. You must forgive me,' I slur and pat the knight on his pauldron. The whole thing gives a wobble and the sword falls with another crash. 'Sod you then.' I point an accusatory finger at the polished breastplate and bend down to unbuckle my shoes.

'Ah, I think you should let me take care of that.' Atticus catches me by the elbow as I sway precariously, staring at the clasps as they seem to dance around my two pairs of feet. He helps me over to one of the chairs and, getting to one knee, releases me from the tight binds of my first shoe.

Atticus takes his time with the second, letting his soft fingertips trace over my ankle. I just begin to doze off when his voice startles me awake again. 'Who is she?'

Peeling open one of my bleary lids, I can just about make out the portrait he has his eye fixed upon. At the very top of the wide staircase, a gold frame towers above everything else in the room. The likeness is of a young woman, draped in ermine furs with a coronet balanced on her fair hair. Standing tall, she flaunts a pair of stern eyes that keep a watch of the whole ground floor, seeming to follow each one of your steps. Nothing in her face suggests a smile. There has always seemed to be a kind of power emanating from its brushstrokes. Her persistent gaze haunts even your consciousness in this room as you live in fear of her perpetual judgement.

'That is Princess Alexandra. My grandmother. Terrifying, isn't she?' I whisper the latter part, afraid of the two-dimensional representation's wrath.

'Incredible,' Atticus breathes, the giddiness of only moments ago entirely replaced by intense seriousness.

'She's only nineteen there but already not a woman to be trifled with. She had grown up through the war, even worked the land at one time, trying to inspire other women at home to do the same,' I add, still slurring slightly. 'I was scared of her portrait as a child. I would always run past her with my eyes closed, just in case she one day barked through the canvas telling me to stand up straight or to not smile with my teeth. Still do it now sometimes.'

'Does that mean that you are in line for the throne? With her being a princess, I mean.' He flicks the fastening of my shoe and it pops open with ease before he gets to his feet and draws closer to the painting.

'My grandmother was. But I'm so far down the list now that something terrible would have to happen to a great many people before I was even a thought in anyone's mind.'

'What about on the Danish side?' He looks at me expectantly, the grin on his face clear as day through my hazy vision.

'Danish side?'

'Didn't you say Felix was your cousin and that's how you set him up with Kitty?' He strides back over to me as I stoop in my seat and he takes my hands in his. 'So surely that means you're somewhere in their line of succession?'

'Oh, I have no idea. I don't even think we're cousins, at least not first, second, or even third. I suppose it's just a weird thing the family do with the European royals to make the bloodline look strong, or just imply that all of the leaders are inherently connected.' Resting my head against a side table, I yawn loudly. 'I don't know . . . who cares. All of this is hurting my brain.'

'I'd say that is most likely the whisky with the port mixer you insisted on being your nightcap,' Atticus declares. Massaging my temples, I hardly take heed of his words as he scouts about the room, running his fingers along my mother's questionable interior design choices.

'I think we should set your sister up with my cousin.' My lips are numb and words seem to tumble from me as though I have lost all ability to gatekeep them.

With my eyes still closed and the room spinning, I'm hardly sure if I am speaking out loud until Atticus replies, 'Is this one an actual cousin, or . . . ?'

'Yes, an actual cousin. My mother's nephew. James, I think his name is.'

'You think? What is it with you trying to play Cupid? You even tried to set up the secretary of state for environment with your father's private security at the charity conference tonight, if you can remember.'

I actually don't remember even meeting the secretary of state, or even what charity the conference was in aid of, and I am struck with the stark reminder of why I don't usually drink. 'Have you ever actually accomplished anything with your meddling matchmaking?'

'Well like you said, Kitty and Felix are one of my creations.' I smile sloppily at Atticus and he rolls his eyes.

'Kitty would date a lamppost if its father was rich. How far were you *actually* involved?'

'Well, I said, "Kitty, this is my cousin Felix. He's from Denmark," and I looked over five minutes later and they were snogging in the conservatory.' Atticus gives me a pointed look. 'Ah yes, I see now.' I wobble to my feet to stand before him.

Stretching up, I kiss him softly. 'I suppose I just love love. Some people just need a helping hand to know where to look. Every good story needs a narrator, or an author. I like to think that's me: penning people's happy endings, giving fate just that little nudge in the right direction.'

'You're so drunk.' Atticus laughs softly, shaking his head. His light hair falls across his forehead with the motion and I lean up twirl a few of the thin strands between my fingers.

'Of course I am. That's the only time I make any sense.' With an overly exaggerated wink I add, 'We can't all be lucky enough to find an Atticus Beaumont.'

'I think you'll find it was me who found you.' He smirks before pulling away and returning his attention to my grandmother's portrait. 'Has anyone ever said that you remind them of her? At first glance I thought it was you.'

'Only in looks. My father likes to remind me on an almost daily basis that that is where the resemblance ends. She was a firm woman, powerful, knew exactly what she wanted and got it. I, on the other hand, have my head too far in the clouds and my nose too firmly wedged into sappy romance books and childish fairy tales to take notice of much of the rest of the world. At least that's what Mother says.'

Atticus only hums in reply. Overcome with the desire to continue to hold his interest, to prolong his stay, I rush off down the hall, calling behind me, 'Wait there one moment; I have a surprise.'

Along the vast corridors of the east wing, each doorway is guarded by a mannequin, draped in various items of ceremonial clothing. It's a rather striking guard of honour that leads to my father's office at the end of the hallway, designed to impress his litany of guests and remind them of his authority. That was my mother's idea, of course. The last headless figure boasts the very furs from my grandmother's painting, and with the gall only a drunken mind can summon, I whip it off and sprint back to Atticus as though my theft would set off a series of booby traps behind me.

Pausing to hook the heavy hide about my neck, I begin to stride past Atticus as if walking down the aisle of Westminster Abbey to my coronation. Ascending the stairs, I stand beside my grandmother, mimicking her pose, though unable to control the smile that takes over my face.

'A vision of perfection,' Atticus calls from the bottom of the stairs, as he takes out his phone and snaps a photo.

'What is the meaning of all this?' My mother's voice booms around the room, startling us both to attention. My father scurries behind her, wrapping himself in his dressing gown and clutching it around his throat.

'Oh my, you did give me a fright. I thought you were the ghost of Mother for a moment there.' My father's wide eyes soften for a split second before the realisation hits him and anger tightens his features. 'Alice, please tell me that isn't what I think it is,' he growls through gritted teeth.

My stomach drops and suddenly the alcohol coursing through my bloodstream seems to curdle – sucking out all the Dutch courage and transforming it into plain old English regret.

An all too familiar feeling gurgles within me. 'Sorry, sir, may . . . may you excuse me for one moment?' I say quickly, my words slurred through my attempts to keep my lips closed for as long as possible. My parents both stare at me, confused, their anger still threatening to boil over. Stumbling across to the nearest mantel, I grasp at my mother's ugliest vase and vomit directly into it.

'I think, Mr Beaumont, that may be your cue to leave.' My mother gives Atticus a hard stare, and though her tone is polite, her expression is far from it.

My boyfriend doesn't need telling twice, and with a look that tells me he will come back for me, Atticus turns on his heel and strides away with as much control as a sober man.

As soon as we hear the latch of the door click, my father mellows slightly. 'You know you aren't supposed to drink with those tablets, Alice. There's no wonder you're in such a mess.'

My mother rolls her eyes. 'I have no idea who you have become these last few weeks. Not long ago, I thought you *almost* worthy of a cape like that; now I feel sick to see it lowered in such a way.' She stomps back across the landing and out of sight as I sway, unable to move my feet from where they stay, rooted to the stairs.

My father descends the few steps between us, and holds out his hand to me. Assuming it to be a peace offering, I take comfort in resting my palm on his, just as I did as a child when the world felt too overwhelming. With an exasperated huff he quickly shakes me off.

'The cape,' he demands, without meeting my eye.

I unhook it wordlessly, lay it across his outstretched arm, and watch as he returns it to its rightful place.

'Get to bed, Alice. We shall speak in the morning.' Father returns after a moment and passes me without stopping, as he heads in the opposite direction to Mother, to his own bedroom.

As I stand still beneath the gaze of my grandmother, my heart throbs so thunderously in my chest that I'm sure even her cold and soulless figure would be able to feel its beat around the room. I know my mother and father cannot think much less of me – that much is a given – but Atticus? How humiliating that in trying to prove myself to him, to appeal to him, he has witnessed me scolded like a child. The common sadness that usually comes at night spreads its cold winds through me again as I stare at Princess Alexandra, the woman whose face I inherited, and wonder why I keep getting it all so wrong.

The evening plays over and over in my head at such an invasive pace that I can hardly manage to catch a breath in between its repetitions. Unsure of how much time has passed, my body regains just enough strength to carry me off to bed before I fall into a deep, dreamless sleep.

Fishing for complaints?
Lady Alice Walpole makes a splash at the Save our Salmon conference where she appeared to be too drunk, on booze and men, to bother—

My clock says eight-thirty when I open my eyes again and read the headline of the newspaper left on my bedside table. It's gone midday before I can bring myself to leave the confines of my duvet. In all the time in between, I just stare at the walls, telling myself that I need to get up, only for my body to remain paralysed, afraid of what darkness awaits me outside of the warmth of my bed.

I am almost grateful for the hangover; at least I'm feeling *something*, even if that something is like a pneumatic drill through my skull.

Dressing hurriedly whilst I have the energy, I dry-swallow the tablets that have been hidden beneath a small blacked-out bell jar on my bed-side table and scurry downstairs, doing my best to plaster a look of complete serenity on my face.

I don't get far until my name is called and I see my mother standing in the open doorway of my father's office. I've never seen her look less than pristine and, despite her rude awakening in the early hours, today is no exception. Her lipstick is without a single smudge; not so much as an eyelash has been permitted to stray out of place. All I do when I look at her is wonder whether she's so organised on the inside, or if her mind is anything like mine: disordered, a series of broken pieces superglued back together in just ever so slightly wrong positions, a constant cacophony of screams. Knowing her, it's probably like the Sistine Chapel in there.

Walking past her and doing my best to avoid her gaze, I cower into the office like a scared dog with its tail between its legs.

'Your mother and I have been talking . . .' my father begins as I take the seat across the desk from where he sits, looking back and forth between me and his wife, his anxiousness etched onto his face. 'And, well, we think it might be best if you take a little . . . sabbatical.'

My mother forces a laugh as she joins him on the business side of the desk, standing over him in her heels, drowning out any air of intimidation he might be prevailed upon to summon. 'Taking a sabbatical implies she has actually done any work, Henry. Considering I had a rather uncomfortable phone call with Lionel from the *Save our Salmon* Foundation where he informed me that you were too inebriated to make your speech last night, I should say you don't qualify.'

One of my jobs as a working royal is to be a patron of, and show support for, charities across the nation. By working alongside them and becoming the face of a good cause it seems to make the rest of the world start paying more attention. A rewarding job, of course, and I have no objections to fulfilling my duties.

I hadn't gone to the fundraiser with the intent of getting drunk either. Save our Salmon is just as worthy as any charity: specialising in the protection of the fish in British rivers and lakes. But the irony in all of this is that I am deathly allergic to seafood. Just a staring contest with one of the slimy things would bring me out in a rash the colour of a salmon with sunburn and a one-way ticket to the nearest hospital. So, becoming the patroness of a species that is one sloppy kiss away from killing me wasn't exactly top of my list of things I'm willing to devote myself to. It was Atticus who suggested one drink, to calm my nerves, but it seemed that no matter how much I drank, my glass remained half full, whilst I became half-cut.

In all honesty, I don't know where my passion lies. I suppose that is half of the problem. Being twenty-two, having just completed a degree in philosophy, where I realised halfway through that I would rather never have a single thought again than read another word of Kant, I have no idea what I want or who I am. I know what is expected of me, of course. That has been drilled into me since the moment I was born. But the thought of spending the rest of my life reciting prepared speeches at events, where I have no idea what half of the things I'm saying even mean, hardly fills me with hope for the future.

Expressing any of these cynical thoughts out loud had my father getting his doctor to prescribe me up to the eyeballs with antidepressants, so there was little point in arguing with mother about my work ethic. As someone who believes wealth is all a person can really ever need, the thought of me being too depressed to make it out of my four-poster bed only makes her roll her eyes. How can one be depressed, when one has everything that one could ever dream of? Something I learnt very quickly, however, is that one cannot balance the chemicals in one's brain with a trust fund alone.

We're not supposed to mention the pills. Royals aren't meant to get depressed, so although almost everyone I know takes them in secret, and my mother could probably use a prescription of her own, they still remain an unspeakable taboo in this family.

'Before you tarnish the family name any further and give the king a reason to interfere, we believe you would benefit from spending the summer in Balmoral.' My father refuses to look at me as his wife lays out my sentencing.

'Scotland?' is my only feeble response.

I am no one without London society. Without love, without parties, what do I have to offer? If I go to Scotland, if I go *alone*, what will become of me? When I have none of the distractions of home? When I have to exist within my own mind, and actually have to stand my own company?

The thought is nauseating and I have to stifle a gag as I cover my mouth with a shaking hand.

'It is the family's furthest and most secluded residence. There will be no way for you to embarrass us from there. No distractions, no way to continue this self-destructive spiral you're on. I would at least hope.' Mother adds her two pennies' worth.

'Alone?' I ask, half pleading for an answer in the negative.

'The family will be popping in intermittently for their summer holidays but yes, far from any *bad influences* and hopefully far enough away that the teenage rebellions you seem to still be making in your twenties don't continue to make it onto the front pages.'

I should fight, I should argue that I am no child, that I am a woman with my own mind and her own desires. But I have no energy left. And I'm hardly sure if that is true anymore. Mustering the energy to brush my hair in the morning is hard enough these days, so trying to convince my parents who are so stubborn in their ways that I am trying, that I will change, that I need to stay, is just futile. They would only remind me that I am dependent on them and their finances, they would only reiterate that I *owe* this family my life in exchange for my privilege, and every word I say in protest will only fall on unbothered ears.

Father looks up at me for the first time. 'It's for the best, Alice darling.'

That is no term of endearment; it is the final killing blow as he pretends that any of this is for my sake.

Isolate the woman who has to fill her empty spaces in the day with music in an attempt to fight off thoughts that hurt just a little too much? Isolate the girl who is desperate for the company of others because she cannot make herself happy? Isolate the child who pines for touch, who just needs a hug?

This isn't for my good, or the good of the family. No, they simply want me far enough away that they don't have to see me spiral.

And spiral I shall.

Chapter 3

Atticus isn't here to see me off. Though I'm sure he is planning something; like storming the train as it passes the border, carrying me from it and taking us both to Gretna Green before anyone notices we have eloped.

I have no doubt that Mother has threatened him. Or offered him something to keep away. But I know Atticus. He wouldn't take it; he's biding his time, I'm sure of it. My mother hasn't come to say goodbye either, but for that I am actually grateful. It has been a week since my fate was sealed, and I have never seen her look so cheery. She was practically dancing around the halls whilst my belongings were gathered together.

I often wonder if she is really my mother. All of the stories you hear, of mothers being the paragon of virtue and affection, who would do anything for their children, have never felt real to me. I believe that part just as much as I believe that pumpkins can turn into carriages. Mothers in fairy tales are these God-like figures, angels incarnate

25

and the greatest tragedy of all for the protagonists is losing her. Mine is the villain in my story.

Often, I think she never wanted a child at all. I suppose it was her duty, as much as behaving myself is mine. Yet if that was the case, why would she be so assiduous about upholding the values of an institution that oppressed her? Why pass her trauma on to me, when she has it well in her power to never allow me the pain she had to go through?

She doesn't love me, and she certainly doesn't like me. I suppose that answers most of my inner musings as I watch the staff carry the last of my things to the car.

'I have arranged a car to collect you from the station in Aberdeen.' My father hands me my handbag, trying not to make eye contact as he shares his message. Walking by my side to the car, he stops me before we reach it by placing a hand on my shoulder awkwardly. Finally, he looks at me. 'Use this time, Alice. Become the girl that I know you are. Empty your head of these fairy tales and begin to find who *you* are, not who you think you want to be.'

Father doesn't wait for my response, but opens my car door for me. Without another word, he strides back into the house and leaves me baffled on the driveway.

'Are you ready, my lady?' The driver startles me out of my daze as my father's words rattle around my brain. In the absence of my mother is he actually attempting to be a parent? The oddest thing of all is the fact that his advice is *almost* good. He's had it in him all along and yet this is still his solution. Keeping his words with me, though putting the worth of them down to being a fluke, I slide into the car without looking back.

26

Though every inch of me tingles with the threat of tears, I can't cry. Crying is a privilege, reserved only for those who deserve their sadness. So, I return to numbness, the empty unfeeling that feels better than feeling everything just slightly too much.

'Ma'am.' The driver cuts through the overwhelming silence as he turns to me once we pass the threshold of my parents' driveway. Staring out of the window, though seeing nothing in particular, I acknowledge him only with a hum. 'There is a gentleman asking for you. Do you know him?'

As though revived by a shot of adrenaline stabbed straight into my heart, I follow his voice, until my eyes settle on Atticus. Stood before the car, a vision of a man determined. He smiles when our eyes meet.

'Yes, yes, lower the window please.' The driver does as I ask, and Atticus strides forward and takes my cheeks in his hands.

'You didn't think I'd let you leave without saying goodbye, did you?' I try and shake my head, but his hands clutch me too tightly, so I squeak out my reply instead.

'I knew you'd come.' He pinches at one of my cheeks as they swell with my smile. 'You need to help me. I don't want to leave; I can't leave. I can't leave *you*.'

Atticus runs his thumb down my cheek and a sad smile overtakes his face. 'You know I would if I could, my princess, but I can't stay long.' My heartbeat pounds in my chest and his hands spread so much heat to my face, I would half think myself on fire.

'I love you,' I breathe, and though I've said it to him since the second night after we met, it still feels like the first time. So overwhelmed with him, his hands, his smile, his affection, my pulse throbs through me and I could almost cry. *Almost.*

'I'm glad.' He grins as he presses his forehead to mine, before planting a swift kiss in my hair. 'I have something I must discuss with you, Lady Alice.'

'My lady, we really should be leaving.' The driver looks at me from the rear-view mirror, his stare knowing, his expression anxious, but I hardly want to take heed of him or anything other than Atticus in this moment. My heartbeat wooshes in my ears, as though my heart already knows what he is going to say and my brain needs only to focus on his lips.

'Lady Alice . . .' are the words his lips mould to: 'will you w—'

'Yes, yes of course.' I rush, giggling through my straining grin.

'—write my speech . . . Oh perfect, I knew I could rely on you.' He kisses me again on the forehead and the fire in my heart crackles and smokes to an ember as though pissed on without remorse.

'Speech?' I can just about squeak out, my cheeks burning with the embarrassment that I had hoped for a weightier question.

'Yes, darling. Daddy has decided to step down from the company and I shall be taking over as chairman by the middle of August and I shall need a speech for the shareholders' meeting they will be hosting in my honour. I know you're always complaining about wishing to write your own.' One flake of ash rekindles at his final words, a glimmer of hope at the thought he might need me returning.

'My lady.' The driver coughs again and Atticus pulls away and presses a note to my palm before turning on his heel and walking back along the pavement as though he never noticed the car to begin with.

Unfolding the headed paper, my heart swells at the smudged lettering: *Wait for me. A.*

It is short, sweet, and it keeps my head above water for the rest of my journey into nothingness.

In an effort to make it seem as though my family care for the environment, I am bustled onto the 10 a.m. King's Cross to Aberdeen train. LNER do try their best but their first class often consists of a slightly less scratchy seat and a complimentary biscuit and a cup of tea from a mug that has seen better days.

The view, however, is one of the few reasons that the train isn't my most detested form of transport. Once liberated from the confines of high buildings and claustrophobic tracks, the country seems to open out. The carriage slashes through open fields, and skirts around the east coast until you are cutting along what feels like a cliff edge, just a seagull's flight from the sea. For the duration of the seven-hour journey, the view out of the window is one that fails to get boring. Most of the excursion is spent just watching it, as the flat lands of Lincolnshire turn to the moors of Yorkshire, and the rolling hills of Northumberland turn to the Scottish glens, and I have some time to lose myself in my admiration of the world around me.

That is, until the older couple beside me, who keep looking down their noses at everyone who passes through first class under the age of fifty, persistently witter to themselves about how 'England used to be a proper country' (whatever that means) all because they have started serving French biscuits from the trolley.

Just as I am fit to fall asleep and we chug through Newcastle, my phone vibrates obnoxiously on the tray before me. Kitty's name lights up across the screen. The thought that my closest friend hasn't forgotten about me as soon as I am out of her postcode settles my nerves a little.

'Alice, my darling bitch!' Her voice comes through my headphones in a familiar trill.

'Hey, Kitty,' I answer and the old couple aim their insulted glare in my direction. I return their intrigue with a churlish sneer and direct my attention to my phone call.

'I hear there is to be congratulations in order.' I can almost hear her grin, and I picture her twirling a skinny cigarette between her fingers as she lounges across her antique furniture.

'Congratulations?' My confusion is evident in my tone, but she only giggles in reply.

'What would you prefer: Lady Alice or chairwoman?' Kitty has a habit of speaking in such a way that I never can tell whether she is being friendly, or just blatantly mocking me. 'Where are you? It sounds a bit fucking noisy on your end.'

'Kitty, are you going to get to the point or not?' I roll my eyes and add, 'I'm on the train.'

'Oh lovely, a little proletariat holiday? Experiencing "real life" are we?' She's definitely mocking now. 'Couldn't Daddy have at least sent you on a plane?'

'Kitty, I'm being sent to the family in Balmoral. I told you this last week.' I can't be bothered to argue with her; in fact, I'm almost glad she didn't care enough to come and see me off.

'Oh, did you? Must have slipped my mind.' She gives a forced titter and continues, 'You will be back for the meeting, I hope?'

'Meeting?' I ask in a bored tone, knowing full well that she has only mentioned it as a way to prove she knows something I don't.

'The shareholders' meeting, silly.' She giggles to herself, though I know she finds no amusement in her words beyond the power she is holding over me. 'Surely Atticus has invited you?'

'Of course he has,' I bluff. He hasn't in so many words but he has asked me to write his speech. That's as good as an invite, right?

'I see.' She seems a little deflated but soon perks up again. 'Well make sure you find somewhere in Ireland that can give you a nice little manicure beforehand.' I don't bother to correct her on the fact that Scotland and Ireland are two completely different countries, and one cannot, in fact, get to said country from London via train. She wouldn't be bothered to understand anyway.

'And why would that be?' I roll my eyes again, though it's only the nosy first-class passengers that are hanging on my every word who are privy to it.

'Well, he will be proposing, won't he?'

Suddenly Kitty's voice becomes the only thing in the universe that matters. The hum of the train, the trundle of the trolley with its shaking teacups, the muttering of the passengers all fall silent as I take note of each of her tinny breaths on the receiver. When only my own shaking ones answer her, she continues, 'Oops. Didn't you know?' Kitty giggles again. 'Atticus's father proposed to his mother at this meeting when he became chairman, and then again to his twenty-four-year-old mistress when it was his twenty-fifth anniversary with the company. It's tradition – something about proving loyalty and stability to the shareholders.'

Proposing? Is that why he mentioned the meeting? Perhaps he doesn't want me to write a speech at all, but rather just wanted to test the waters, to leave a hint, send me away clinging to the knowledge that in just one month he shall be down on one knee in front of everyone important to him, and I shall no longer be alone.

Only when the car purrs to a halt do I take much notice of my surroundings. I hardly remember getting off the train at all, because my mind has only thought of one thing for the last few hours: Atticus. Realising that we are not yet arrived at Balmoral, but in fact parked up in the car park of a pub called 'The Balmoral Arms', I call politely to the driver for the first time this whole journey from Aberdeen, 'Excuse me, why have we stopped at a pub?'

'These are my instructions, ma'am,' he says, only glancing at me momentarily through the rear-view mirror.

'Well then where are we?'

'Braemar, ma'am.'

'Well, there must be some kind of mistake. We are

supposed to be going to Balmoral *Castle*, not some pub with a slightly similar name.'

Before I have time to hear his response, my door is pulled open and a woman stands before me, a riding crop in hand, and wearing wellies, muddied to her knees. 'There is no mistake, unless you are not Lady Alice?' she says, her Scottish accent thick. Her tone is clipped, and she has a no-nonsense air about her as she stares at me as though I should know exactly who she is.

I begin to feel my pulse throb erratically in my neck. Am I being kidnapped? Is this all Mother's plan? Stage a kidnap, put a bag over my head, and send me to some camp where they shave my head and straighten me out? 'A lady should not divulge her identity to a stranger.' I try and keep my voice as level as possible, showing no signs of weakness. 'I wonder if you may be able to help me. My driver seems to have gotten lost on his way to Balmoral Castle. Do you know the roads?'

'I know every blade of grass in the Highlands, my lady. But your driver is not lost. I have been sent to fetch you.' She finishes with a little breathy laugh, though there is no real amusement behind her stoic face.

'Fetch me? But I am already in the car.' I scan my eyes up and down her attire. Focusing again on the riding crop in her hand, I wonder how I can wangle the weapon out of her hand if needs be. 'I am quite content here, thank you.' I sit back into the seat and cross my arms over my chest.

'You mistake me, my lady. The king is rather fond of the clean air around these parts, and the environment is his pride and joy. He has insisted that no cars must enter the grounds of Balmoral unless for emergencies or matters of state. As your arrival is neither, I have arranged for us to go on horseback.'

'Excuse me?' I choke out my response, too dumbfounded to try and mask my emotions.

'I should introduce myself. I am Mrs Buchanan: housekeeper of Balmoral Castle.' Pride flows from her as she stands up even straighter than before.

'You could have opened with that,' I whinge, too overwhelmed with whatever is happening right now to trouble myself with more false politeness.

'What was that?' Though richly Scottish, Mrs Buchanan's tone reminds me of that of my grandmother; she is neither loud nor angry but so firm, so controlled, that I am startled into submission.

I slide out of the car to meet her face to face, and she glances up and down, shaking her head at the sight before her.

'Now, I shall make it known from the off that although I have worked for your family almost thirty years, I am no servant. Your father has also insisted that you are not to receive any special treatment, so you will do well not to expect any.'

'I didn't ex— I wasn't—' Mrs Buchanan cuts me off before I can figure out what I am trying to say.

'You know how to ride I assume?'

'Yes, but—'

'Perfect – you shall take Hamish.' She points to a white stallion tied to the fence. Though I spent much of my childhood learning to ride horses, as every good posh girl does, the size of this particular beast intimidates me. 'We need to get moving before the rain sets in. It is a two-anda-half-hour ride for a skilled horsewoman—' she scans me up and down once again '—but I have left us four.'

'None taken.' I roll my eyes, though she is right. Living in Central London in the century of Uber, I have had very little need for a horse in recent years, so I must say I am a little out of practice. 'Do you have anything I can change into before we set out?' I look down at my outfit. I definitely didn't wake up this morning expecting a hack through the Scottish wilderness on a chilly July afternoon, and the summer dress I wear proves as much.

'Didn't you bring anything suitable in your luggage?'

I think of the array of dresses, pretty pastel socks, and latest shoes straight off the fashion week runway tucked away in my suitcases and admit defeat.

'Never mind, I am no stranger to riding in a dress.' A minor face-saving fib, but I hike up the skirt and tuck half of it into the belt around my waist, exposing my leg to the elements. The Scottish air kisses down my calves until a trail of goose bumps are left behind. 'What shall I do with my bags?'

'You may carry whatever you can on your saddle now, and then we shall send someone to collect the rest of your things when they next come into town.' Deciding not to give Mrs Buchanan the satisfaction of ruffling me any further, I stuff the saddle pouches with my underwear and pyjamas (my most important possessions) and set the stirrups to the right length before climbing onto the fence and mounting my steed with ease.

Mrs Buchanan gives a huff and I grin widely for the first time since we met. 'Shall we?' I give my stallion a little tap and I set off at a canter. After a moment with the wind in my hair, I turn about to see Mrs B and my driver still laughing with one another at the car, making no attempt to join me. Manoeuvring Hamish back around, we both come to a stop before them.

'What's the hold-up?' I ask, thoroughly irritated. 'And what's so funny?' I add when all they do is continue their childish giggles.

'Balmoral is that way, my lady.' My driver points to the opposite direction than I had just flown off to and my cheeks redden.

'Well, how was I meant to know?' I complain and sit up straighter in the saddle. The housekeeper swings a leg over her mare and doesn't wait for me before speeding off down the track.

'I know every last thread and sock in that suitcase. If anything goes missing or ends up on any sketchy websites, I will know about it,' I say to the driver, trying my best at a stern face before I follow suit and race through the breeze to catch up to my guide.

As though sent to punish me, it takes less than five minutes of riding in silence before the heavens open and I am given the royally Scottish welcome I'm sure I deserve. Hamish plods on, unperturbed by the downpour as I shiver against his saddle.

Thoughts of Atticus are the only things that warm me, the only reason I'm not currently sobbing into Hamish's mane. In just six weeks, I will be agreeing to be his wife. He will make all of this right. I know he will. Because he truly loves me, everything will be okay.

Chapter 4

The chill has soaked into my bones and with every jolt in the path, it feels painfully like my skeleton is made of ice. Hamish still plods on at a pace that thankfully doesn't require me to move my limbs or digits past a twitch, though somehow Mrs Buchanan still trots on, high in her seat, as though the clouds have just rained around her. She only slows down when we cross the river and draw up to a gatehouse three and a half hours after we set out.

'Welcome, my lady, to the grounds of Balmoral Castle.' Mrs Buchanan hops down from her horse and brushes some of the rain from her croup with her gloved palm. 'The Scottish seat of the British royal family since 1852 when Prince Albert purchased it for Queen Victoria after she fell in love with the Highlands.'

'I assume she was at least granted the privilege of a carriage.' Dismounting, I speak more to Hamish than Mrs B, but she scowls at me anyway. Perhaps my appreciation of seeing the place for the first time would be greater were

I not shivering and unable to distract myself from the all-encompassing smell of wet horse.

'Ah, Mr Campbell, late as always.' Mrs Buchanan shifts her attention from me to the stocky older gentleman who has emerged from the gatehouse with his shotgun hooked casually over the tweed sleeve of his jacket.

'Mary, always a pleasure.' He tips his flat cap with a coy smile, and she rolls her eyes. At least I'm not the only one getting a frosty reception. 'You must be Lady Alice, ma'am?' Mr Campbell turns to me with a friendly smile and stretches out his hand for me to shake. I oblige him. 'My word, my lady, your fingers are frozen solid.' He clutches both my hands between his rough palms and rubs them affectionately. 'You've made the poor child ride all this time in the rain without so much as a pair of gloves?'

'King's orders,' is all Mrs Buchanan can reply as she fusses with the reins of the horses.

Mr Campbell leans forward and speaks in a low voice from the side of his mouth so only I can hear him. 'Since that old bat is too rude to introduce me, I'm James Campbell, groundskeeper. You can call me Jimmy. Everyone does, except Sourpuss.' He gestures his head towards Mrs Buchanan who stares at the both of us with her arms folded.

'It is a pleasure to meet you, Jimmy.' The warmth of his hands and the kind, jesting tone of his voice comforts me, and I find enough strength in me to return his smile.

'Would you like to come in and warm up with a cup of tea before you head up to the castle? I can stick the fire on?' His wispy eyebrows twitch with his broadening grin and the way his wide brown eyes seem to glow as they reflect the clouds that blanket the sky reminds me of roasted chestnuts at Christmas.

'We have much to get on with thank you, Mr Campbell,' Mrs Buchanan answers for the both of us.

'Who said I was asking you, Mary hen?' A cheeky glint crosses his face as he forces another huff from the housekeeper.

'Mr Campbell, please be so kind as to take the horses round to the stables and I shall finish the task that I have been ordered to do and deliver Lady Alice to the castle and get her settled into her lodgings.' She hands him the reins and Jimmy gives her a wink once she crosses into his personal space and I am almost certain that I see her blush.

'Do I get a say in any of this?' I ask, twirling a few strands of Hamish's damp mane between my fingers.

'No,' Mrs Buchanan replies bluntly.

'Didn't think so.' She turns on her heel, and sets out towards a pair of gates embossed with the cyphers GVR and MR side by side: the mark of King George V and his wife Mary.

As I trail along behind her, my shoes squeak with the puddles that have collected in the soles. Trees line the limestone path and only the sound of their applause as their leaves blow and clash in the wind escorts our crunching footsteps. The whispering breeze follows us through the grounds, so subtle, so silent, my nervous breaths are the noisier accompaniment, for even the birds must be hiding from the weather.

After another ten minutes of walking, I finally see it: Balmoral. Tucked away in a clearing of trees, the granite of the castle stands proud against the perfectly manicured lawn. Its beauty isn't dampened by the wealth of grey cloud surrounding it, but rather the contrary. The turrets and gables, each so sharply pointed, seem to slot so perfectly into the damp scene, it's as if the castle sprung from the ground as naturally as the maples and oaks framing it did. For the first time, I realise what all the fuss has been about.

'Queen Victoria once called it her "dear paradise in the Highlands" in her journals.' Only when Mrs Buchanan speaks do I realise I had stopped still, at the mercy of the drizzle, to take in the scene before me. Her voice is softer than it has been all day, and she too takes a moment from her determined strides to breathe in its air, and truly appreciate its image.

'Beautiful,' I breathe and she almost smiles. Ivy scales the walls, peeping politely into the windows, though smartly pruned enough to not encroach on the bright white of the panes. The deep emerald leaves ornament the stone, as though all of it belongs to the landscape and we are all just Mother Nature's guests. Not another manmade structure can be seen for miles, at least not above the sea of green as the forest stretches for leagues. It could be its own kingdom, a castle from a fairy tale, enchanted to appear only when the seeker truly needs its magic.

With rekindled strength, I reach the entrance as though an invisible force pulls me through its doors.

When within its walls, the housekeeper moves through the hallways and passages as though renewed, charged almost, by the energy of its interior. Trailing behind her at a pace that leaves me stumbling over my feet, I am unable to appreciate any of the castle's intricacies and leaving a breadcrumb trail to find my way back out again is certainly out of the question. Drawn deeper and deeper into the labyrinth of tartan carpets and taxidermy, I am well and truly lost when Mrs Buchanan finally stops at a white door, in a long hallway of white doors, and tells me it is to be my room.

It's bright, just full of too much air and empty space. A green tartan carpet matches the curtains in a slightly overwhelming reminder that I am no longer in London. Only a large bed, wardrobe, and desk occupy the room, all overlooked by a rather sorry-looking stag's head mounted on the back wall.

'Is there any way that we could take Bambi's dad down at all?' I look between Mrs B and the stag that just seems to pout and grow more glassy-eyed the more I stare at him.

'No, my lady. Balmoral's interior is largely unchanged from the Victorian period. And we shall not be starting now.' From what I have seen so far, I know she is telling the truth. 'Well, if that is all, I shall leave you to get settled. Dinner is at six-thirty in the dining room of the west wing. It is veal tonight, and I shall have one of the kitchen staff leave you a menu in the morning for the rest of the week. Any questions?'

Parting my lips ready to ask how exactly I can find the dining room, I don't even get the chance to utter a syllable before she leaves the room and closes the door behind her.

With nothing to unpack besides the throngs of wet

41

underwear that I still manage to cling to, I have little else to do aside from peel off my damp clothes that stick to my body like a second skin. Finding a robe in the wardrobe, I sling it around my limbs that ripple with goose bumps and perch on the end of the bed, telling myself that I'll shower in just a moment.

For the first time in what feels like forever, there is complete and utter silence. There is no hustle and bustle in the house, no sirens wailing at perpetual emergencies, not even the low distant hum of an aeroplane. For the first time, in not long enough, my thoughts are the loudest thing in the room. It doesn't take long for them to go from innocent observations of the decor, of the way my chest rises and falls with my breath, of Atticus, to something vile, twisted and gnarled into a rat-king of self-destruction.

Staring out of the tall windows, I no longer see the vast landscape, the paradise of what only five minutes ago was as exciting as all of the stories I've read about in my book of fairy tales. Literally, I can see, of course, even if it is just a mass blur of every hue of green, but my eyes are unfocused. It is as though I am looking in on myself, watching everything that has ever worried me, hurt me, plagued me, on repeat like some highlight reel of my very worst moments.

This is nothing new, of course. These thoughts, these feelings, have followed me through my life, grown with me over the years, and yet each time they surface, they feel as scary as if it were the first time. Logically speaking, I know I am safe; I know I have it easy, and yet my body battles me at every turn.

42

It got slightly easier when Kitty introduced me to all of her friends. Knowing I'd be under their scrutiny, knowing the depths of their judgement, I masked everything, it became easier and easier to pretend that I wasn't feeling anything at all. Becoming someone else held off my sadness for a while, distracted me from these thoughts that seemed to appear in my brain to keep my happiness in check. But it always gets bad when I'm alone again. I can't pretend with no one around. I have to face myself. I have to face an overpowering sadness of which I can't seem to ever find the source.

A soft knock sounds around the room and for the first time, I notice that the sun is setting and the light is almost all gone. Snapping out of my thoughts, I clear my throat to tell the knocker to enter.

A small mousy woman, no older than me, peers around the side of the door. Each one of her features is petite aside from her brown eyes that seem to hold the whole expanse of the room in the reflection within them. She doesn't say anything, only stares at me with a pinched smile, a broad air of expectation in her gaze.

When another moment passes, I finally speak. 'Are you just here to stare at me? Or do you have something you wish to share?'

She visibly swallows and shifts around the door so the rest of her aproned body can be seen. Her dark hair is braided down her back, although loose wisps of it tickle at her brows and cheeks and she twitches her head in what is seemingly an attempt to stop their constant tickling, though her hands remain stuck firm behind her back.

'Sorry, my lady. Mrs Buchanan told me I was not to speak unless spoken to.'

'I see she does not like to stick to her own rules,' I muse with a slight smile, and the girl gives a nervous twitch of her lips. 'Don't bother yourself with that nonsense around me. I would rather hear you talk at me constantly.' *It might drown out my own thoughts,* I add, though only to myself.

'Thank you, my lady. I, er, well, it's just that you missed dinner. I wondered if you might prefer to eat in the privacy of your own room.' She stands aside to reveal a trolley, laden with several plates and cutlery.

'What is your name?' I ask, warmed by the thoughtfulness of this stranger, and relieved to have some friendly company at last.

'Sophie, ma'am – sorry, I mean, Miss Sophie Chorley. I'm just a maid, not kitchen staff, but I was clearing away and noticed you hadn't had so much as a bite and thought you must be hungry after your journey. My lady.' She adds the final honorific in a hurry, looking nervous.

'Do you have the time, Miss Sophie Chorley?' I ask, and she looks down at her watch so quickly I almost worry the movement will leave her with whiplash.

'It's 8.30 p.m., ma'am.' I have been sat, on this bed, in this dressing gown for almost four hours. I haven't showered. As if on cue, my stomach lets out an obnoxious gurgle and I am reminded that I haven't eaten anything since the train nearly ten hours ago. Sophie hears it too and rushes into the room with the trolley and begins unloading platefuls onto the desk.

'It is a little cold now, ma'am. But still lovely. All nice and fresh, I promise.' She bustles around and is soon heading for the door with her empty trolley and a rushed goodbye.

'Sophie?' I say.

'Yes, ma'am.' She wheels around, and stands to attention at the sound of her name.

'Would you like to stay? For a chat, I mean?' I pick up a floret of broccoli with my fingers and plop it as casually as possible into my mouth, attempting to reclaim a little of my mask before this stranger.

'With me?' she asks, her accent growing stronger in the slipping of her guard.

'Of course, you. Unless you have anyone else more exciting to suggest?' She can't know that I *need* her to stay, that I cannot stay here alone, not right now.

'Oh, yes, ma'am, it would be my pleasure. My shift was just about to finish anyway.' A bitter swirl of guilt sloshes in my stomach at the thought of her giving up her free time for me, but the selfish desire for distraction overpowers it.

'Perfect, have a seat.' She stands bolt upright before me and I gesture to the chair tucked under the desk. She slides it out cautiously, watching my every twitch before sitting down before me as I pick at the food. 'Tell me about yourself, Sophie.'

'What would you like to know, ma'am?' She tries her hardest not to make eye contact and I can almost see her thought processes as she attempts to control herself.

'Anything you'd like to tell me. Who are you? How did you get here? What makes you tick?'

A grin she has been trying to suppress overtakes her

face and, at the sight of it, I know it means she will oblige in distracting me, and that relieves me immensely.

'I suppose I should start from the beginning then . . .' Sophie pinches a macaroon from the desk and with a powdery mouthful, commences her story. 'I live in Braemar – I assume you passed through it on your way. It never gets any bigger, but I haven't quite outgrown it yet. My grandmother was housekeeper before Mrs B. I spent my summers here when I was a child, under her feet mostly. When she passed, I decided I wanted to be just like her . . .'

Sophie talks, and talks, and talks, until all that concerns me are thoughts of her and the twenty-one years of her life in her tranquil corner of Scotland.

Chapter 5

Light streams into the room as though the sun has shifted a thousand miles closer overnight. I don't remember falling asleep but when I pry open my lids, I notice that all of the pots and plates that Sophie brought last night are gone and not so much as a crumb has been left behind. For a moment, I have to ask myself whether I dreamt the whole thing, but my bleary brain is soon stunned into motion when the piercing screech of what I can only describe as a fight between a Pegasus and a donkey forces itself through my cracked-open window.

Leaping out of bed at the commotion, I fly to the window, clutching the dressing gown around my chest as though it would in any way protect me from the sound. Sliding up the pane, it isn't hard to find the source. The piper stands at the very foot of my window; his red Balmoral tartan kilt, with matching hose and bonnet, and a black military jacket are a stark contrast to the green morning. His pale cheeks are flushed with the exertion of his playing. His broad arms almost swallow the instrument.

'You do know if you loosen your grip on a squealing animal, they usually cease their crying,' I call out the window just as the mouthpiece falls from his lip and his clutch on the bag loosens enough for me to be heard above the droning song.

'They are bagpipes, ma'am,' the piper calls back. 'I can assure you that I'm not harming anyone.'

'Except my ears, of course. I dread to think the shock my body is under after such a rude awakening.' I laugh down at him, attempting to show him that I only mean it in jest. He continues his grave, obedient stare. 'Is there nowhere else that you can practise?'

'I am not practising, ma'am. It has been specially requested by your father that I wake you each morning.' His voice is gruff, and though I can hear him from a storey away, he still sounds as though he is mumbling.

'Is this Scotland's answer to an alarm clock? I thought we were past such stereotypes.' He isn't amused by the joke, only repositions his fingers on the chanter and sucks on the mouthpiece as he prepares for his next onslaught. 'Look . . .' I speak quickly before he can begin again '. . . look, I appreciate the sentiment, respect the culture. It's a fascinating history. It's just that I had a long journey yesterday and was hoping to spend much of today unconscious, and this really, *really*, isn't helping.' Hoping a sweet smile might persuade him to leave me in peace for the rest of the morning, I grin at him from above. The longer I sleep, the less time for my consciousness to battle against me. When my whole being isn't vibrating with the sound of bagpipes, the silence of this place will be too much. I know it already.

'I apologise, ma'am. These are my orders. Your father knew how fond the late queen was of being woken to the sound of her piper and made a special request. It is the Balmoral experience, and I must follow my commands.' Before I can protest, he begins again, drowning out the morning call of the birds with another slightly too upbeat song that I can hardly distinguish from the other.

With a huff, I slam the window down, and crawl back under my duvet. Both movements prove futile as neither succeeds in muting the noise outside. After tossing and turning in my bed for at least another ten minutes, I throw off my covers with a grunt and submit to the piper and his persistent piping.

Heaving myself out of the dishevelled bedclothes for a second time already this morning, I have nothing else to do besides head to the bathroom to finally take the shower I have been procrastinating. The powerful spray slapping my skin and sloshing against the glass is exactly what I needed to dull the relentless crooning and I soon find the sound almost tolerable when accompanied by the hissing of hot water.

Once the smell of damp horse is well and truly scrubbed from my skin, I re-emerge to silence. With my towel looped around my dripping frame, I glance out of the window briefly to find my early morning caller departed and peace restored. That is until I realise that all of my clothes are still a four-hour horse ride away and even the underwear

I managed to smuggle is heaped in a soggy puddle on the floor.

With nothing else to do, I pull out my phone, hoping a message or two will distract me for a time. Not a single name fills the screen, not Atticus, not Kitty, not even my father asking if I have arrived safely. The emptiness hits me again.

Atticus will have an excuse. He's probably on his way as we speak, or making arrangements at the blacksmith's shop in Gretna Green, unable to wait another few weeks. Plus, he's hardly ever on his phone. Perhaps he has sent me a handwritten letter and the post here is just a little slow. Yes, it will be something like that, I tell myself.

Desperate for some distraction, anything at all, I settle on breakfast as the answer. Clad only in my fluffy towel, I walk along the corridor, my hair leaving a trail of perfumed drips behind me. High walls, thick with frames, seem to stretch on forever. The inhabitants of the portraits watch on as I become exactly the person my mother and the press think I am.

My bare feet pad down the carpet to a chorus of muffled gasps. The bustling household seems to slow to a stop, like a flock of birds shot down mid-flight.

'Good morning.' I address each wide-eyed member of staff with a blinding smile, as though my heart isn't currently pounding hard enough to punch through my chest, or I'm not fighting with each breath. Many of them can't scramble together a response, whilst others struggle to mask their shock in their unintelligible replies. Though there are some, surprisingly the older generation, that seem

na

50

almost entirely unfazed. They simply bow their heads respectfully, or return my greeting with a slight curtsey.

It is Mrs Buchanan who is most undisturbed of all, standing like a sentry at the end of the corridor, arms folded, smirk twitching at one side of her thin lips. 'Lady Alice, how good of you to join us. How nice to see you making yourself so at home already. I trust everything is to your liking?'

Another member of staff flicks a nervous look back and forth between us as it becomes clear that the housekeeper is attempting to get me to crack, to even just mention the fact I am one draughty hallway away from flashing my bare arse to the whole household.

'Absolutely wonderful.' I grin, not giving in to her. 'Although . . .' I begin, and Mrs Buchanan's triumphant smirk begins to show more plainly. 'If you could ask your piper to give me at least another half an hour in the mornings if he insists on giving me such a wake-up call, it would be much appreciated.' Finally, she scowls, opens her mouth to speak and when nothing comes out, turns on her heel and marches back down the hallway with her sharp nose upturned.

With my confidence taking a nosedive once the adrenaline begins to wear off, I am grateful to see Sophie singing to herself as she walks seemingly aimlessly down the corridor towards me. Only when she ceases her subtle dancing does her mind return back to earth and she notices me. For just a single second she is a deer in the headlights, until she breaks out into the most chandelier-shaking laughter I have ever heard. It's infectious. She is bent double, and soon I too am clutching my chest, with tears clouding my eyes.

'Already running around in the scud? Amazing,' Sophie says between breaths. 'I did wonder why Mrs B was scampering about looking like she'd been licking piss off a thistle.'

I burst out in another fit of laughter and she flushes red. 'I mean . . .' she stammers, 'looking like she's been licking uri— no— pish— no . . . sorry, my lady.' She curtseys, her pale cheeks burning so hot, even her neck begins to flame.

'Oh hush,' I reassure her, still giggling at the image. 'That's the best laugh I've had in a while.'

Sophie smiles shyly again. 'I've never seen her so frazzled,' she half-whispers and a glimmer of pride washes over me.

'Sophie, could you possibly do me a favour?' I finally compose myself enough to ask.

'You'd like me to find you some clothes, wouldn't you?' Amusement glints across her whole face.

'Yes please.' Finally, it's my turn to blush – my true colours finally on show.

'Leave it with me. I'll see what I can do.' She's serious this time, and there's such a soft kindness in her thick brows that I know I can trust her, 'Oh, and Lady Alice?' I nod. 'I'll find someone to bring your breakfast to your room whilst you wait.'

After just about sprinting back to my room, I am glad when Sophie finally returns under a heap of fabric.

'Now,' she begins, tossing the pile onto my bed, 'I can't

promise couture or whatever, but I have found a few bits and bobs lying about.' She picks out a few pairs of jodhpurs, too many tartan garments, and a jumper or two. 'I couldn't find you any,' she leans in to whisper, 'knickers. I'm afraid we don't usually have too many spares lying around and I'm not sure the queen would like to share from her selection that she keeps here. But I was going to go swimming in the loch tonight with a few of the girls from the village, so I've got my cozzie you can borrow whilst I send yours down to be washed, if you like?'

'You'd do that for me?' I look at her wide-eyed, and she nods, handing me the bright floral swimming costume. 'But then you won't be able to go swimming with your friends.'

'Haven't you ever swum in just your scants?' she replies casually.

'Scants?' I enquire, bemused.

'Scants? Keks? Pants? Undies?' She gives me a teasing look that proves she already knows the answer.

'I can't say there are many places that I could do that in London without having an audience.' I chuckle as I imagine jumping into the pond in St James's Park and becoming the most taboo photo in a hundred people's holiday album.

'We definitely don't have that sort of trouble around here. Aye, if you ever fancy letting them hang free and getting a good cold splash of nature about you, Loch Muick after five . . .' She taps the side of her nose as though she has just revealed the identity of Jack the Ripper. Hearing her talk so bluntly, so coarsely, is a breath of fresh air through my

53

stiflingly stuffy life. I'm not sure that anyone has ever said exactly what comes to their mind to me before, at least not before perfectly polishing it first in an effort to make it more palatable. It seems that honesty, no matter how brash, is far nicer.

'I'll keep it in mind.' Chuckling, I pick out a knee-length tartan skirt and the jumper that looks the least itchy and decide to make of it what I can. Changing quickly in the en-suite, I have to shimmy into Sophie's bikini bottoms and though they chafe at my legs, anything would be better than going commando in a castle for a second time today.

My outfit is about as flattering as could be expected. Sophie stands beside my bed, refolding the copious amount of fabrics that she had unloaded onto it. 'I can leave a few bits here if you like? I'm not sure Mrs B is in a rush to fetch your things from the village.'

'Thank you, Sophie,' I say sincerely. 'I'll get your *cozzie* back to you as soon as I can.'

'Don't bother yourself with that. Take it as my gift from me to your ladyship.' She's teasing but I know she isn't mocking me. 'Who knows, you might have some more use for it in the next few weeks.'

I don't bother to tell her she'd never catch me dead in a freshwater lake; the sentiment itself is sweet and I don't wish to expose my snobbery even further.

'Anyway, I must be getting on. Your knickers don't wash themselves.' She laughs but a pang of guilt slides through me.

Chapter 6

Without Sophie and her *interesting* conversation, the silence of Balmoral resumes. It itches, the silence. It starts out as a tickle, like a loose hair kissing at your neck with irritating persistence. Then it begins to crawl all over you, in an inescapable attack, pinning you down and subjecting you to your own personal hell.

When the only sound more torturous than the sound of my own thoughts reaches me for the second time today, I am almost grateful. The distant hum of bagpipes seems to float through the castle like tinnitus, stubbornly burrowing its way into my thoughts until the inability to focus on anything else begins to drive me insane.

With nothing else to occupy me, I decide to follow it. Retracing my steps down from this morning, I am thankful when it seems as though the house is at rest. There is no movement aside from the rattling of ornaments along sideboards as my bare feet pad down the carpet. Not a single creature stirs as I creep down the stairs; I'm watched only by the soulless taxidermy that lines each wall, and my heart throbs in my throat. I'm not doing anything wrong, at least I don't think I am, but the thought of being perceived, of being caught out in my curiosity, forces me to tiptoe in a way reminiscent of my childhood, creeping around the hallways at home to read books in Mother's library after dark.

The music flows louder. A few discordant notes echo through the empty hallway until they suddenly terminate, leaving only a straining hum behind. Just as I reach the kitchen the jarring sound of voices blends with the grating clash of crockery, a sure sign of life heading in my direction. Before I am caught, I slip off through a side room and into a tall doorway. The white-painted wood creaks under my touch but I remain undetected, watching through the crack in the door as a member of the household trundles past with a rattling tea trolley.

Releasing my breath as soon as he has passed, I finally take notice of the high ceilings of the room I have stumbled into. More stag heads accompany the coving in a crown of disembodied antlers, and I wonder if there are actually any left to roam the wild, or how many generations of the poor unfortunate souls are strung up there to gather dust forever.

Just as the thought begins to well and truly lower my spirits, a horrisonant screech almost renders my heart as useless as my furry friends. Finally drawing my eyes away from the nearest paintings and trefoil designs, I look about the room and notice for the first time that I stand in the corner of the ballroom. At the far end, beyond the great glass-enclosed candelabras that hang from the ceiling like giant bell jars of fireflies, a pair of parallel stairs lead up to a grand door. The rich mahogany forms a sort of pulpit structure, and one imagines the king standing over its banister, raising a toast to his guests across the ballroom. It is not the king who stands there today, however.

The Piper to the Sovereign, relieved of the confines of his uniform, stands proud over the room, his mouthpiece tucked between his lips, an almost playful smirk threatening to grace them too. 'Are you trying to give me a heart attack?' I enquire, once my blood pressure has returned to a non-life-threatening level.

'No, ma'am,' is his only reply.

'What happened to a simple "good morning"? Or even a friendly "hello"?' I cross the floor to gauge him with a closer look. His hair is dark but when the light catches it from the wide windows, it twists with threads of red.

'I must not speak un—'

'—unless spoken to.' I finish for him with an eyeroll. 'What a boring rule. Is there any way we can swap it for: do not announce your presence with what can only be described as a chicken's battle cry?'

He tries to control the smile that tickles at his mouth but the deep dimples in his freckled cheeks give him away.

'My apologies, ma'am.' He bows his head. His civilian clothes cling to his body in a way that his uniform tries to hide. Thick arms embrace his instrument, and his broad chest is pushed out proudly with his pristine military posture.

'Oh and the ma'am thing too. People in London only

call me ma'am to take the piss. My mother named me Alice; you're welcome to use it.'

'Aye, of course, ma'am.' Those dimples make a return as he looks down at me bashfully.

'What is your name, Piper?' I fold my arms over my chest and raise an eyebrow.

'Well, ma'am —'

'Alice,' I moan, my voice echoing in the ceilings.

'No, it's actually Fraser, Fraser Bell.' The subtle grin surfaces again as he teases me.

'Hilarious.' Fraser sets down his bagpipes and they groan with the motion. Looking down at me from his stage, he leans casually against the banister, his wide arms folded over his chest.

'Is there something I can do for you?' His thick Scottish drawl reverberates about the ballroom, and for a moment I can't seem to find any words. 'I had chosen the room furthest from you to rehearse,' he continues, noting my silence. 'My apologies if I have disturbed you.' For a moment I am taken aback. He has changed his plans to one that would irritate me least.

I am used to having households rushing around at my every beck and call, but such casual consideration is so unfamiliar that I have no idea how to process it.

'I was just having a look around, gathering my bearings.'

I'm not sure why I lie. Why I don't tell him I was looking for him, chasing the sound that has been occupying my mind? I have a reputation to uphold, after all.

'Is everything to your liking?'

'I suppose it is adequate. I mean aside from that

incessant noise that seems to travel through the place. Are we sure there are no feral cats trapped in the walls? Or perhaps a disgruntled phantom?'

'My granny would turn in her grave to hear an English lass voice such an opinion. She hated the pipes, of course. But she hated the English slagging them off even more.' Fraser descends the steps and meets me in the middle of the hall. 'I guarantee after a couple of weeks here, you'll be asking me to teach you how to play.' The piper is so close now that I can see the light patch of red strands under his chin that he must have missed with his morning shave. His irises are knots of green, with a thread of amber woven through and suspended like the stained glass of a marble.

'It's lucky that I shan't be here that long then, isn't it?' The reminder of Atticus pangs through me in a painful strike and I have to take a step back from Fraser to try and recover some of my composure.

'My mistake, my lady, I was told you'd be staying with us for the summer.' He too, takes another step back, as though realising how close he had drawn to me without thinking.

'Yes, well not if I can help it.' My voice comes out in a grumble but I know he has heard me. Fixing a taut smile onto my face, I try to mask the seriousness that had overcome me for a moment. 'I had best let you get back to your practising. Sorry for the interruption.'

I turn abruptly on my heel, and my feet slap along the floor as I head back the way I came.

'I'll see you in the morning,' Fraser calls, and I can almost hear the smile in his voice.

'Can't wait.' I roll my eyes and fire a sarcastic thumbs

up over my shoulder, though I catch myself beginning to smile. Turning back to say something, anything, Fraser is already halfway back up the stairs. With another second unseen by him to gather my thoughts, I push back through the door and leave him in the ballroom, chased out by his bagpipes in a sound that is already becoming too familiar.

Unafraid of being caught this time, I return proudly through the halls, taking a moment to absorb my surroundings properly for the first time. The whole place is a masterclass of Highland design. Though all of it was pretty much rebuilt through the nineteenth century, there's still that feeling of authenticity there, as though you can picture a Scottish laird plodding up and down the halls, admiring his game, or straightening the plaid curtains.

Though outside of the windows the sun is clouded over, the place doesn't feel dull. If anything, it feels brighter, at least brighter than London, where you're always overlooked by one building or another casting shadows over each street corner. No, here the cloud seems to keep all the radiance of the summer sun, without the harsh glare, the squint-inducing stare. Light diffuses across the sky and all the land around it seems to glow, as though not one point is worthy of the sun's spotlight, but every tree, crag, and sprig of heather shines as though the world has always wanted your eye to land upon it specifically.

Jimmy, the groundskeeper, strides across the lawn, his fox-red Labrador trailing at his heel. Watching him for a moment, I take note of the lightness of his step, of the way that in spite of the drizzle dampening his flat cap, he seems so genuinely happy. Even as Mrs Buchanan pursues him with a familiar sour expression, a skirt almost identical to the one currently itching my thighs flowing behind her as she chases after him, he only grins at her. Standing before him, berating him for something or other, whilst nervously itching away from his dog that keeps attempting to lick her fingertips, Mrs B has a face like thunder and yet as soon as her back is turned, Jimmy watches her all the way back to the castle as though struck by lightning.

With my mind once again falling to Atticus, I rush back to my bedroom. After several wrong turns and at least four dramatic entrances into rooms that aren't my own, I finally get the right one and grab my phone from the desk. What is the use in waiting to be saved? Calling the only man who has ever told me he fell in love with me at first sight, my heart thumps in anticipation with every unanswered ring.

'Hello, you've—' Atticus's voice flows through the speakers.

'Atticus! Oh, I can't tell you how glad I am to hear your—'

'—reached Atticus Beaumont. Either I cannot take your call right now, or I am ignoring you. I shall let you decide which one you think applies to you . . .' His answering machine continues and I end the call, and redial straight away. You never know, he might have lost it down the crack of the sofa and by the time he found it, it had rung out.

When the same pre-recorded message answers the third time I ring, I give up. The kernel of hope fizzles out and I deflate into my bed.

Chapter 7

When Fraser Bell plays the bagpipes at 9 a.m. under my window each morning for the next week, it is the only time of the day that I get out of bed. On the second day, I told Mrs Buchanan I wasn't well, which is half true, just the kind of ill that her constant supply of Lemsips and Balmoral honey can't really fix. Worried that our damp hack where she forced me to brave the Scottish elements in just a summer dress was enough to destroy my weak, spoiled, city-girl immune system, she at least let up with her comments after the third day.

At first, the only reason for my getting out of bed was to close the window. With no threat of being woken by sirens at 3 a.m., I had left the window open overnight so I could fall asleep to the rhythmic drip of rain against the sill. But now, as I find my brain growing more disordered, more noisy, I stand behind the netted curtain and allow the harshness of the melody to overwhelm everything else. Drown out the constant reminders that Atticus still hasn't returned my calls, that Kitty seems to have forgotten I ever existed, and that my father has seemingly been communicating strictly with Mrs Buchanan, using her as a way to pass on his messages without having to be troubled by whatever I have to say in return.

Fraser stands below me this Tuesday morning, in his familiar uniform, playing his familiar melodies, allowing me a moment's peace in the few seconds where music overthrows this place. When a distinctly dissonant note punctuates the end of the musical phrase, it startles me forward, out from behind the anonymity of the curtain. Upon seeing me, with his expression one of complete seriousness, and not a hint of a dimple in sight, Fraser bows his head, about-turns, and marches back down the garden path.

'Knock, knock.' A soft voice accompanies a rap at the door. Sophie's face peers around the doorway, her dark plaits swinging against the frame. 'Are you decent?' she asks, already stepping in and busying herself by picking up the various items of clothing strewn across the floor.

'Well, would it have made any difference if I was?' My voice is hoarse from the lack of use, but I almost manage a smile in her direction when she shrugs in reply. Sophie goes to pull down the pair of trousers that I had thrown over the stag's head and I place a hand on her arm to stop her. 'I don't like him looking at me in bed.' I cringe, and she gives an understanding nod.

'I've been sent to get you ready.' She plucks out various items of clothing before scurrying off to the bathroom. Only returning after the sound of running water and a soft cloud of steam follows her out, Sophie looks at me expectantly.

'Ready for what?' My brain seems to take a while to shift into gear, and all I can do is stand in the middle of the room, wrapped in my dressing gown, feeling completely and utterly lost.

'Well, I say I've been sent . . .' she blabbers, 'that might have been a lie. Today is my day off. I'm taking you on a tour.' She doesn't bother to look at me, only continues to buzz around the room, returning it to an almost human standard.

'A tour? A tour of what?'

'Of here, of course. The people, the secrets, the best spots to get the Wi-Fi. You know, all the important stuff.' She stops her fussing for a moment to look at me. 'Now get yoursel in that bath because – no offence, my lady – you're absolutely honking.' For the first time in seven days, I crack a full smile, and cannot keep in the spluttering laugh that bursts from me.

Sophie pushes me gently towards the bathroom, handing me a hairbrush as she goes. 'You know, Sophie, just because you say "no offence", or use my title, it doesn't simply negate all of the insult of your sentence,' I say, still laughing.

'Well, you needed someone to tell you the truth. If your hair gets any more feral, we'll be having to put a pair of trousers over your head once they've mounted you on the wall.' Handing me a towel, she shoves me into the bathroom and closes the door behind me.

'Charming!' I say to the wooden backside of the bathroom door.

'Hurry up, there's lots to get through.'

I don't need telling twice. Washing myself quickly, I allow the warm water just long enough to seep into my skin, thaw my bones, and get the blood pumping back around my body to kick-start my motivation once again. Afraid of Sophie's wrath, I don't give myself long enough to let my mind wander as it usually does, and as soon as I feel almost presentable again, I re-emerge. After dressing in the clothes she has laid out for me on the side, I leave the bathroom to find the room returned to an unlived-in state. The only proof I have been rotting in this room for a week is the pair of culottes, still draped over the stag. Sheets have been changed, not a speck of dust has settled on any surface, and not a single pair of underwear remains on the carpet.

'You did all of this yourself?' I stare at Sophie as she straightens a few of the trinkets on the chest of drawers.

'Oh God no.' She chuckles. 'We're a bunch of worker bees in this place.'

'I didn't even hear you,' I say, a little disturbed at the thought of more than just Sophie rooting through my things.

'Of course you didn't. That's exactly how we're trained: never be seen or heard, finish the job with maximum efficiency.' She grins and her thick dark eyebrows slope in a way that makes her whole face look soft and welcoming. 'It's likely that you'll never see half of the people who work here. You'll only see those of us who aren't that great at our jobs.'

We have staff back in London, so I am regretfully used to such things: my room is cleaned whilst I am out, the rest of the house is taken care of when none of us are around. To give the illusion that the place is just so naturally well kept, we don't see them, and to make sure they have no interactions with us that they can sell to the papers, they hardly see us either. Balmoral feels different, however. There is a hum within it, as though it is alive and breathing. Most of all, however, Sophie is different. Always told I need not socialise with 'people like her', now that she stands before me, all smiles, I can't help but feel as though I have missed out on some happier company.

'Are you ready?' Sophie asks and I look down at myself. Another scratchy jumper, paired with some ever so slightly too small jodhpurs, and my dripping blonde hair make for a rather interesting outfit, but I don't have the energy to change any of that now.

Nodding my head, I slide on a pair of slippers and follow her out of my room for the first time in too many days. Sophie gives me a whistle-stop tour of the castle, not bothering to delay to have a good look in any of the rooms and giving a little more information beyond which prime ministers have stayed in which of the fifty-two bedrooms and how many of them she believed would have been visited by *Wuthering Heights*-esque spirits.

'Now, I think you should be made aware of some of the politics of this place.' Her face is deadly serious, and I worry for a moment that this is some sort of Scottish initiation. 'There are those of us who are permanent Balmoral staff – you know, your standard, housekeeping, kitchen staff, garden staff. And there are the staff who travel with the household. Think Montagues and Capulets, if they were all trapped together on a remote island. And that is putting it politely. The staff that the royals bring always think they are superior, know the best way to run things, enjoy stepping on our toes, telling us how to do our jobs. And we detest them. But that doesn't stop all of the royal footmen getting off with half the housekeeping staff at the Ghillies Ball and refusing to talk about it again until the following summer.'

'The Ghillies Ball?' I ask through my amusement, more than enthralled to be privy to palace gossip that, for once, doesn't include me as its subject.

'You know? The annual ball for the family and the staff?' Excitement seeps from her. 'We all get really pissed and have a ceilidh with the king and queen! Surely you've heard of it?'

'Can't say I have. Although, I am very upset that I have been deprived of such an evening for so long.'

'Well Queen Victoria and Prince Albert started the tradition. It's essentially an evening for the royals and us staff to mingle as equals. My grandmother once danced with the crown prince, and she told us that story every Christmas until she died. It's a night where just about anything goes. Well, at least that's everyone's excuse for getting off with the people they have spent the summer swearing they hate.' She skips a little further down the hallway before stopping dead at the next window. The tall frame is almost double her height and floods her with light, illuminating the grin that grows across her face.

'What is it?' I ask tentatively, a little unnerved by the sudden look of mischief that crosses her face.

67

'Speaking of . . .' Sophie raises a cheeky eyebrow and gestures out of the window. 'Have you ever wondered why the Buchanan has a particular distaste for Jimmy, when he is perhaps the only fella in this place who I've never heard say a bad word against anyone?'

The two of them are where I saw them on the lawn last week. The groundskeeper with his familiar smile, the housekeeper with her scowl. As she chases his dog across the damp grass, I see that Mrs Buchanan's pinafore is stamped with muddied pawprints, and Jimmy is bent double with laughter. 'I had always thought it just part of her constitution,' I reply, intrigued. 'I thought she took the same unwelcoming tone with everyone.'

'No, you see, she does like to act as though she is miserable and scary. She might mother you, but with good intentions. Most of the time. No, with Jimmy it's different.' Sophie wiggles her eyebrows, and we watch as Mrs B shifts her attention from the dog, to Jimmy, pointing her bony finger at him as she unleashes her wrath.

'You don't mean . . .' I begin to understand the meaning of her dancing eyebrows and the delighted stare in her eye.

'Oh I do.' She can't control her laughter as it echoes through the stone halls.

'Mrs Buchanan, and . . . Jimmy?'

'Snogging in the billiards room. Caught them myself two years ago.' She looks so proud of herself as she tells the story. 'They've hated each other ever since.'

'Isn't she married?'

'Widowed. Few of the older lot say she used to be happier when her husband was alive. He was the fun one.

Stable master. Never said anything with a straight face. She got all uptight after he died apparently.'

A pang of pity rushes through me as I watch her now with Jimmy. A woman hardened against happiness. They say that to love is to be changed, but what happens when your greatest love is lost, and there's no way of being who you once were again? To have to go through life with your favourite part of yourself missing must be like relearning how to crawl as a caterpillar when you're already a fully-fledged butterfly.

Although I shan't be here long, I decide in that moment that I shall make it my mission to leave some semblance of a fairy tale behind in this lonely castle. If I am to return to London to spend forever with the love of my life in just five weeks, it's only right that I put this short time that I'm here to good use. Everyone deserves to be loved, even miserable old housekeepers whose faces have forgotten what it feels like to smile.

'Sophie . . .' It's my turn to look at her with a brazen grin. 'I think I've come up with an idea that may just help me pass my time here.'

'I reckon I'll like where you're going with this.'

Chapter 8

'Okay so usually after breakfast, the Buchanan heads into the scullery to read her *Take a Break* that she hides between the pages of the same copy of the *Times* that she's had since 2003.' Sophie sits on my bed as I pace up and down the room in front of her, tapping my finger against my chin. She seemingly forgot all about the tour of the castle as soon as the scheming began yesterday, and, though I appreciated knowing a little more about the place, I am more than happy with the diversion that has taken us almost seamlessly into the following day. As is she, by the way she lounges across my duvet with a grin. 'She's usually in there for about half an hour by herself before inspecting the kitchen and laundry.'

'And where is Jimmy at this time?' I stop pacing to ask her.

Sophie thinks about it for a moment, her face straining as though she's physically rifling through her brain. 'Well, he and Fraser usually head to the stables in the morning after Fraser has finished piping.'

'Fraser?' She nods. 'Perfect.' As if on cue, the carriage clock on the mantel ticks softly to 9 a.m. and I cross to the window.

As punctual as ever, he is already there, beneath the vines, assembling his instrument under his arms. For the first time since I arrived, I am waiting for him, and I steal a moment to watch him when he believes himself unperceived. He's deep in thought and his fingers twitch against his kilt, as though already playing the songs he has lined up in his mind. The serious expression on his face, lined by his furrowed brows, relaxes ever so slightly as he draws in a breath and releases it shakily. The thought of a man who is usually so composed calming his nerves beneath my window makes me smile, and I fantasise for a moment that he is a prince come to serenade me with a prettier instrument than the bagpipes.

Only when he looks up to take another breath for his opening note does he actually see me. The novelty of seeing me at all, let alone already fully dressed and ready for the day, seems to make him falter for a moment.

'Are you well, my lady?' He breaches his protocol to call to me first.

'I need your help.' Setting down his pipes without another second's hesitation, he marches down the garden path towards the castle entrance.

'Pipe Major Bell.' Fraser about-turns at the sound of my voice. 'Where are you going?'

'You need my help,' he replies bluntly.

'Well, yes.' He waits just long enough to hear my affirmation, before turning again and entering the castle.

'I just assumed it would take a little more convincing than that,' I babble to myself.

'What's going on?' Sophie asks as I retreat from the window.

'I believe Fraser is on his way up here.' I shrug, still unsure of what exactly it is that I want him for.

'Fraser? Fraser Bell? The piper?' Sophie's eyes widen and her face flushes.

'Is there another one?'

'Well, no, not that I know of.' Her brows knit together and the heel of her shoe taps against the rug as she bounces her knee nervously.

'Is there a problem?' I haven't yet seen her so ruffled as she picks at the hem of her dress.

'No, no, no problem. It's just Fraser Bell doesn't really socialise with us inside lot very often,' she whispers and tracks her eyes erratically across the room as though he is already hiding in the walls. 'I only ever see him alone or with Jimmy and the horses. I've been here half a decade and I don't know if he's ever said two words to me.'

'Well, that's perfect for us. If he can help us get Jimmy in the right position, we stand more chance of putting him in Buchanan's path.' I grin. My scheme is falling together.

'I, er, well, I went to school with his sister,' Sophie stammers out, as though revealing an embarrassing secret.

'Excellent?' I reply, a little confused, and am grateful when a firm knock finally sounds. 'That will be him.' Rushing to open the door, I don't fail to notice how Sophie straightens and smooths out her hair and dress.

When I reveal Fraser on the other side of the door, he

is stood to attention, hands firm at his sides, his uniform pressed perfectly against his frame.

'Are you well, my lady?' He repeats his initial question, his eyes flicking across my face and then scanning into the room behind me.

'I am quite well, thank you.' His attention darts back to me, his forehead creasing beneath his cap.

'You no longer require my help, ma'am? Not ill? Or in danger?' His chest rises and falls softly with each of his breaths.

'Danger? Christ, no.' I chuckle. The piper doesn't crack a smile. After pulling him by the wrist into my room, I close the door quickly before imparting our plan to him. 'We need your help setting up Mrs Buchanan and Jimmy.' Fraser seems to lose control of his expression for a moment as his face contorts in bewilderment.

'Hi.' Sophie breathes heavily and raises an awkward hand in a greeting before he can fully process my words. The single contraction paints her cheeks a brand-new shade of crimson as soon as it leaves her lips.

A confused Fraser nods in reply, and looks down at my hand wrapped around the cuff of his jacket. 'Is this a joke?'

'How is Eilidh?' Sophie covers her mouth as soon as she speaks, as though trying to stop any other words from slipping out.

'She's well, thank you,' Fraser answers politely, though still quite considerably perplexed.

Opening my mouth to speak again, I can't get out a word before Sophie is blabbering once again. 'We went to school together. I'm Sophie.'

'Aye, I know.'

'Wait, you know I went to school with your sister or you know my name? Did she tell you?'

'Of course I know your name, Sophie; we have worked together for four years.'

'Five, actually, but who's counting, right?' She chuckles awkwardly.

'Right, moving on from whatever *this* is . . .' I cast a side glance at Sophie and remind myself to return to this topic with her later in the day. 'Will you help us or not?'

'Sorry, ma'am, but I'm not exactly sure how I come into this?' Fraser looks between myself and Sophie, a glimmer of what almost looks like fear in his eye. 'I'm just here to play the bagpipes.'

'That's exactly what I need you to do.' Now it's Sophie's turn to look confused. 'Buchanan reads her magazine in the scullery because it's quiet, right?' Sophie nods as I continue reciting my plan. 'Well then, why don't we make sure that she gets absolutely no peace? And she has no choice but to take her reading to the garden? And . . . who else will be alone with her in the garden?'

'It won't work,' Fraser pipes up after I have given myself a little giddy round of applause at the climax of my plan. A little ruffled by my hard stare, he continues, 'Well, if you want her to cross paths with Jim, the maze will probably be your best shot, no? It's more secluded too.' Sophie and I share a glance as though neither of us can actually believe we have roped Fraser into this, and are both now champing at the bit to find out why he would choose to describe it as 'secluded'.

'How will we get them both into the maze?'

'It'll be easy enough. Jim spends most of his time in there at the moment, getting it ready for the king coming in August. He's become just a little obsessed, as the king's "brand-new thistle-shaped maze" has been the talk of all of the royal circles since they planted it last year.'

'He might not have to be so anxious. I, thankfully, haven't heard a peep in any of my circles.' I snigger, amused at the idea of Jimmy taking a pair of scissors to the hedgerows to perfect each manicured point of the giant thistle.

'Aye, well, if you'd like to get him alone, then the maze is where he will be.'

'I, for one, think that's a brilliant idea.' Sophie grins at Fraser before turning back to me. 'Mrs B will do anything to make sure things are perfect for the family coming for their holidays, especially when it involves bossing old Jimmy around.'

'That's settled then.' Moving to the window, I can just about make out the tops of the yews that have not a single leaf out of place. 'Now we just need to figure out how we get Buchanan to actually go inside the maze.'

'Oh, if there's any sign of Jimmy, she won't be able to help herself. I reckon we can use Flo to our advantage too.' Sophie joins me in looking out of the window.

'Flo?'

'Jimmy's dog,' Fraser answers for her as he draws up to my other side and the three of us watch as the man and his dog stride across the lawn, the latter running off ahead before circling back obediently when called.

After another half an hour ironing out the details, the plan is finally set. Sophie and I watch Fraser from across the garden as he takes his position just outside of the window to the scullery.

'Sophie?' I whisper to her as Fraser begins his opening melody. She hums in reply, keeping her doe eyes firmly locked onto the piper. 'He's great, isn't he?' I encourage, sensing another match on the cards.

'Who?' she asks, though still unable to tear her eyes from him.

'Fraser, of course.'

'Yes, yes, brilliant. I can't believe he actually agreed.'

'Handsome too, right?'

'The whole family are, they're like the hot Hollywood version of what everyone thought Scottish royalty looked like.' Finally tearing her eyes away, she looks at me with an animated glow across her cheeks. 'They all have that dark red hair too, like sunlight through a ruby.'

There it is – all the proof I need is right there in her dilated pupils and cherry-brushed cheeks. Since Sophie has been nothing but good to me, it's only fair that I repay the favour: by the end of the summer she and Fraser will be my most successful match to date. If there is one good thing I can do whilst I'm here, it's bringing her a little happiness. From this day forth, I'll make it my mission to get to know everything there is to know about Fraser Bell, find out what makes him tick, what makes him smile, what will make him fall in love.

Before I have the chance to comb over the fine details of my plan, Mrs Buchanan comes huffing out of the kitchen door, shaking her head in Fraser's direction, her tattered copy of the *Times* tucked under her arm.

'She's going the wrong way,' I whisper to Sophie as Mrs B comes strutting around the path in the opposite direction to the maze.

'Leave it with me. If there is one thing the Buchanan hates more than Jimmy, it's being pestered on her break.' Sophie stands up from behind the bush we are crouched in, brushes down her dress and strides towards her with a bounce in her step. 'Mrs B?' She waves a manic hand in the housekeeper's direction. With the speed and ease of a reflex, Mrs Buchanan draws her phone out of her pocket, holds up a silencing finger and turns in the opposite direction to take the call that miraculously came at the sight of an interruption.

Stifling a giggle from the bushes, I almost give the game away when Sophie turns around to shoot me a wink and a thumbs up. Once our target has moved out of sight, I emerge from my hiding place and rejoin Team Cupid in the middle of the garden. Fraser's playing slowly diminuendos until the peaceful silence is restored to the Balmoral gardens.

'Those bagpipes have never sounded so sweet,' I tease. 'Who knew they'd actually have a use.'

'My lady, I'm going to say this in the politest way possible.' Sophie turns to me with uncharacteristic seriousness. 'Only those of us who have spent too many PE lessons at school being forced to learn Scottish country dancing as the popular kids all laugh when their pal has to hold your hand for Strip the Willow are allowed to slag off traditional Scottish music.'

I hold my hands up in surrender. Both Sophie and

Fraser chuckle and the nervous thumping in my chest quickly subsides.

'We'd better make sure Flo is in position.' Sophie returns to her usual jolly demeanour as she tries to peek around the side of the house for any sign of our targets.

'Do you still require my services or may I be excused, ma'am?' Fraser straightens and returns to his usual air of seriousness.

A little taken aback, a small part of me aches at the thought that he has only joined us this morning as he believed it to be some royal order. 'You're welcome to join us as a friend?' As soon as the words leave me, I know he would only ever accept so as to not upset his bosses. I wonder for a moment if Sophie too is only here for fear of her job or reputation.

'I have some other duties to attend to. I work in the stables in the afternoon, ma'am, and the horses will need me since Jim is in the maze.'

'Very well. Thank you for your services, Piper Major. You are dismissed.' The excitement of my scheme seems to dwindle as Fraser bows and marches back down the garden path and out of sight.

'Shall we?' Sophie interrupts my ruminations as she shakes a packet of custard creams in front of me. Nodding wordlessly, we follow back along in the direction that Mrs Buchanan took off in and tread carefully along the limestone walkway.

From behind some of the perfectly manicured foliage, we spy the housekeeper sat in one of the shaded corners of the castle muttering to herself as she skims through her magazine.

'Okay, here's the plan,' I whisper to Sophie. 'You lure Flo out of the maze for just a moment with the biscuits, just as I tell Mrs B that there is a dog digging up the lawn and causing trouble. If all goes as predicted, she will storm right over, find Jimmy, and if there was something about one another they couldn't ignore once, it has to still be there now. We shall leave it up to them for the rest.'

Sophie nods her head like a solider given an order to fix bayonets and scampers across the garden, her custard creams clutched in her hand. With as much poise as twenty-two years of pretending to be someone else has readied me for, I strut over to the housekeeper and unleash my best finishing-school acting.

'Do you get many strays around here, Mrs Buchanan?' Though I keep my tone as casual and level as possible, she snaps her attention from her magazine so quickly that one would think I've told her that Hamish the horse is walking on his hind legs singing 'Zadok the Priest'.

'Strays?' she rushes out. 'Stray what?' Scanning across the lawn, she is half hunting spaniel herself before she regains her composure. 'My lady,' she adds as an afterthought.

'Why, stray dogs of course.' I give her one of my best jeering Kitty titters, and Mrs Buchanan leaps up from her seat.

'Where? Where is she?' Scanning across the garden again, she rushes back along the path and I have to trail behind her.

'Last I saw, she was digging up the flowerbeds near the maze.'

'No, no, no.' She hums to herself as she redirects and

storms towards the maze. 'I'll have that eejit's guts for garters.'

It doesn't take us long to see the mess. Flo is nuzzling in the loose earth and every now and again crunches one of the concealed biscuits between her jaws. Out of the corner of my eye, I spy Sophie, crouched behind a white stone water feature giving me a sly thumbs up.

'Mr Campbell!' Mrs Buchanan screeches as she rushes over to Flo. 'Mr Campbell.'

The groundskeeper rushes from the maze as fast as his wobbly legs can carry him, his eyes wide and panicked at the sound of her call.

'Mary? What is it, hen?' He places a tender hand on her elbow and she snatches it away as though stung by his touch.

'What is it? What is it? Your mindless mutt is what it is.' She points at Flo who sits obediently now at her master's feet, a mud-smeared grin on her face. 'The king will be here next week and look at this!' She points at the decimated marigolds that are now littered across the pathway. 'His pride and joy!'

Mrs B scrambles to her hands and knees and attempts to shove the shredded petals back into the soil but her efforts are futile.

'Mary, please. Let me.' Jimmy kneels beside her and tenderly takes the roots from between her dirtied fingernails. 'I don't know what's come over her – it's not like her at all.' Jimmy gives Flo a long, sad stare and the sight of all three of them, filthy and miserable, causes my gut to tremble.

The feeling doesn't subside. Mrs Buchanan grows more agitated, as Jimmy's shoulders round even more in a defeated hunch and all I desire is to go back in time and never have come up with this foolish plan.

'Please,' I splutter forth, 'allow me.' Dropping to my knees beside Jimmy only causes the expression of panic to deepen on his face.

'Lady Alice!' Mrs Buchanan cries. 'See here, Mr Campbell, what has become because of your beast! You have Princess Alexandra's granddaughter knee-deep in filth!' She lets out an exacerbated cry and runs her hands over her face, leaving behind a thick streak of mud.

'My lady, there you are!' Sophie rushes out of her hiding place, a guilty expression on her face. 'I have been looking for you. Come on, we must be off.' She tries to pull me to my feet but my shame keeps me rooted.

'I just need to help—'

'Ma'am.' Sophie gives me a pointed look and tugs at my wrist as gently as she can whilst still sending me the message that I must move now. 'It is quite urgent.'

Looking back once more at the chaos I have created, a coldness spreads through me until I no longer fight against Sophie and allow her to drag me away.

Chapter 9

The guilt continues to gnaw away at me for the rest of the day. Watching Jimmy from my window, replanting until long after the sun sets, unable to even look at Flo, makes me feel utterly rotten.

Sophie assured me that I would only make things worse by getting myself involved again now, as even if I admitted to my meddling, both parties and their pride would never allow me to take any of the blame. The self-repulsion only mounts when night falls and both Fraser and Sophie join Jim in the flowerbeds once they know they're free from the prying eyes and bitter tongue of Mrs B.

'*I have no idea who you've become.*' My mother's words ring round and round in my head and for the first time in my life, I actually agree with her. In the last few months, it's as though I've lost the little grip I had on my life and everything has just seemed to spiral out of control. It's not as though until now I have been particularly prosperous, just clawing my way through the days for as long as I can remember. Now even that doesn't seem to be enough. Feeling blistered and bruised, I'm surprised I can still breathe correctly. Part of me is almost disappointed that I still can.

That thought only makes me hate myself more. Here I am, sitting in a bloody castle, with my haircut alone costing more than a family of six's weekly shop, the maker of my own misery, and I'm feeling sorry for myself whilst my friends are sent to clear up all of the messes I make. It's repulsive.

Rifling through the clothes I have managed to accumulate from all of the lost property across the castle, I dig out a pair of jeans and a woollen jumper that have been thrust to the back of the drawers.

Sneaking my way through the castle (finally on a good errand this time), I steal a pair of wellies at the kitchen door and make my way across the grass in the twilight hellbent on fixing my own mistakes. Drawing close to Fraser and Sophie, I can hear their soft chattering whilst still remaining unperceived. My confidence faltering for a moment, I stop and listen to what they're saying. The thought of eavesdropping sits sour in my stomach but as soon as their voices come into range, I hold my breath to hear.

'It's nice to have a bit of excitement around here for once, isn't it?' Sophie whispers. Fraser doesn't reply, only looks at her dirt-covered skirt and face. 'Yes, okay, I wouldn't say that *this* is particularly exciting but having *something* new around here is what we've needed for so long.'

'Trouble, you mean?' is Fraser's quiet response.

'She's not trouble.'

'She causes it. Seemingly without trying.'

I realise that it's me they're talking about. It's nothing new – I've had the world gossiping about me for decades – but something about Fraser and Sophie discussing me makes me itch.

'Jim says that her mum was exactly the same. She sent your gran round the bend back in the day.'

Well surely that part can't be about me. My mother and I have never so much as had a similarly positioned freckle in common, let alone her behaviour resembling mine in any way.

'For years we've washed the same beds, played the same tunes, been to parties with the same people. Trouble is exactly what we needed. The castle may be perfect and pristine, but the culture of the place is crumbling. I think she will be good for us.' Her words warm me and calm the turmoil that was threatening to boil over in my stomach.

'She isn't here for us. Just remember who she is, Sophie. She will never and can never be a friend.'

Fraser's Scottish drawl renews my pain, and the desire to denounce all that I am cuts through me and leaves me rooted on the spot. Though it hurts, I can't stop myself from listening.

'I know that,' Sophie replies, but her tone has shifted and she sounds deflated. 'She will have plenty of friends like her; she won't need us when she leaves. But I think she needs us right now, as much as we need her.'

I think of Kitty, Hugo, even Barty, and I realise I would

not associate a single one of their names with the word 'friendship'. People like Kitty don't do friendships, they do partnerships. Every one of their relationships are formed with the single object of gaining something, bettering themselves, their families, their businesses. In fact, all of my relationships are 'give and take'. Even my father; I take his financial support and family name, and in return, he gets a daughter he can use to expand his empire, or sell the image of his family that he wishes to portray. At least, that's likely what he hoped for and is now bitterly disappointed. At least I have Atticus. I have nothing to give him except my heart, and he's held on to that since we first met, and I have possessed his just as long. Perhaps he is the only real friend I have.

'She will forget us quickly enough once the summer ends.' Fraser's voice cuts through the moment of silence that had fallen across the garden.

Almost determined to prove them wrong, I finally regain control over my body and decide I have eavesdropped long enough. I wander into their line of sight as though only just stumbling across them.

'Lady Alice!' Sophie is startled when her eyes finally land upon me. 'What are you doing here?'

'I'm here to fix the problems that I've caused.' Sophie opens her mouth and begins to protest, but I cut her off quickly. 'I absolutely insist and shall not change my mind.'

'If those are the lady's orders, we must oblige,' Fraser drones, thrusting his trowel into the loose earth.

'No, there is no order, no obligation. You may both walk away and leave me to it if you so desire, or wake the house to have Mrs Buchanan berate me. I am here, as an equal, and perhaps one day as a friend, if you both shall have me?'

Sophie and Fraser look at one another, the latter's cheeks pinking at the knowledge that I may have heard a little of their conversation. The former only smiles, hands me a pair of polka-dot gardening gloves, and pats the space of grass beside her.

Getting straight to work replanting, I speak without looking at either of them. 'This really wasn't exactly how I envisaged it going,' I say, hazarding a chuckle. 'I'm sorry.'

'It's okay,' Sophie says quickly. 'You had good intentions.'

Fraser stays silent.

'I hope Jimmy is okay,' I whisper after Sophie tells me how the ageing groundskeeper had called it a night just before I joined them, complaining of a sore back.

'It will take much more than the Buchanan to trouble Jimmy.' Fraser speaks for the first time after a prolonged silence. 'I'm just not sure that Balmoral is ready for love.'

Sophie and I catch a glimpse of one another, a shared look of surprise crossing each of our faces.

'This place was built out of love,' I can't help but gush once I have gathered a little of my composure. 'Prince Albert purchased the place, redesigned it and had it rebuilt himself all because it pleased his wife. Queen Victoria loved the Highlands, and he loved her, so he created this to be the perfect Scottish paradise. Every inch of this place was created in the image of love.' I grow more and more excited as I recall the little that I already know about the place.

Clambering to my feet, I get a little overexcited as I stare at the grey stone castle shimmering in the moonlight.

Sophie and Fraser watch me, an amused glint crossing the former's face. 'The thing everyone gets wrong about love is they expect it to happen miraculously. Sometimes it's written in the stars, but sometimes fate is actually just hard work and a little meddling.'

'Shouldn't it be for the couple to decide if they wish to be in love?' Fraser is surprisingly serious but this is the one topic in which I don't doubt myself.

'Love creeps up on us all so slowly – there is no decision about it. If one has to decide to be in love, it is simply a practicality. No, what I mean is that sometimes one needs a little push in the right direction, to untangle that self-doubt from the inexplicable yearning and to finally have the gall to take what one truly desires. Romeo and Juliet fell in love but without the help of the nurse or the friar, how could they ever have done anything about it? Who knows what would have happened to the star-crossed lovers had they never had help.'

'Do you not think they might not have died if their teenage crush was just left to fizzle out?' Sophie swoops in with the reality check. 'I'd say their help was actually pretty irresponsible.'

Fraser and I chuckle in unison.

'She has got a point to be fair.' Fraser's face lines in amusement as he battles against releasing his laughter.

'Okay, okay, maybe it was a bad example. But my point still stands: fate always needs a hand and Balmoral should always be full of love.'

When all of the grandfather clocks in the house chime midnight at ever so slightly different times, the three of us call it a night. After saying goodbye to Fraser at the kitchen door, Sophie and I leave our muddied boots by the pantry and creep back through the corridors before parting ways at the stairs. Sophie goes down; I must go up.

When I am alone again in my room, before the haunting thoughts have time to return, I get to work on this tale's auxiliary plot. Already, in failing to bring together my intended protagonists, I have mistakenly brought the supporting cast closer together. For the first time in years, Fraser and Sophie were alone and grasped the opportunity of developing their passing acquaintance and unrequited crush into the beginnings of something rather more exciting. Now, all I need to do is keep up the momentum.

If it's my mistakes that have forced them together, then perhaps the way forward isn't to curb my mischief, but rather redirect it.

'Sophie?' I find the young maid in the dining room the following morning, polishing the cutlery on the table. She drops the silver knife in her hand, and it clatters against a neighbouring plate as she greets me with a friendly grin, then quickly rushes to inspect the fine china for any signs of chipping.

'Good morning, my lady. Did you sleep okay?' she enquires politely.

'Same as usual,' I reply, 'I just about reach the deep sleep phase and then Pipe Major Fraser Bell keeps his time better than Big Ben and I'm awoken to his screeching. I at least thought the excitement of yesterday would have made him oversleep by a few minutes but alas!'

At the mention of his name, Sophie lays down her cloth and cutlery carefully to hand me her full attention.

'He is rather annoying for that. But Mrs B runs this place down to the second and when I hear him playing for you in the mornings, I know that's my cue to stop whatever I'm doing and have the breakfast room prepared. He's quite an effective alarm to be honest.'

'What time does your day begin?' I ask, realising I don't actually know too much of what Sophie is *supposed* to be doing here aside from babysitting me.

'Well, contractually it's six, but Mrs B likes us all up and mustering in the kitchens at five-forty-five, just to leave a buffer for any silly business.' Shame curdles in me, like a drink turned sour in my gut. Whilst I moan about not quite achieving my nine-hour sleep target, Sophie is already on her fourth chore of the day. She would never be able to lose a whole week to her bed, forget how to function, disregard every one of her responsibilities. She must think me as spoilt as Buchanan does, except she stands here, right now, her smiles bringing me comfort.

'What was your dream, Sophie?' I see my question takes her off guard. It takes me by surprise just as much.

'It was an odd one to be honest,' she begins as I grow increasingly intrigued. 'I was hoovering in my old school hall and all of a sudden this man came in and just poured a big vat of chip shop gravy all over the floor.'

I allow her to finish without interruption, and then

the maid shakes her head, as though her unconscious annoyance has returned. 'I meant your life's dream, Sophie,' I say, chuckling.

'Oh, aye, right.' Blushing, she pauses to muse for a moment. 'I haven't put much thought into it recently.' Her slim fingers twirl the ends of her hair. 'I used to want to open my own youth club, in the village. I didn't have much to do growing up; we didn't live anywhere busy enough for them to bother building anything cool nearby. Don't get me wrong, getting out in the fresh air, building dens in the woods, swimming in the lochs was great, but come winter, it would've been great to have something to do with your pals indoors.'

'What did you do instead?' I ask, and she looks at me as if the answer is obvious.

'Caught a lot of colds.'

Chapter 10

'Why the bagpipes?' My sudden question startles Fraser and he drops the hoof pick he was holding as he swivels around to find me at the stable door. Brushing his hands down his trousers, he fusses with the sleeves of his flannel shirt that he has rolled to his elbows in an attempt to straighten himself out.

Though it is I who sought him out, I swallow at the sight of him, my mouth suddenly dry upon stepping past his threshold. Trying to think nothing of it, aside from questioning whether I have acquired a hay allergy in the last few days, as my neck begins to itch, I clear my throat in an effort to get the piper to speak.

'Ma'am.' He bows his head, still tugging at his sleeve.

'Fraser.' I give him a pointed look, and he is flustered again.

'Yes, ma'am?'

'What is my name?'

'Lady Alice? Ma'am?'

I chuckle at his bumbling attempts to figure out which title shall please me most whilst knowing that I wish for him to call me by anything but. Fraser's pale cheeks flush a deeper shade of red. I continue, 'Now, Fraser, tell me what made you choose the bagpipes.'

Moving across the stable, my dress drags in the hay as I approach the mare Fraser had been caring for when I arrived. I hold out my palm, and the mare presses her pink speckled nose against it before allowing me to slide my fingers through the thick strands of her mane. Fraser soon joins me in rubbing a wide hand across her flank, and the affectionate horse presses her head hard against him in encouragement. The piper visibly relaxes and lets out a contented sigh before speaking again.

'My dad held this position before me. When I was a wain, he would be practising all hours of the day to be perfect for the late queen. Drove my mum round the bend. Made it even worse when he taught me everything he knew, so even when Dad was working, I'd be at home skirling away.' Thoughts of a tiny Fraser, with a shock of red hair, hopping around the house with bagpipes the same size as him, make me smile and I reach for a brush to hide my grin.

'She will love you for that. Proper spoiled lass is this one.' Fraser chuckles as I slide the brush down the already pristine coat. 'You're just a wee princess aren't you, DeeDee?' He presses his forehead to her muzzle and plants a kiss against her nose that makes her snicker in approval.

'You always wanted to be a piper?' I ask, hidden from his view by DeeDee.

Fraser sighs so softly that I'm surprised I hear it at all. 'I joined the cavalry, initially.' He doesn't elaborate further, and for a moment I stand in silence deciding whether to ask him more.

'The army?' I say to fill the gap, though from his position here I already knew that was his basic role. 'Would you ever go back to more active service stuff? Instead of this ceremonial posting I mean.'

'In all honesty,' he begins, his cheeks flushing, 'I didn't join the cavalry to join the army. It was the only job with horses that someone like me could get a decent wage for. I reckon I'd have run off with the circus when I was sixteen if they let me ride a horse for most of the day.'

I'm unsurprised at his reply as I watch him now. In his presence, DeeDee seems at ease, perfectly tranquil, as though under a spell from his touch. Perhaps such magic is the reason why I feel so at home in his company. Falling into a comfortable silence, I picture him, galloping through the glens, racing through valleys, smiling into the breeze. The image is so pure, so natural, that suddenly the stuffy uniform and bagpipes don't suit him anymore.

'So why are you now startling young women out of their beauty sleep with your bagpipes?' I chuckle, trying to inject a little humour into what has become a pretty serious conversation. 'Your dream doesn't seem too crazy to me. Why give it up?' I can't help myself. When I look at Fraser with DeeDee, I see a man where he belongs. Though my question is brash, bordering on rude, I can't stop myself from speaking.

Fraser is silent. Only when he moves further around

DeeDee and is totally obscured from my view does he speak again. 'My position here was only supposed to be temporary. I was brought in last minute five summers ago to cover for my dad whilst he recovered from a sudden illness.'

He doesn't need to say any more. Fraser's prolonged presence here fills in all of the other gaps for me. My gut stirs with pity and, almost instinctively, I rest my hand on top of his where he has it frozen mid stroke along the mare's back.

'I'm sorry,' is the only pitiful response I can stir and Fraser draws his hand away at the sound of my voice, as though its sudden interruption brings him back into the room.

'Is this your dream?' Fraser asks me this time, shifting his expression, as though switching out the sad seriousness for a playful smile.

'Standing ankle-high in horse dung in a Scottish stable? I can't say it was ever one of my life goals.'

He laughs softly and the sound warms the chill of the Caledonian twilight.

'You know what I mean.' The piper seems to relax as he manoeuvres himself to stand before me.

'This is every little girl's dream, isn't it? Being a royal?'

No one has ever asked me such a thing before.

'Maybe.' Fraser's eyes track across my face, trying to decipher my expression that even I am struggling to comprehend. 'It's always seemed a wee bit stuffy to me.' His candour is a relief. For the first time in a few weeks, I feel as though I don't have to think about what to say, or how to phrase it, or how to stand as I deliver it.

'I have everything I could ever need.' I think for a moment, and Fraser leaves the silence undisturbed until I am ready to continue. 'But it does get a little lonely, I suppose.'

'Nae shit.' Fraser slaps a hand over his mouth, shocked at his own expression. Only when I laugh, does he visibly relax. 'Sorry,' he babbles with pinked cheeks. 'I just meant that I'm sure it's impossible to have a genuine conversation, isn't it? So many rules, so many mistakes to make.'

'I know that all too well.' I half-laugh, and then am reminded of my intentions for coming here. 'Sophie has been a welcome respite from it all. I don't think she is capable of having a false conversation.'

Fraser hums. 'She's a good lass.' Then his face cracks with a smile. 'My dad loved her, and her gran. She was at both of their funerals, and somehow, she still managed to make everyone smile.'

His words only make me surer than ever that I've finally got something right. Sophie deserves this; they both do. No matter how badly I can't stop watching his strong hands hauling around stable equipment, or can't stop peeking behind my curtains to catch a glimpse of him in the mornings, Fraser shall be Sophie's Prince Charming, and I shall return to marry my own in just a few weeks.

'So, what *is* your dream?' Fraser persists. 'I told you mine; it's only fair.' He shrugs with a cheeky grin.

How do I tell him that the thought of having a dream has never crossed my mind? What would he think if I told him my life was planned out for me before I was even born so I was never taught to dream? My dreams are childish.

My only dreams are to find someone to love; my only desire is to just be happy.

Looking about the stable, I wonder what I can tell him. Fraser Bell doesn't need to hear my self-pity. It is clear he has had enough hurt in his own life.

'My dream is to see a foal,' I reply, returning his smile. I know it isn't the answer he was looking for, but the light in his eyes tells me he doesn't mind. 'I have only ever seen fully trained adult horses. They come to my family perfect. I'd like to see those first weeks of a foal's life where they're stumbling around on their gangly legs, trying to figure out how to run.'

Before he has the chance to ask more questions, I turn to leave and track back through the hay-covered floor to the stable doors. As I go to step over the threshold, I have just one niggling thought in my mind that I haven't quite managed to shake from last night: *Jim says that her mum was exactly the same.*

'Fraser?' I begin to speak, preparing to ask him what he meant. The piper ceases all he is doing at the sound of his name, and his undivided attention rests on me so heavily that the weight of his gaze is like a boot on my chest, making it almost impossible to breathe.

'My lady?' he presses, his words constricting my airflow even further.

Unable to admit to my eavesdropping, unable to form any coherent words at all, I stride from the stable without another breath and rush down to the gatehouse to find my answers from the source.

What on earth just came over me? It was like for a

moment I had lost all sight of myself; all sense had flown out of the window and Fraser Bell – his plaid shirt, his arms, his tender drawl – was rendering me thunderstruck.

Physically shaking such treacherous thoughts from my head, I reach Jimmy's little house, finally composed enough to find the words to ask him all about my mother's history with this place. Before I reach the door, however, the sight before me forces me to stop dead, and sends a little excited tingle bouncing from my fingers to my toes. Mrs Buchanan stands outside of the cottage, peering into one of the front windows, chewing nervously on her lip.

When she finally spots me, she flees from the scene before I can so much as utter a greeting.

'Mrs Buchanan?' I call after her as she attempts to slip inconspicuously into the treeline. The housekeeper stiffens, wedged between an oak and an overgrown rhododendron, giving me enough time to catch up to her and see her flushed cheeks up close.

'My lady.' She gives an uneasy nod all whilst attempting to unhook her skirt from a particularly poky branch.

'Do you require any help?' She tugs again at the pleats before releasing a defeated huff and nodding reluctantly.

With a little of my aid, she is soon free and stands before me with her harsh face dappled with a blush. 'Thank you, ma'am.'

'Were you here to see Jimmy?' I ask and her composure is quickly ironed out.

'I am not here to *see* anyone, my lady. I was simply coming to tell Mr Campbell that his, um, services are required in the orchard this afternoon.' She struggles to hold eye contact and, for the first time, I think I am seeing her without her scales and armour.

'His services?' I press, intrigued at this whole spectacle.

'Yes, my lady. The apples are beginning to drop so we need them tidied before the king returns, and the wasps make themselves at home.'

'I see.' Tapping a finger against my chin, my mind swirls with new ideas. There is no way that I was wrong about those two, and Mrs Buchanan's bashful eyes and slightly glossed lips just prove that. 'Well, I was just going along to see Jimmy, perhaps we can catch him together?' I know she can't refuse me; she is contractually obliged to bend to my whims. Usually, I'd feel guilty for such a fact, but my desire for positive mischief far outweighs it today.

The disinclination is written on her face but still she follows me back through the clearing to Jimmy's stone gatehouse. Chapping the door loudly, it's Flo who answers first with a defensive bark, and soon Jimmy's gruff telling-off quiets her. As soon as the door is swung open and he sees us both, however, his tone quickly changes.

'Lady Alice!' He grins and pats me on the top of my arm. 'What a pleasure and privilege.'

'Good afternoon, Jimmy, how are you?' It's impossible to not return the smile that still shines from him as he tries to stop Flo from charging us down and smothering us with welcome kisses.

'All the better for seeing your beautiful face. And you brought Mary with you too.' He gives me a cheeky wink. 'To what do I owe the pleasure?'

'I am here strictly on business, Mr Campbell, not

pleasure.' Mrs Buchanan's hard exterior returns, though Jimmy still gazes upon her with his characteristic softness.

'When you love what you do, Mary hen, all business is pleasure.'

The housekeeper makes no attempt to hide the way she rolls her eyes. 'I need you to pick up the rotting fruit in the orchard.'

'You spoil me.' Jimmy grins.

Huffing, Mrs Buchanan turns to walk away. 'I expect to see it looking perfect before dinner tonight. Bring any of the salvageable fruit to the kitchen and I shall have the cook make a pie.'

'It's a date,' Jimmy calls as she returns along the path with a hurried step.

'It most certainly is not,' she calls, without stopping to look back.

'Always playing hard to get that one.' Jimmy titters under his breath playfully. 'Did you want to come in for a cup of tea, my lady?' he adds, stepping aside and allowing Flo to give me the full force of her fuss.

'I'd love nothing more.' I cross the threshold and note that the small cottage is exactly as I'd expect. With low wooden beams across the ceiling, the place is thick with all kinds of plants and greenery. Mismatched armchairs are dotted around the living room, all facing Flo's bed in front of the open fire, with no television set to be seen. The only thing that seems to use any electricity at all is his radio plugged in on the sideboard, which hums quiet tinny Gaelic tunes around the small space. A cabinet of old photographs takes pride of place in the very centre of the room, positioned to be the first thing one sees as one enters. The multitude of sepia faces greet one with beaming smiles and Jimmy's same jolly gaze. It's a beautiful little home, with his character and his love woven into the tartan throws, and every knick-knack and trinket.

Taking a seat in one of the armchairs, I take a moment to really soak in my surroundings.

'Sorry about the mess,' Jimmy says shyly. 'No room to swing a cat in this place,' he adds apologetically, although all I can think for just a moment is how much beauty there is in a space so small. Where the furniture is so close it feels like a caress, like the very house itself is constantly reaching out to offer you affection. There is no empty space here; every inch is filled with a memory, or something that Jimmy once found endearing enough to bring home. Even the clutter tells a story. A half-dissected train set is piled in a corner; clearly, he had made an attempt to fix it, but got waylaid and it was forgotten for a moment. It's the first time I've been in a house and known what the word 'homely' actually means. It's personal, it's comforting, and it is a place dusted with happiness.

Jimmy returns from the kitchen, an old kettle in hand. 'How do you take it?' He shakes the scratched appliance and its contents slosh.

'Milk, two sugars please,' I say, and he toddles off to the kitchen, before taking the seat opposite me to wait for it to boil on the stove.

'Now, what can I do for you, hen?' Jimmy gives me the tender look of an aged grandfather.

'First of all, I wish to apologise. It was my fault that Flo was in the flowers. I never meant to get you in trouble.' Chewing on my lip, I watch Jimmy nervously for any sign of anger, but it never comes. He only raises his eyebrows for a split second, then shrugs nonchalantly as though he has already gotten over it.

'Oh hush. Never you mind any of that.' He chuckles a soothing titter. 'Anything else on your mind?'

I pause for a moment, thinking of how I can phrase my question. 'I overheard something the other day and I just wanted to ask you about it. If you don't mind?' Jimmy's smile falls ever so slightly as a mild crease of concern crosses his brow.

'On you go.' He nods.

'Has my mother been to Balmoral?' I speak quickly, and once it comes out it I feel silly that it ever felt weighty at all.

'Oh of course, several times. Both of your parents used to come for a weekend in the summer when your grandmother was alive, God rest her.'

'Am I anything like my mother?' is the real question that I can't help but squeak out. Jimmy takes a moment's breath and leans back in his armchair, his eyes tracing over my face.

'Well, there was one time when she was here on her honeymoon. She must have been about your age—' he begins but is cut off by the piercing squeal of the kettle in the kitchen, and just in case we hadn't already been deafened by it, Flo gives a loud bark to draw our attention to it. 'Ah, tea. Give me one moment, lass.'

He returns a few moments later with a rattling tea

tray and hands me a mug with the words 'I'm sexy and I mow it' painted on it alongside a rather pretty likeness of a lawnmower. Taking the handle, I thank Jimmy as he returns to his armchair.

'Where were we?' he witters, offering me a biscuit before dunking one of his own in his tea.

'My mother?' I remind him, my gut stirring as I attempt to predict what he's going to say. What if he says that we are alike? But what if we're nothing alike? My body can't seem to decide which outcome is more anxiety-inducing, and the bile rising in my throat means I have to leave my half-eaten Bourbon on the coffee table.

'Ah yes, your mother was ever such a character.' Jimmy looks off at his cabinet of photos with an absent smile. 'I'm surprised she sent you here after her honeymoon. I was always under the impression that she hated the place.'

'That will be the exact reason why she sent me here.' I can't hide the sadness that seeps into my voice, though I try and cover it with an eyeroll.

'Mrs Buchanan would probably be the better person to ask. If I remember correctly, they became quite friendly over that summer. She wasn't the housekeeper then; she was a relatively new maid. They were practically inseparable.' He smiles as though remembering both stern women in their carefree youth. 'Much like yourself and young Miss Chorley.'

My mother and Mrs Buchanan? Did they bond over their shared love of misery? Or who can make the most people wince with just one churlish look? I can't imagine either of them as 'friendly', let alone with one another. He must have made a mistake, misremembered or something.

Jimmy doesn't elaborate any further, and I can tell from the way he quickly begins to talk about his allotment that he is trying to change the subject. After we finish our cups of tea and his gardening chat, the groundskeeper suddenly remembers the orders of the housekeeper. Apologising profusely, he takes his flat cap and dog down to the orchard, leaving me to take the long walk back to the house alone.

Left alone to ponder Jimmy's careful words, I realise how little of my mother I actually know. Knowing only her sternness and cold shoulder, just the thought of her in this context, having friendly words with anyone, let alone a member of staff, feels foreign. Jimmy definitely has it confused; he must be thinking of someone else.

This is why I like fairy tales: the binaries. It is easier to understand the world when it's black and white. Shades of grey only make things confusing. One is either good or evil. My mother can't have been both. It would be like finding out the wolf from *Little Red Riding Hood* used to be a paediatric nurse: it just wouldn't make any sense.

Chapter 11

'Phase two, Jimmy and Buchanan.' A week later, I find Sophie in one of the guest bedrooms, preparing the fresh linen, and I join her in stretching the sheet across the mattress and tucking it. Despite trying my hardest to make sure not a wrinkle is left on display, Sophie still has to come to my side and redo it.

'Are you sure?' Sophie looks at me from beneath her thick brows, her usually bright irises dulled with a hint of concern. 'It's just that it didn't exactly go to plan last time . . .'

Thinking back to the maze fiasco, the way our previous attempt at matchmaking ended in more arguments and resentment, a knot of guilt pulls tightly in my stomach. 'I've read enough books to know that things have to get worse before they get better.' I push down the feeling and bulldoze on. 'They are in love. I have never been more certain of anything. If they aren't, then I know nothing of the word.' Reminded of her blushed cheeks and glossed lips, peering into Jimmy's windows only last week, I am surer than ever that I am not barking up the wrong tree here.

A muffled voice interrupts us from the other side of the window. Mrs Buchanan fusses around the garden, ordering about furniture and any poor member of staff who dares get in her way.

Tomorrow is the day that the king arrives, and the first item on his agenda is the pheasant hunt. Various high-ranking guests are also supposed to be filtering in and out so, of course, the whole household is on red alert and Mrs B has been even more assiduous than usual. All week she has been barking orders left, right, and centre, having things dusted, polished, and repolished.

Having hardly heard a peep from anyone this week, I trail behind Sophie like a needy toddler lingers in their mother's shadow as she continues all of her various jobs across the room. She thrusts a basket of bath salts towards me. I take it obediently and am subsequently loaded up like a packhorse, one item at a time until I become her walking, talking cleaning trolley.

'Mrs B gets particularly crabbit this time of year, Alice. Maybe stick the matchmaking on hold for a wee while eh?' She shakes out a tartan throw with such ferocity that I almost feel sorry for the thing.

'One last attempt and then I'll set my sights elsewhere.' Shifting a decorative pillow from the top of the basket, I give her my most childlike pleading look and she gives me a pointed one in return. I have less than a month until I am gone, less than a month until the shareholders' meeting, less than a month to bring everyone else love whilst I wait to return to mine. With another week passed without word from Atticus, I need this distraction more than ever.

'What did you have in mind?' Sophie sets down her duster and faces me, arms folded, a curious expression lifting her brow.

'Well, yourself and Fraser each accompany the Buchanan and Jimmy respectively. The former in the kitchen as she prepares the afternoon tea, and the latter on the hunt. Both of you spend the morning telling your wards how much the other has been talking highly of them, flatter them to the high heavens. Then, when the picnic is set, you insist on sitting beside Fraser, and Fraser will insist to Jimmy that the Buchanan has requested his company. Leaving them together, in front of the king and his guests, they cannot argue.' *And it gives you and Fraser space to be alone too,* I refrain from adding.

'Have you run this by Fraser?' she asks, still unsure.

'Not yet,' I admit. 'You've all been rather difficult to get a hold of these last few days.'

'Sophie Chorley, your grandmother did not give birth to your mother in the downstairs lavatory, so she didn't miss the great spring clean for her only granddaughter to slack off, chit-chatting, the very day before the family arrives.' Mrs Buchanan storms into the room, her words firing from her before anyone can even see her, and Sophie shrinks into her apron.

As quickly as the bad-omen housekeeper comes, she has floated off again, her bark being heard, aimed at another poor staff member just down the hall.

'I'm sorry, my lady.' Sophie looks at me apologetically. 'I really would love to help you, but with the family coming, and the Ghillies Ball so close, Mrs Buchanan would sooner hunt us for sport than admit she has any feelings at all, let alone romantic ones for Jimmy. Perhaps you should set your sights elsewhere.'

Before I can utter another syllable, she dusts off her apron and piles herself high with her baskets before making off in the same direction as Mrs B. Whisps of her hair hang loose from her plaits as they swing behind her until she is out of sight.

As I walk back through the castle, bodies rush by me like a Saturday night in A&E and I feel completely and utterly hopeless. With all of my distractions too distracted, my mind instantly leaps back to Atticus.

What must he be doing? If you love someone, how could you ignore them? One day is being too busy. Two days is a worry. But almost a whole month? You surely can't forget about someone you love. In fantasy, fae wait centuries for their lover. Monsters and men alike scale the heavens and earth to find the one they love. In fiction they fight wars, pine through decades, and sacrifice every last bit of themselves just to be in with a shot at love. So, can it truly and honestly be love, if they can't so much as text you back? It's hardly asking for a Shakespeare-quality sonnet every day. Just a 'hello' would suffice.

There will be a good explanation though, I am sure. And none of this will matter anyway when we're married. I'm sure we will laugh about it one day once he tells me all of the Darcy-esque plans he has been making in secret.

I crawl back into bed. The heat of the summer sun through the window makes me sweat under my duvet. There I stay for the rest of the day, disturbed only by the hushed voices of the busy household away down the hall.

The king and the rest of my family arrived yesterday, and with one desperately dull dinner to say their hellos have very much left me to my own devices since. With the queen now taking priority, even Fraser's wake-up call has ceased from under my window and I hear him now, his muffled pipes waking the opposite side of the castle.

Searching each linen cupboard for Sophie, it is as if she – and most of the rest of the household – have vanished. 'Excuse m—' I try to catch another member of staff who rushes by, but he passes by with a breeze. It's as though he doesn't see me all.

With hardly another human in sight, I turn my attention to the stables, then if I don't manage to catch Fraser on his rounds, at least Hamish and DeeDee will provide a little of the companionship I need. But as I cross the gardens, it seems that even Jimmy has been erased from the landscape. The silence seems even more overbearing than usual, as though even the birds and squirrels are on their best behaviour for the king.

The horses are alone when I reach them and, though I still hear him piping faintly in the distance, I try to push down the disappointment of not finding Fraser in their company.

'We've all been shoved down the priority list then, eh?' I scruff Hamish's jaw and he gives a little whinny in either appreciation or agreement. 'To think I'm actually jealous,' I scoff, the wordless creatures the perfect interlocutors for my only opportunity for an honest conversation, 'of someone else being woken up by the bloody bagpipes. I actually miss them . . . and that is exactly how I know that this place is sending me crazy.'

DeeDee throws her mane back and forth at the gate. 'You better not tell Fraser.' I give her a pointed look before laughing at the absurdity that I have felt so lonely these past few days that I have resorted to chatting with horses. DeeDee flaps her lips as I pass her, dappling me with her saliva. 'You're hardly helping me to turn this into a Cinderella story with that kind of behaviour now, are you?' I chuckle, wiping a hand down my dampened nose.

Pacing the stables, I look for something to busy my twitching fingers. My eyes fall to DeeDee's reins hooked up next to her, and without thinking too much about it, I take them down and tack her up. She stands perfectly still, as though royally rehearsed, and soon I am leading her out of the stable and into the warm breeze of August. Having never actually saddled my own horse, I decide against attempting now and instead climb the mounting block and sit high on the dark coat of her back.

Determining on a tranquil hack through the woods, I'm sure no one will mind me taking her out. In fact, I'm almost certain that no one will even notice. Cantering off down the track, the woosh of fresh air that flicks through my hair sends a chill of pleasure down my spine. Wrapped up in the thrill of freedom, of the animalistic joy of racing through the country as the summer sun glitters gold through my hair, I spur my mare on faster. Racing down paths, leaping over fallen logs, I realise why my ancestors took so much joy in the company of such beasts.

'Lady Alice!' A voice slices through the silence with an urgent boom. Looking over my shoulder for the source, I catch a glimpse of Fraser pursuing me on a horse I haven't seen before. With the motion, my hair whips around my face, obscuring my vision of the piper and his urgent expression.

Before I can draw DeeDee to a halt, the sound of distant voices distracts me, followed by the echoing boom of simultaneous gunfire. Throwing my hand up to my chest as my heart pummels in my chest, DeeDee bucks as she shares in my fear. Slipping from her back, I crash to the mossy floor, and all I can do is watch the black beauty scramble back through the woods before everything goes dark.

'You're lucky that Pipe Major Bell spotted you when he did or who knows how long you'd have been lying there.' Mrs Buchanan's wrinkled lips are the first thing I see as I open my eyes and squint through the blearing light.

I'm only able to grunt in response. A splitting pain shoots through my skull and I groan as I lift a heavy hand to touch at the tenderness. Sucking in a pained breath, I screw my eyes closed once again and hope my greatest headache, the housekeeper, is gone when I reopen them.

As I pry one lid open slowly, it's Fraser's figure that I notice, looming over the armchair in the corner of the room. For a split second, I panic that I am hallucinating, until his stern features crack into a shy smile and he gets to his feet. He draws towards me, and I toy with the idea of closing my eyes again and just pretending that I'm still asleep. But he moves so swiftly to my bedside that I can't bring myself to tear my gaze from him. Fraser doesn't say a word; he only holds a glass of water to my lips tenderly to allow me a much-needed sip. The cool water wets my tongue and soothes the dryness of my throat and I look up to Fraser, his bright green eyes and furrowed brows, and give him a grateful smile.

'Are you okay, my lady?' he whispers, the soft vibrations of his deep voice almost soothing on my pounding head.

'It's no worse than the usual headache I have when I wake up to the sound of bagpipes,' I try to joke hoarsely, and Fraser chances a smile. 'What happened?'

'You charged head-first into the king's pheasant shoot on the back of a skittish horse. You should be thankful you only fell and weren't shot.' Mrs Buchanan reminds us of her presence as she huffs to herself, pacing the room and fussing over every bit of mess and clutter.

'I thought the shoot was yesterday.' My voice is quiet, and I'm grateful when it's Fraser who answers.

'It got extended. The Duke of Oxford hit nothing in the afternoon so they had to add another day to give him a second chance. Did no one tell you?'

'No,' I say before sinking back into my pillows.

'It's my fault,' Fraser says reproachfully. 'I should have warned you about the hunt, and warned you that DeeDee is an old mare who throws her riders for sport.'

'You weren't to have known that I'd be a fool. Plus, you've been busy; it's not your job to babysit me.'

'It is my— our job to keep you safe, however, and on that account I have failed.' Fraser returns to the armchair, unable to look at me any longer.

'Has anyone informed Atticus? Or my father?' I force down any of the peculiar feelings his words have stirred in me and think of my love instead. The embarrassing thought crosses my mind that perhaps a hint of peril might actually encourage him to break his silence.

Fraser remains silent, so Mrs Buchanan answers, 'Your father sends his best wishes.'

'And Atticus?' I push. My father's lack of concern will be easily overcome with a single word from Atticus.

'No one could reach him,' Fraser replies bluntly. 'A message was left, but has not yet been returned.' Grabbing his jumper from the back of the armchair, Fraser moves to the door. 'If my lady is well, I shall resume my duties.'

Too numb for words, I nod, a sharp pain pinging through my head, and Fraser leaves the room without a second glance.

Chapter 12

In this part of the world, so isolated, so unspoiled, the moonlight feels different. It seems so pure, a bright white beacon of the night as opposed to the dim, outshone light of London, which seems yellowed like an insomniac's eye in comparison. Alone again in my room, I watch the moon's pale face as she casts a stream of silver across the lawn. Though beautiful, her light is icy, and I too grow colder as the night draws on.

Without the distraction of Sophie, of the hustle and bustle of the castle, of attempting to construct my own enemies-to-lovers trope in real life, the emptiness fills my chest again after three more weeks of being alone. Milligram after milligram, no amount of synthetic serotonin can ever quite plug that space. Diversion has been my only successful treatment so far, but even that wears off, the night falls, and sadness returns. I hate the night, I hate the moon, and I hate being alone.

Summer melts away in the silence of my bedroom.

With more stuffy dinners and quietly pompous small talk, my existence here feels hardly different to how it looked in London, though somehow even more lonely. As the whereabouts of my suitcase is still a mystery, and Mrs Buchanan continues to insist that since I am fully clothed finding it is not on her list of her priorities, even my clothes aren't my own. At least in London I was miserable in style, now I'm just depressed *and* frumpy.

The rest of my life is cleaned up around me whilst I sleep, and the pipes have been too busy at various parties and the waking of other guests, so I haven't seen Sophie or Fraser for longer than a passing smile for weeks. Though I have known them only weeks, I feel their absence in almost everything I do. I hardly noticed how much I needed them until my days began to feel so incomplete without them in it.

The closer we draw to the Ghillies Ball at the end of the month, the more savage Mrs Buchanan becomes as she barks her orders and is never seen without a sweat on her brow. Thankfully, in all of her stress, she has been too preoccupied to hassle me. Although, at this moment in time, I would kill to see her sneer at me. At least someone would be looking at me at all.

Unable to stand any longer, absorbing the darkness from outside as though it's infectious, I pull on one of the slip dresses that came in the pile of clothes that Sophie had lent me from the castle's wardrobes and sneak along the empty corridors. With the high windows, the moonlight floods the hallways, as though the place itself is designed for adventures in the dead of night. Silence is thick in the air, not a single creature seems to stir inside the castle, and all I wish to do is cut through the stillness with a bloodcurdling scream that I'm sure will relieve whatever this feeling is within me for just a moment.

Unsure of what compels me, I leave the castle and trek my bare feet across the lawn until my skin feels as cold as my blood in the Scottish midnight. My body still aches from my fall with every step, but I push on. Haunting the hedgerows of the maze, I follow its high green walls step after step, until the path ends and I am face to face with a leafy portcullis and can pass no further. Time slips away into the night and only the slow throbbing in my feet informs me of just how long I have been moving like a ghost through the maze.

'Lady Alice?' A familiar voice cuts through the ruminating silence and I jump at the unexpected sound.

Fraser Bell turns the corner, white shirt glowing in the twilight. Here he feels like Theseus and I his minotaur. I am weak, ready to be defeated.

'Are you okay?' He speaks again after words fail me.

'What are you doing here so late?' I ignore his question as I return one of my own.

'I could ask you the same question, ma'am.' Fraser gestures towards me.

'Does no one in this place realise that simply adding an honorific to the end doesn't negate the insolence of a statement?' I chuckle as a warm glow brushes over his cheeks. Fraser opens his mouth to speak, his brow sloped in such a way that I know the words that are about to come out of his mouth.

115

'I'm—' he begins but I cut him off before he can finish.

'Please do not apologise, or call me ma'am.' The blush deepens on his face. 'I give you a free pass to be as brazen as you like, just as long as you call me Alice. And just Alice. Just, *please*, speak to me like I'm your friend. If only for tonight.' I practically beg, and Fraser clears his throat.

'Are you not cold, m—Alice? You'll catch yourself a chill running about like that at this time of night.'

'Malice?' His slip of the tongue entertains me. 'You know what, I'll take it. At least it's better than a stuffy title.' The brief expression of panic on his face melts into timid amusement. 'To answer your question, I am utterly freezing, but I am committed now; I must find the middle of this bloody maze.'

'And waiting until the morning wasn't an option?'

'Absolutely not.'

'Come on, I'll take you.' Fraser nods his head to the path behind him with a shy smile and sets off slowly. Following the luminosity of his shirt, he becomes my guide and I copy each of his steps as we travel further and further into the maze. 'So, may I ask again, why you are in his majesty's maze at midnight?'

I am grateful that he doesn't turn around to speak to me, only continues to lead me through the winding paths. 'I felt like being alone.'

'Were you not alone in your room? I would have thought everyone in the house is asleep at this time?'

'I was, but it's different, isn't it, being alone and choosing to be alone. By deciding to be alone elsewhere, it's like it's been my decision all along. Opting to be alone

116

doesn't feel quite as lonely as simply being left by oneself.' The words tumble out of me before I can really think of them, and I am glad when Fraser keeps his eyes locked forward. 'That probably makes no sense.' I cover up my anxious turn with a laugh, but the piper doesn't choose to laugh with me.

'I think it makes perfect sense.' For just a split second, he glances at me over his shoulder and smiles in a way that the moonlight catches his teeth and for the first time all night, the shimmering glow doesn't feel so cold. 'Here we are.'

Wandering out into a clearing, we have finally reached the heart. The once endless yews make way for granite statues and obelisks and, for a moment, I am transported back to London and its galleries. Tracing my fingers along the cool stone, each groove, each corner seems to radiate with life.

'It's beautiful,' I breathe.

'I've always said there's a certain special charm about them at night. There's almost something saintly to them.' Fraser puts into words the sensation I couldn't quite explain. Standing side by side, we watch them in silence, as though we are both waiting for one of them to speak, or cry, or reach out a hand. Only the breeze moves around us and I am drawn out of my head with a bone-rattling shiver that I can't quite suppress.

'Here.' Fraser disappears into a shadowy corner of the maze and picks up a thick woollen jumper from a bench and hands it to me. I open my lips to protest, but it's his turn to cut me off. 'If I am not allowed to call you ma'am, you aren't allowed to argue with me.'

With a soft shake of my head, I accept the jumper with a gentle smile and a timid 'thank you' before sliding the thick fabric over my head. Smelling faintly of hay, horses, and the musky scent of an aftershave still lingering in the fibres, it's clear from the fraying sleeves that this has been a common feature of his wardrobe for many years. Despite the rawness of the wool, it is actually rather soft. Well-worn threads tickle rather than itch, and I am warmed almost instantly.

'Why are you out so late then, Piper Major? Don't you have to be up early to disturb the peace of those of us who'd actually rather like a lie-in?' Fraser's deep laugh fills the silence of the night in a song more beautiful than those he wakes me up with.

'I, er, struggle to sleep.' Fraser avoids my eyes, and speaks to the granite statue of the late queen instead. 'Instead of lying in bed tossing and turning, I find it's nicer to have a wander. See the parts of the world that most people miss whilst they're sleeping.'

'And what parts might they be?' I ask, genuinely intrigued by his candour.

'The stars, the wildlife, the quiet of three o'clock on a Monday morning. There's no peace on earth quite like it.'

'This place is always silent. Too silent.'

'Then you're not listening well enough.' He turns to me with a smile and pulls me softy by my arm until we both sit side by side on a cold stone bench in the middle of the maze. 'Listen right now . . .' He pauses for a moment and the silence envelops me again. 'Can you hear it?' I shake my head, but it doesn't dull the excitement that crosses his face. 'Right there.'

Focusing all of my energy into my hearing, I close my eyes. At first, all I hear is the breeze as it slides through the leafy fingers of the trees and rustles at the rhododendrons. Then, there's a faint call from an animal in the distance. It's a high-pitched cry, though not like that of a bird, or deer. Before I can focus any deeper, the sound is drowned out by soft breaths. The velvety melody of them, though almost silent, makes it impossible to hear anything else besides. With each breath in and out, another tight patch of tension in my body seems to ease as my chest instinctively follows its lead, rising and falling in harmony.

Snapping open my eyes, I am met with Fraser's clear green irises watching me closely. Reddening at the thought of him perceiving my moment of weightlessness, I speak quickly. 'What is it?' I ask, referring to the animalistic cries in the darkness.

'Red squirrels,' Fraser whispers with a grin. 'All but extinct everywhere else, but here they thrive.' The soft cry cracks through the silence again and we both smile at the sound. 'Things are never quiet with them around, but I'm glad of it. If they're quiet, it means they're all gone.'

A soft hoot drawls through the night and instinctively, my attention shifts back to Fraser, as though waiting like a patient child for him to label the asynchronous sound. 'Now I know that one's an owl but that's where my expertise ends.'

'Tawny,' he says softly. 'But we have a few different kinds through here. You can always tell the tawny though –

they're the ones that make the classic "too-wit, too-woo" sounds.'

Fraser sits beside me grinning at the moon and her stars. The unabashed joy that lights up in his face, at each distant call of all of the nocturnal lovers in nature, sets him apart from anyone I have ever known. It's like all of his secrets are laid bare right there on his face and he makes no attempt to hide them. Fraser Bell isn't an open book, he is a song in perfect harmony and I intend to learn him by heart. For Sophie's sake, of course.

Though my mind swims with questions to ask him – his favourite animal, his greatest fears, his favourite colour – for once, I cannot bring myself to infiltrate the comfortable silence that has settled between us. Instead of thoughts of myself, I think of him, whether he's ever been in love, whom he may admire most, if he has ever had his heart broken, and my mind swims with all of my predictions. When those thoughts have run their course, I listen to the trees, to their inhabitants, to the city of nature that hustles around us.

So at peace, I no longer shiver with the cold, nor fight the heaviness of my lids, without a second thought, I find my stooping head pressed against Fraser's shoulder and his rhythmic breaths pulling me to sleep.

When I open my eyes again, I am no longer in the maze, nor in the garden. Sprawled across the top of my bed, my duvet beneath me and a throw tucked around my legs, I am still clad in Fraser's woollen jumper – the only clue that last night wasn't a dream.

There is another thing that makes this morning different from all others. Checking the carriage clock beside me, I see that 9 a.m. has long gone, and without a peep from my regular alarm, whether that is beneath my window or that of the queen. I have slept entirely undisturbed until almost half past ten, and unless I have somehow managed to sleep through the bagpipes, Fraser hasn't yet been to wake the house.

Am I to blame? Is he in trouble? Will he be in trouble now? Everywhere I go, I somehow manage to derail all that is good, as though I have the reverse of the Midas touch and all of the gold that surrounds me suddenly turns to dust and scatters as soon as I get too close.

Hopping out of bed, I rush to open the curtains and to my immense relief, there he stands in his spot beneath my window, his bagpipes in their case at his feet, and his tired eyes fixed upon me. As soon as I reveal myself to him, he leaps into action, awakens his instrument and commences his opening song.

Rushing to the door, I pause at the handle. Having lived in plenty of households such as this one, I know that a lady running around in the piper slash stableboy's jumper is enough gossip to keep everyone excited for weeks. Whipping it off, and dragging on an outfit compiled from all of the discarded garments on my floor, I toss Fraser's jumper back onto my bed before racing down the stairs and out in the garden to see him.

Though I'm no longer there, he still faces my window, his cheeks flushed from the force of his breath. Standing in the doorway to the castle, I watch him play, take note of how his fingers skip across the holes and his whole body seems to contract and tense with each new note. When the familiar tune begins to draw to its end, I close the distance between us and stand face to face with the piper who falters on his very final note at the unexpected sight of me.

'Are you okay?' Today, I am the first to ask the question.

'Am I okay, ma'am?' Fraser looks at me a little gone out, as though he never expected such a mundane sentence to fall from my lips.

'Fraser.' Folding my arms over my chest, I narrow my eyes at the title he consistently punctuates his responses with.

'Sorry, aye, I am very well. Thank you?' His tone is almost questioning, as though still confused at my meaning, though to me it is obvious.

'You aren't in trouble?'

'Why would I be?'

'You're late. I— Well I didn't know if last night had anything to do with it?' Looking around nervously, I await an interruption from Mrs Buchanan storming across the grass to berate him, but she doesn't come.

'I am late because of last night,' he says bluntly. 'But—'

'Oh bloody hell, I'm sorry. I really didn't intend— I really didn't mean to—'

'Alice?' Fraser interrupts me and for the first time my name crosses his lips. The syllables fall so naturally that I begin to question why anyone would wish to be called anything other; the whole world would be full of Alices if they heard how the name sounds from the mouth of Fraser Bell. 'I am late on purpose. You were so tired yesterday that

122

you fell asleep in the maze.' He leans in closely to speak under his breath. 'I, er, carried you back to your room and thought I'd wait until you woke up organically before I woke you myself.' He scratches at the back of his neck as the blush begins to creep up mine. 'I apologise if I overstepped. It was clear to me, as someone who sleep rarely visits easily, that you needed as much as you could get.'

I am unsure of how to feel. Until now, I foolishly hadn't put much thought into how I had actually gotten into bed. I knew it was very unlikely that I would have found my own way out of the maze alone but the thought of Fraser carrying me such a way – across the garden, up the stairs – to deliver me safely back makes my heart heave in my chest. Imagining his arms wrapped under my legs, circling around my back, sends a shiver through me, and before the image can fully form, I shake it out of my head as though allowing it to fully fledge would be heretical. The thought that Atticus would never do such a thing fills the space instead and my guilt only mounts.

'What about the queen?' I suddenly panic. I am no longer his priority; he doesn't work to my timings anymore. In thinking of me, his true role has gone unfulfilled.

'Her majesty has requested not to be woken on a Sunday morning any longer.' He struggles to hold eye contact and his freckled cheeks pink in the damp of the mid-morning.

'So today should be your day off?' Guilt throbs in my gut all too familiarly.

'Yes, ma'am. But I wished to check if you were better this morning after your restless night. I apologise for my disturbance.'

'No, no, I should be thanking you. I don't know what came over me, must have just been the excitement of the day.' Chuckling breathily, I run my hands through my hair, and the way it snags on my rings in the process reminds me that I am probably not much of a sight at this moment in time. I wonder what my mother would think of me: sneaking about in the gardens in the middle of the night with the 'staff', parading around in public without so much as running a brush through my hair beforehand. I think it would be enough to send her into shock. Kitty and Hugo also cross my mind for the first time in a while. Their sneers are so vivid in my mind that for a split second I am sure I can smell the sickly sweetness of Kitty's perfume, as though she is haunting me in spirit.

Straightening out, I return my features to their rehearsed hardened state. 'Thank you, Piper Major. It shan't happen again.'

Fraser's expression roughens too. Standing to attention, he simply salutes me until I turn and walk away.

Chapter 13

'I concede,' I say to Fraser, my arms folded over my chest in the ballroom, watching beneath the balcony as he finishes off the final phrase of his rehearsal.

'And what may that be in reference to, my lady?' His face is flushed with exertion. As his clear eyes widen, his bright irises catch every bit of sunlight that flows from the high windows.

'When I first arrived here, you told me that I would find a space in my heart for the pipes and would soon be begging you to teach me to play. Now, the former is a work in progress. But the latter . . . I am so bored that I am in desperate need of a distraction. Do you perhaps have a little time today?'

My heart beats irregularly as I await his reply but soon it falls into a pretty little up-tempo rhythm when his freckled cheeks pull into a winning grin. 'Hey, don't be getting too excited. You have yet to convert me; this is purely to combat the boredom that is bordering on terminal at this point.'

Shaking his head with a smile, Fraser's low voice echoes softly through the high ceilings. 'It would be my pleasure.'

Clapping my hands together, I skip up the stairs to join him. Once face to face, I notice how his lips are slightly swollen and rosy from his morning of playing and I quickly divert my attention to the pipes, before my cheeks blush the same colour.

'Where do I start?' I smile excitedly, if a little bewildered at the array of pipes.

As I reach out to touch them, Fraser gently diverts my hands with his own. 'Not these ones, and not here. I don't think the king and queen would appreciate you skirling all through the house. It's enough when it's just me, and I actually know how to play. No, we'll head out to the treeline by Loch Muick this afternoon and then it's only the deer you'll be disturbing.'

'Perfect. I'll see you there.'

By the time the afternoon rolls around, I am the most excited I have been for weeks. My day gets increasingly intriguing when I find Sophie, sitting alone on a bench behind the kitchen, smoking neurotically as though she has just witnessed a murder.

'Sophie?' I ask quietly and she snaps her head up to look at me, with a great fear in her eyes. 'Are you okay?'

Noticing it's me, she visibly relaxes and gives a hearty sigh. 'Fancy a bine?' She offers me the packet of cigarettes and I politely decline. Sophie runs a hand over her weary face and sighs again before speaking. 'The Buchanan is going to be the death of me.'

'What has she done this time?'

Sophie scoffs. 'What hasn't she done? The Ghillies Ball sends her doo-fecking-lally. She's gone aff her heid this time I swear.' Her accent thickens with each syllable she utters and she takes another drag to steady herself.

'Do you fancy bunking off?' I proposition her. 'I'll take all of the blame, of course.'

Sophie doesn't even think about it for a second. Stamping out her cigarette, she gets to her feet and leaves her apron on the bench. Following beside me for a few moments, she finally asks, 'Where are we going?'

'Loch Muick. I've convinced Fraser Bell to teach me to play.' The familiar light returns to her eyes as she gives me a mischievous glance.

'You? Learning to play the bagpipes?' She chuckles and glances at me with a disbelieving look.

'What, like it's hard?' Wiggling my eyebrows playfully, I grin until Sophie shakes her head with another laugh.

'For any particular reason?'

'What else does one expect a woman to do to occupy herself whilst she's locked in a Scottish castle?'

Sophie diverts her path to head towards a small collection of sheds I've never seen before. 'Where are you going?'

'You didn't think we'd walk all the way to the loch did you? That'd take you all day.' Pulling out two rusted bicycles from behind the shed, she hands me one and slings her leg over the other. 'They're a little old, but they do the trick.'

Wobbling up onto the seat, I push down on the pedal and a screech follows the strained motion. These bikes must be at least fifty years old, if not older, and yet Sophie flies off down the path, her braids freed and flowing behind her. Racing to catch her, I push through the burning in my legs and soon we're both goose-pimpled and our mouths are dry from smiling too wide into the headwind.

By the time we come to the small collection of trees on the edge of the loch, we're both laughing maniacally, and Fraser – already arrived and set up – watches on in a mix of awe and confusion. Sophie's hair sticks up in every direction; her bobbles only cling to a few strands as the rest have escaped to kiss about her face. I can't imagine that I look much better at this point either.

'I was about to send out a search party, but thankfully I could hear you both giggling from a mile away so I knew Miss Chorley would have something to do with it.' Fraser grins at the both of us, and right here, just a couple of miles from the confines of the castle, each one of us seems to have left some of our reservations behind. Here in these trees, I am just a girl, laughing with her friends. Though the wind is biting, I am warm to the core as both of their smiles seem to fulfil the part of my life that I never realised I was missing. Sophie and Fraser are my friends.

'Shall we crack on?' Fraser says after a little while of small talk, as he pulls out a different set of pipes from his own and hands them to me.

'Aye,' I reply with a strong nod as Sophie and Fraser share a proud smile.

'Oh, I cannae wait for this.' Sophie lays down her scarf on the woodland floor and makes herself comfortable.

* * *

'I cannae listen to this any longer,' Sophie groans an hour later. 'Are you sure those things are in tune?'

'You know it takes about six months of practice just to start being able to make the right sound out of these? That's before you even start trying to play a tune.' Fraser chuckles, then grimaces as I make another animalistic screech. 'Although I'm not sure I can say you were blessed with much natural talent.'

I collapse to the ground, the pipes screeching with my motion. 'I am bushed. I wasn't told this would be a full-on workout. I thought it was a little blow, a little squeeze, move your fingers a little and there you have it: "Scotland the Brave".'

'Sounds strangely like losing my virginity.' Sophie lies back against the earth with a smile. 'Who fancies a swim?' She props herself up on her elbows and side-eyes the loch.

Fraser and I share a look. 'I'm not sure—' he begins to protest, but is quickly cut off by Sophie stripping down to her underwear and splashing into the water with a shriek.

'Come on, ya big jessies. It's lovely.' She splashes in our direction, and she looks so free. Her hair clings to her face and there she stands like the Lady of the Lake, glowing with exhilaration.

Looking around, just to make sure my parents aren't lurking around the corner or the whole of London's high society haven't magically appeared in the middle of the Scottish countryside in the last hour, I remove my jumper timidly.

'My lady?' Fraser faces away from the both of us, finding the bark of a nearby hawthorn tree particularly interesting.

'You don't have to do anything you don't wish to. Sophie is a menace for peer pressure.'

Smiling at his worry, I strip down to my underwear and join Sophie with a splash. The coolness prickles through my body in an almost pleasurable attack. It awakens every inch of me in places I never knew had lain dormant, and for the first time in years, I feel alive.

'C'mon Fraz!' Sophie shouts. 'Shitebag if ye dinnae!' Still, he shakes his head, trying not to look at the both of us, half naked, just metres before him.

'Come on you wee . . . wee . . . fanny?' I try my best at a bit of Scots and silence falls through the countryside. Worried I have offended him, panic begins to rise, until both Fraser and Sophie burst out into the most melodious laughter I have ever heard, and not even the singing of the thrushes could sound any sweeter.

Convinced by my teasing, Fraser pulls off his shirt and shorts and races for the water. Splashing in beside us, the only sounds the three of us can make are that of unstoppable laughter, as Sophie splashes each of us in turn.

Swimming up beside me, the pale skin of Fraser's torso glows above the surface of the water, dappled with little droplets as they glide over the red hair of his chest.

'Fanny, aye?' he asks with a smirk, and I feel my cheeks heat.

'Aye,' I reply with a shy grin.

'And who taught you that?'

'I may or may not have heard Mrs Buchanan calling Jimmy that last week for getting mud in the hallway.'

'Of course you did.' He looks off into the forest, his cheeks pinching in amusement.

'They are in love, you know.' I swim around Fraser, getting a good look at the circumference of his figure.

'And you've reached that conclusion because she called him a fanny?' He watches me closely. 'Does that mean you're in love with me?'

Unable to formulate a coherent reply, I splash a little water in his face and dive beneath the surface to hide and soothe my hot cheeks.

'I wish to make a bet with the both of you right now,' I call to Sophie who had swum out a little further, refusing to make eye contact with Fraser again.

'A bet?' Sophie splashes back towards us, intrigued.

'I bet you both that by this time next year, Jimmy and the Buchanan will be a couple.'

'And what do we get when you inevitably lose?' Sophie raises an eyebrow.

'The loser has to . . .' I think for a moment '. . . streak through the maze.'

Sophie outstretches her dripping hand. 'Deal.' We shake with a splash and I turn to Fraser with that Machiavellian glint in my eye.

He hesitates for a moment, but then cautiously takes my hand in his and squeezes it softly. 'I can't wait to see you lose.'

Too overcome to address him directly, I call out, 'I'll race you both to that rock.'

'I wouldn't do that if I were you – you'll wake the beasties.' Fraser grins mischievously.

'Beasties?' I look down into the dark water, the abyss below almost never-ending as my feet flap back and forth to keep me afloat.

'Well, everyone's heard of the Loch Ness monster of course, but Nessie is only scratching the surface. Haven't you heard of the kelpies, or the Bean Nighe?' Still smiling, the piper floats on his back, stealing a glance at me out of his periphery.

'Let me guess, something is lurking below ready to swallow me whole?'

'Oh no, far worse.' Fraser swims close. 'The kelpies may look like pretty little horses when they're stood beside bodies of water but they're far from it. They haunt the lochs and rivers, waiting for passers-by to mount their beautiful hides. Once they have riders on their backs, the kelpies refuse to release their prey, dragging them into the water where the unsuspecting victim becomes their latest meal.'

'Okay, note to self, don't go mounting any strange horses near bodies of water,' I say, looking around the loch for any sign of such a creature. 'I'd say that's a pretty simple ask.'

'You may think so, but you couldn't help yourself with DeeDee and look where that got you.' Fraser winks and my cheeks flush again.

'Yeah, yeah, well, lessons have been learnt.'

'At least the look of the Bean Nighe is hardly going to coax you closer. She is a small, gnarled washerwoman who lurks at streams and lochs washing blood from the clothes of those who are about to die. Fated to spend eternity working, she was once a woman who died in childbirth and is now a terrifying omen of death.'

'Lovely and cheery.'

'Isn't it just.'

'Don't you have any nice creatures in your mythology? Like some sweet little fairies, or something from the fairy tales, and I don't mean the Grimm versions.'

Fraser ponders for a moment. 'There is the Ghillie Dhu. He's often thought of as a lonely forest faerie.'

'Okay, I like the sound of that. He's not wanting to eat me? Or tell me I'm going to die?'

'Nope. He's the guardian of the forest. Though he may look wild, he has a kinship with nature, protecting wildlife and nature and any inhabitants from harm. Supposedly he has a soft spot for children and lost travellers, so if you ever lose your way in the forest, know that the Ghillie Dhu will be protecting you.' Trying to picture the creature in my mind – benevolent, wild, protector – the only image that manifests is Fraser, striding through the clearing behind me after I lost my grip on DeeDee. I try to shake the image, but my imagined version of the events when Fraser carried me from the maze to my bed, clad in his own jumper, plays over and over in my mind instead. Fraser Bell, the piper, the protector, the thing of myth. It would be a privilege to tell his story over and over.

Lying on the bank, drying off in the breeze, the three of us haven't said a word for some time. Listening to the way the water slowly laps against the shore, I am almost ready to fall asleep.

'What is the date today?' I ask into the air. I have lost all track of the days, as though time has slipped through my fingers and flushed away into the lakes and rivers.

'The 27th?' Sophie asks, though seemingly unsure.

'The 28th,' Fraser corrects her, and I leap to my feet. 'What is it? Are you okay?' Fraser follows suit and the two of us stare at one another, half naked and goose-fleshed.

'It's tomorrow,' I say, filled with horror.

'What is?' Sophie too gets to her feet in a panic.

'I had completely forgotten. How had I forgotten?!' Pacing the bank, I collect my clothes and drag them on erratically.

'Alice.' Fraser catches my elbow, slowing me to a halt.

'The conference,' I breathe. 'I had forgotten about the conference.' My friends both look at me gone out; Fraser still clutches my arm softly. 'I'm supposed to be getting engaged tomorrow. And I'm five hundred miles away.'

Fraser releases me and his hand falls to his side as he takes a step back.

'Engaged?' Sophie asks, brows furrowed. 'To that Atticus guy?'

I nod, desperately trying to pull my jeans up my damp legs.

'The one you haven't heard from in over a month?' Fraser's voice is rough, foreign from his usual soft depths.

His words cut me. 'That's not fair.'

'What's not fair, Alice, is that the guy hasn't shown you a single bit of care the whole time you've been away, and now you're going to rush off to marry him at a *conference*. Surely you must know he doesn't love you.'

Fraser takes the knife and plunges it ever deeper.

'You don't know a single thing about me.'

'And you don't know a single thing about love.' His

words gouge at my chest, and an icy breeze seems to pass through the spaces between my ribs.

Sophie watches on, open-mouthed as I pick up one of the bicycles and begin to pedal back down the footpath. 'Alice! Alice, wait!' she calls to me, but I don't look back.

By the time Balmoral is back in my sights, the sky is beginning to blemish in bruises of purple and gold, like a peach left too long in the sun. The sweetness is sucked dry from the scene, and all that is reflected over and over in the ivy-framed windows are Fraser's words. They fill every space in my mind until my head throbs with the weight of it all.

The castle is silent aside from the clinking of cutlery and muted tones of polite chatter coming from the king's dining room, and I sneak through to my bedroom entirely unobserved. Peeling off my loch-dampened clothes, I stand, naked and alone, repulsed at the feeling of my own skin. Rifling through my drawers for something to wear, something me, and not these itchy jumpers, tartan skirts, and whatever regal façade I've been attempting to wear these last weeks, my fingers slide against something sharp, which slices through the tip of my ring finger. Dragging in a hissing breath, I suck the injured appendage, until the metallic taste of blood glides over my tongue in a bitter attack.

Upon searching out the guilty party, my eyes land on a thick sheet of paper, tucked into one of my socks. Drawing it out, the *Beaumont & Sons*–headed slip only adds insult to injury.

Wait for me. *A*. Scratched in Atticus's perfect

handwriting are the words that have cut me. The note he'd handed to me the day I left, the last words I had from him, renew my melancholy all over again.

I am tired of waiting. I am not Cinderella, waiting for the prince to fondle her perfect feet. I am not Snow White, nor Sleeping Beauty, awaiting the kiss of a man to wake me. I am not going to wait to be saved. I refuse to wait at all.

Chapter 14

Perhaps I should have waited.

As it turns out, there isn't actually much romance in stealing a royal horse at midnight and attempting to canter through the Scottish wilderness whilst your nipples are almost tearing holes in your shawl with the cold. And when it isn't simply a filler sentence in a book, one certainly feels the length of every moment of the saddle digging into one's coccyx and the smell of horse dung that seems to cling to the air despite the trail beginning a mile and a half back. Once again, I find myself miserable on the back of Hamish, thinking of Atticus to get me through.

Trying to use Google Maps to navigate a horse is not easy at the best of times I'm sure, but trying to gather just enough signal to at least find out whether to travel north, east, south, or west, is borderline impossible. The one redeeming quality, and the reason why I am not yet quaking in my boots, is the fact that the moon is full tonight and my path is well lit in her silvery glow. Oh, and knowledge that if a handsome prince who had been cursed to live as an even sexier beast wished to kidnap me for trespassing on his land, I wouldn't mind much either (as long as he stayed as the beast, of course).

Have I thought any of this through even just a little bit? No. Is it likely to work at all? Probably not. Do I have any idea of what I'm going to do once I reach London and stand face to face with the love of my life after trekking through earth, wind, and East Coast trains to get to him? Absolutely not. But this feels exactly like something a hopelessly in love heroine would do, so perhaps if I do it too, it may suppress those little seeds of doubt that Fraser – with his silly bagpipes, and his habit of breaking protocol to tell me some stinging truths – has sewn.

Close to lying down in the middle of the path in hopes that the kind Ghillie Dhu finds me before the Dog Fairy or some other evil creature of mythology tears me apart, I finally see the dim lights of Braemar village in the distance. After I rouse Hamish, we race through the last stretch, until we reach the Balmoral Arms. All of its lights are extinguished, with the pub and its patrons all in bed for the night, but I don't yet lose hope. I tie my tired steed to the fence, make my bed in the stone doorway of the pub, and hope that the milkman comes early this morning.

I don't realise that I have nodded off until the rough clearing of a throat startles me awake. 'Cannae sleep there, lass. My regulars would trample ye to get their elevenses pint, no matter how pretty you are.'

Jumping to my feet, I brush myself down and stand before the landlord with an apologetic smile. 'So sorry, sir.' And just as he moves to enter his establishment, an uncommon shot of confidence pings through my arm and I outstretch it to stop him. 'May I . . . Would you perhaps . . .'

'I don't do handouts. No free pints, certainly no free pies,' the bearded man gruffs.

'No, no, forgive me, I was wondering if you knew where I could get a lift to Aberdeen train station? I can pay.'

'Can ye now?' He rubs his beard, suddenly interested. 'How much?'

I draw out a few of the notes I have stuffed into my pockets, no idea how much a taxi across rural Scotland at dawn is meant to cost. The landlord's eyes light up, and I know I have shown too many of my cards.

'I'll take you. I was heading that way to the brewers anyway.' Unlocking the door, he pushes it open to reveal a hearty country pub. The fireplace is emptied of its ashes in the very heart of the room, and little groups of mismatched tartan armchairs sit around it. A cowhide rug spreads out across the wooden floor, with the creamy oak reaching up and wrapping around the bar that overhangs with hand-drawn beer-tap labels. The back wall of the bar is wallpapered in various amber bottles of whisky, all of them giving way to frame a large portrait of Balmoral Castle itself.

Taking pride of place on the corner of the bar is an old photograph of my grandmother stood beside a young boy in the corner of the pub, which hasn't much changed since.

'Princess Alexandra.' The landlord notices me looking at the photo and draws up beside me. 'She used to be a regular here when I was a wee lad. She'd just waltz right on in like any other Tom, Dick, or Harry and sit and have a sweet sherry in that old chair by the fire.'

I would never have even believed that the figure I remember looming around like a ghoul during dinner parties, staring down her bespeckled nose with a scowl every time I laid a finger out of place, would even know what a pub was, let alone frequent one. She lived and breathed royalty, and anything else besides is strictly not spoken about.

'Her son and daughter-in-law stayed with us a couple of nights too. Apparently, they were holed up in the castle on their honeymoon and couldn't breathe for the stuffiness of it all, so had a weekend as a couple of "normal" newlyweds right here.'

Trying not to think about my parents consummating their marriage in the bedrooms just above me, I try to figure out if this is simply a rural landlord's way of creating his own tales to sell his pints. Yet, nothing in his face would suggest anything other than genuine pride, and my family are hardly the exciting royals. If I were making up stories of royal patrons, I certainly wouldn't choose my miserable mother as the poster girl.

'I have a photo of them here somewhere.' The landlord, unperturbed by my silence, rummages around in a back room before re-entering with a photo album that bursts with little slips of paper and various other knick-knacks that have been hoarded over the years. Flicking through it, trying not to let the thing explode in a sea of memories on the bar before me, the landlord hums with satisfaction and he turns the photograph he was looking for towards me.

My father, dressed in a tweed blazer with matching flat cap, grins at the camera, a small scruffy dog at his feet. My mother leans against him affectionately, not bothering to look at the camera, only gazing lovingly at her new husband. In jeans and riding boots, she is muddied to the waist, and a great smear of mud across her dimpled cheek doesn't cease her smile. I had never even known that she had dimples. There is no denying it is her, however. Her bright blonde hair glows on the paper, that same blonde hair that's always restrained, caged in a sleek, perfected bun, but this time her wisping curls are feral and floating in the breeze. My mother looks wild, and . . . free.

'She's beautiful,' I can't help but breathe.

'Isn't she just,' the landlord agrees. 'The upper-middle-class naval officer's daughter, marrying the son of a princess – caused quite the stir back in the day. Apparently, Princess Alex sent them up here to get them out of the limelight until the news all blew over. The new Duchess Fran Walpole hated it, locked up in a stuffy castle, thrust into the life of a lady after being used to the carefree party life whilst still at uni. She still swore just like a sailor back then too. I heard she wreaked havoc up at Balmoral just to entertain herself. A true free spirit that one.' He chuckles affectionately.

'The Highland air must do funny things to people,' is all the reply I can muster, unable to break my stare from my mother's photo. Why couldn't this woman here, with the smiles and life, be the one who raised me? Why did I get coldness and solitude, whilst all along there was once someone capable of showing me affection? What could have happened between these photos and the day I was born? My parents even look in love. The people in this photo wouldn't sleep in separate bedrooms, or treat public displays of affection as strictly work-related. How can one go from being so in love, so full of life, to being a shell of a human being? A walking, talking rule book?

'Or is it the air down south that oppresses them? And only when they come here can they truly become who they wish to be?' the landlord murmurs as though he too is deep in thought and my mind flicks back to the loch, to Fraser Bell and his broad chest, to Sophie and her melodious laughter, to the easy feeling in my heart that has overtaken me as though until I got here a weight had been slowly crushing it.

'Perhaps,' I hum.

'Here, I've just thought, don't you look the spit of the duchess down to that wild shock of blonde hair and all?' He pauses for thought as he scans my features with a curious dark eye.

I chuckle nervously. 'I can't say I see it.' Fiddling with the fraying hem of my jumper, I am impatient to change the subject. 'Would we perhaps be leaving soon, sir?' I remind him of our initial errand.

'Oh aye, aye, the train station. I'll just grab Rose and we'll be aff.' Scooting off again into the back room, he re-emerges with an old dog plodding beside him. Her chocolate coat is greying but she gives a sprightly wag of her tail before leaving a sloppy smudge against my trousers with her jowls. 'Just this way.'

Back out in the car park, I give Hamish one last fuss,

hoping someone from the castle will be passing through soon enough and recognise him, and hop up into the landlord's beat-up Land Rover Defender. Lifting Rose into the seat beside me, she soon makes herself comfortable with her head on my thighs and her snores rattling right through to my bones.

'I never got your name, lass,' the landlord says once he strikes up the truck that makes an almost wheezing splutter.

'Allie,' I reply, deciding against using my own name now that the reality sets in that I am alone in a car with a total stranger I met outside of a pub less than an hour ago.

'Aye, good to meet you, Allie. Callum.' He outstretches one of his hands, keeping the other on the trembling steering wheel, and I shake it in my own.

After breaking down thrice, listening to Callum's interesting impression of Celine Dion that played on repeat in the tape deck for the last hour, and finally caving and telling the old man about Atticus and my plans in London, we finally arrive in Aberdeen. I thank my new acquaintance, and he ruffles my hair in an affectionate goodbye.

'Look after yourself there, Allie.' He gives me a smile as I fuss Rose again beside him. 'Come into the pub any time if you ever find yourself back up that way. There'll always be a sweet sherry waiting for you. Aye, and bring that fella of yours with you too. Best of luck, hen.'

'Thank you, Callum.' Grabbing the small bag that I had packed to bring with me, I race through the train station, hopping on the first train I see headed for London. Already bursting at the seams, I trundle up and down each carriage hoping for a seat, but proving unlucky. Finally discovering one in first class, I sit down and hope to rest my weary head and gather my strength to see Atticus once again.

'Tickets please.' The conductor startles me awake as the rolling hills turn to wide open sea just out of the window. 'Ma'am, tickets please,' he says again, as I stare at him blankly, my brain still catching up with the rest of my body.

'I'm sorry, I don't have one. I was in a rush. May I buy one now?' I try to plead but the conductor only tuts.

'You don't have a first-class ticket?' Now the whole carriage seems to have stopped tapping on their laptops, or clinking their glasses of Prosecco to watch this drama unfold.

'No, sir.' My cheeks are on fire and I think for a moment of prying open the doors and jumping off the train right here, right now.

'Then I'm going to have to ask you to exit the first-class coach.'

'There are no other seats. Can I please just stay here until the actual occupier of the seat boards?'

'Nice try, hen. First class is for first-class patrons only.' He looks me up and down. 'We have standards to uphold.' Gritting my teeth to prevent myself from having an outburst of *don't you know who I am*', I get to my feet and do the walk of shame back down the carriage. I have no other choice than to make myself comfortable on the floor next to the toilet, which will every now and again swing open to reveal an unsuspecting user halfway through peeing, like the prize on an Eighties game show. The conductor escorts me the whole way.

'That will be £350 to London King's Cross.' He smirks, as though the money is to go directly into his pocket.

'How is that possible? I don't even have a seat,' I splutter. I know I am hardly down to earth enough to know the price of a pint of milk, or a bus ticket, but I know for a fact that paying three hundred and fifty great British pounds for the privilege of sitting next to a toilet on a stained and itchy carpet is taking the piss, literally.

'It's either that or you're off at the next station.' The conductor shrugs and I suppress the urge to scream in his face.

'Fine.' Drawing out my credit card, I reluctantly hand it over.

'That's all gone through – have a wonderful journey.' He hands me my ticket and saunters away.

The experience of the train from my space on the floor reminds me a little of the twelve days of Christmas. I've seen six ladies weeing, five pissed-up hens, four screaming kids, three cokeheads, two fluffy dogs. All that's missing is the partridge in a pear tree.

When the train pulls into King's Cross at 3 p.m., reality begins to set in. I'm going to make it. In just one short tube journey, I shall get to see him again, down on one knee, confessing his love.

Chapter 15

Though everything is going to plan so far, I can't shake the sickness that settles in my stomach the further I descend into the tube station. Perhaps it's being back in London after so long, the air, or the memories? Until Balmoral became my home for the summer, the cacophony of London, its hustle and bustle, never really bothered me. Yet now I find myself pinging through the public like a deer too far from the comfort of open fields and sheltered forests.

Or perhaps it's something I've forgotten? Have I got the wrong date? The wrong time? No, this date has been playing on my wind for weeks; I can't have gotten it wrong now. Unless it has changed, and in all the time I haven't heard from Atticus, he hasn't told me. But why wouldn't he tell me it had been rescheduled if the main purpose of the evening is our engagement?

No, Alice, you fool. I stop dead on the tube platform as the reminder finally hits me. In getting so wrapped up in my excitement for the engagement Kitty told me about, I have overlooked the fact that the conference isn't for me, or our relationship, it's for his relationship with the company he is inheriting. The conference is to prove his power to the shareholders, to give a speech that will inspire and impress them. A speech I was supposed to write.

Selfish, self-obsessed, love-brained Alice strikes again.

One job, I had one job, one thing he asked of me, and I was too preoccupied with the thought of a nice shiny engagement ring and a public declaration of love that I let it slip my mind.

Scurrying onto the next tube that comes, I type furiously into the notes app on my phone, trying to piece together some semblance of a speech. He hasn't given me any bullet points to work from, nor asked me for a draft before now. Perhaps he's done it himself? Or he was thinking, as I do, that his love would surprise him and save the day. Refusing to disappoint the man I love, by the time the carriage pulls into my station I'm sweating from the stress as I weave together some 'thank yous' and flattery and hope for the best.

Rushing out of the station, I find his office building with some difficulty but soon I am neck-deep in suits and aged male faces and I know I am in the right place. Drawing up to the doorman in my muddied skirt and tatty hair, I am sure I look a sight, so it is no surprise when he stops me to ask my business.

'I am here with Atticus Beaumont,' I say, chewing my lip, impatient to get inside.

'Name,' the doorman says with a bored tone as he flicks through his guest list.

'Lady Alice Walpole,' I say proudly and stand up straighter, remembering one of my first conversations with the man of the hour all those months ago in the Kensington side street: '*Your title is your crowning glory*'.

Smiling softly at the memory, it quickly falters as the behemoth of a man speaks again.

'Not on the guest list.' Without looking at me, he turns to the next guest and allows them to pass without question.

'Well look again, good sir,' I persist. 'Mr Beaumont will be waiting for me. He won't be happy if you make his future wife miss her own proposal.' Trying to force myself past him, he outstretches a tree trunk of a bicep and stops me dead in my tracks before I can get a toe in the door.

'Not on the guest list,' he grunts again and I can only give an exacerbated huff in reply.

Turning to walk away, I take a deep breath to calm myself. There is no way that I'm hacking through the wilderness, hitchhiking across Scotland, and sitting next to a train toilet for six hours just to be turned away at the door. No big beefy bloke is getting between me and the man I love.

With the kind of speed only the adrenaline of love can summon, I sprint past the doorman, get chased through the reception, and slip breathlessly into the lift. Pressing the buttons to the floor labelled 'Beaumont & Sons' erratically, I can finally breathe a sigh of relief as the doors close before the security staff can reach me.

I am here. I am seconds from seeing the love of my life.

They've begun without me, so I slip into the conference as quietly as possible. With my heart wide open, and my stomach still gurgling with nausea, I allow myself to turn to the stage, and take a look at my Atticus Beaumont for the first time in weeks.

My Atticus Beaumont . . .

Everyone assumes that when you have depression, all you do is cry. For me, it's the opposite. Don't get me wrong, I feel like crying, constantly, but the tears don't come. It's like feeling a sneeze but it never comes out, just tickles incessantly at your nose until it drives you insane.

Even now, as I stand here, watching who I thought was the love of my life, down on one knee in front of a woman I've never even heard of, humiliating me in front of his world, the tears don't come. It's like my emotions form a bottleneck in my chest, and before they can reach my eyes, they explode over my heart, numbing me to everything good, filling me only with that cold throb of a broken heart.

Standing at the back of the room smelling a little of Hamish, and looking a little like Princess Diana if she'd had a fight in a knitted jumper factory, I am drowned out in a tide of smart suits and receding hairlines, and no one else notices me except *him*. Every eye in the room is fixed upon the great Atticus Beaumont as he takes on the role he was born to fulfil, with his new, glowing fiancée by his side. His perfect, beautiful fiancée who isn't me.

The woman beside him now is what I expect my mother and father wished I was. Looking just enough like his sister to please the gentry, but just different enough that they will make beautiful children: it is a match made in upper-class heaven. With the posture and figure of a mannequin, with the smile of a beauty queen and an aura of grace and intelligence, I see only my flaws within her perfection and another shred of my self-esteem chips away. Perhaps both best and worst of all, I have never seen her in my life.

Seeing as I don't seem to have the maturity and propriety of the woman up there, I give myself two choices. Number one: storm that stage, punch Atticus square in the face and tell all of the shareholders what a lying cheat he is. Or number two: turn around without a word, run back to Scotland and pretend none of this ever happened.

My parents cross my mind for the first time all day. I wonder what my mother would say if she could see me now. She'd laugh, more than likely. Or use this as an opportunity to prove that mothers know best and try to argue that it is my punishment for disobedience. 'None of this would have happened if you'd only done as you were told,' she'd say, with a subtle eyeroll just like she did when I was six and fell and grazed my knee running in the halls at home after she had told me to stop. Mother would make sure I'd remember this moment for the rest of my life just to keep me straight. Father would think and say whatever Mother told him to.

My anger mounts at the thought. Though I know option two would please Mother most, I can't bring myself to follow it through. I can't think of Scotland without thinking of *him*. What would Fraser say if I returned with my tail tucked between my legs? 'I told you so'? That thought alone is the one that sends me over the edge, and I have to clutch my throat to prevent myself from vomiting across the cream carpets. In feeling so much at once, I feel nothing at all. Only a cold oblivion fills me and I am as soulless as charcoal on canvas. Unable to choose either fight or flight, I stay fixed in position, watching as all that I had planned comes crumbling down around me, and I am crushed beneath the rubble of what could have been.

Atticus speaks into the microphone, his eyes unmoved from my face, but I hear none of what he says. Nor do I hear the applause as he exits the stage, or the calls of congratulations as he passes through the crowd towards me.

'Lady Alice.' Atticus bows his head, so casually that it's almost as if he invited me here himself, and this is his royal blessing. How is he so calm? How is this not fazing him? Is he so sure that I won't make a scene and damage his reputation that he is arrogant enough to waltz over here as though nothing is amiss? Unable to bring myself to speak, Atticus simply smiles at my appearance. 'It's nothing personal.'

The voice that I have spent months longing to hear makes me physically recoil as soon as he speaks. Being so close to him now, finally having what I have desired for so long, should fill me with joy, should make me feel at least a fraction of the happiness I felt just hours ago in the depths of the Scottish Highlands. Staring up at him, I scan his face, desperately trying to find the same man I once found so handsome, that I swore was the love of my life. I see none of that in him now. Unable to draw a full breath under the weight of such a realisation, I can just about gather enough air to scoff, as I struggle to fight of the endless waves of nausea.

'Honestly, Alice, I did like you. But come on, prince consort of Liechtenstein . . .' he points to his future wife, waiting demurely in the corner '. . . was an opportunity that I, and the business, just couldn't refuse. Don't you think it suits me? Prince Atticus?'

Something in the smirk punctuating his sentence sends ringing through my ears, like the bride of *Kill Bill*, scouting out her target for revenge. Wincing, I try and take a step back, but my feet are rooted in place. The more he speaks, the more my body begins to throb all over, as though tiny wounds are opening up from head to toe and a cold draught is able to whistle its way through the gaps they leave behind. Everything about him in this moment repulses me and I curse myself for my blind stupidity these past months.

Now it all makes sense. The 'love at first sight', the obsession with my lineage, his refusal to call me by anything but my title. There really is no true love when you have a title; it's just business. I was always just business.

Except, I know full well that any of his business partners would have been treated with far more respect, not just replaced without even so much as a text.

I should be used to that feeling – of knowing that the benefactors, the public, and our images come before any of my needs. But here and now is when I want to know why. Why my parents, my lovers, my friends, have always prioritised everything but me. Why my feelings have never mattered as long as reputations remain intact. What have I done to not be worth the same respect as a contract or an article in a magazine? Why do people assume that just because I was born into this life, I am fine with the same coldness they all seem to revel in?

My heart races in my chest. The seeping, self-pitying sadness turns sour until I am blind with rage and clawing at my throat to keep my screams within.

Closing my eyes for a moment, I imagine myself back in Loch Muick, allowing the cool water to lap against my arms, feeling the plants slide between my toes, listening to the silence of true peaceful nature. Soothing my burning heart. I look at Atticus once again, his gaze scanning my face for any hints of anger.

I lean up to place a tender departing kiss on his cheek. He relaxes against my touch, just enough for me to jab my knee right into his little princelings.

He doubles over in pain, and Atticus's groans are enough to summon the attention of all who had chosen to ignore me until now, but it's his screaming of the word 'bitch' over and over that really sends them running.

Placing my hand on his shoulder, I lean down so close to him that my lips ghost over his ear as I speak. I have no idea how I manage to formulate any words at all, let alone with all the tranquillity of a woman well and truly over it all, but I say with all my strength, 'Have the life you deserve.'

And I walk from that conference, from Atticus Beaumont, with straw in my hair and fire in my belly.

Chapter 16

Though my mother may, once upon a time, have been the woman in those photographs, she isn't anymore. As much as I wish I could run to her and have her stroke my hair like those girls in the books with broken hearts, my reality is very different. The thought of her does the opposite of comfort me, and the thought of returning to my parents' home just miles away to admit defeat is like fleeing the lion's den, only to fling myself into a circle of vultures. No, I can't face them.

The longer I stand outside of the *Beaumont & Sons* offices as the world rushes past, and the noise builds and builds and builds, I realise that I can't face London either.

I always thought that if I could find love, I'd find my home. So now I have no love, and no home, where am I supposed to run to? Where am I supposed to turn when I belong nowhere?

'That's her.' An overly posh voice disturbs my ruminating and I see one of Atticus's little suited minions pointing at me with a particularly acrid expression as he stands sheltering himself behind the giant doorman. When security starts in my direction, I take that as my cue to get as far away from here as possible.

My brain doesn't register where my body instinctively takes me until I reach King's Cross Station. Scouring the boards, I realise there is only one destination I'm searching for, only one where I can think to go that I know I will be safe: Aberdeenshire.

For the whole seven-and-a-half-hour journey, all I can bring myself to do is stare out of the window and watch the world go by. My skin itches, and my throat tickles with a pain that doesn't quite manifest and I actually relish in the discomfort of it all.

The journey melts away, and though night melds into day before my eyes, it feels as if no time has passed at all. So preoccupied in my own head, trying not to spiral in front of an abundance of strangers, so focused on keeping my head above water, I hardly notice when we pull into the Highland station.

Sitting still in my seat as the other passengers bustle around me to get off, I wonder whether I should just stay here, travelling the railways back and forth until I end up somewhere that might actually bring me some joy. The desire to disappear, to just start again with a new name, a new history, throbs through me, and the genuine hatred I have for myself, for who I am, is almost enough to break me once and for all.

Staring out of the window at the train station, seeing

families reunited, seeing friends rushing to one another, and plans in action for home or holiday, my glassy eyes fall on a familiar face.

Mrs Buchanan stands on the platform, the same scowl on her face and her arms crossed tightly over her chest. Despite her fearsome look, the sight of her comforts me. She is an accustomed evil. I don't feel so out of my depth in the wake of her wrath, and I know that although I will get the telling-off of a lifetime, I am safe with her. I am safe here.

As I step down from the train at last, the housekeeper meets me at the door. Preparing myself for an onslaught of reprimands, I wince as she steps towards me. But all she does, after a disappointed sigh, is pluck the wayward pieces of straw from my hair, and smooths it down behind my ears with the tender, almost affectionate touch of a grandmother.

'Is Hamish okay?' is my first question. The housekeeper nods.

'Callum called me as soon as he dropped you off, *Allie.*' She gives a breathy laugh, and I blush as I realise my lie to the landlord was all in vain. 'Pipe Major Bell had worried himself silly about that horse, however.' My chest heaves at her words. I had never meant to affect anyone else in my stupidity. The specific mention of Fraser fills me with an overwhelming feeling as I grapple with my guilt and, most of all, my shame.

'I'm sorry,' I say. Grabbing my bag from my hand, she begins to walk away and I trundle behind her in the station, like Paddington, desperate to find my home.

Half expecting to see a pair of horses waiting outside, I

am relieved when she walks up to a small, rusted car and opens the door for me to slide in. Mumbling a thank you, I sit in the passenger seat in silence as we set off back to Balmoral.

'The king shall not know about all of this tonight.' Her words catch me by surprise after we have spent the best part of an hour driving in silence. 'But you must show your face at the Ghillies Ball, or else he shall ask questions.' She looks over to me and . . . smiles?

'Why are you being so kind to me?' I blurt out. The feeling is foreign. I want her to shout at me, rebuke me, call me a fool – I know how to handle that. But kindness? I don't deserve it, and I certainly don't know how to accept it.

'I know that what you must be feeling is punishment enough.' She keeps her eyes on the road as she drives recklessly through the country.

'You have no idea what I'm feeling,' I mumble like a disgruntled, unguarded teenager, afraid of having her emotions perceived.

'That's okay, I don't need to. I just need to allow you to feel it.' I don't have the words to respond but she continues cautiously, 'Your mother was the same, on her honeymoon. All she needed to do was to feel; all she truly needed was to cry. Balmoral is a quiet place to cry. No one has to see you if you don't wish for them to.'

'I don't need to cry.'

'Perhaps not, but your soul does.' Pulling into the long driveway, she tucks the car behind the kitchen and we both rush through to avoid being caught. 'One thing you absolutely need to do is have a shower and get dressed. You look and smell boggin'.' She turns away and grabs me a towel from her pile of fresh linens.

For the first time all day, I manage a smile. She returns it gently. 'I have asked Sophie to lay out a few options for you but I have requested that she meet you in the queen's dressing room. The queen will already have been dressed by then; hopefully they will be too merry to notice you arriving late.'

'Mrs Buchanan?' I call softly as she begins to walk away, and she turns back. 'Thank you.' My voice comes out in a whisper and she nods in acknowledgement before leaving me.

When I arrived here nearly two months ago, I would never have known this would become a place I'd run to when everything else feels too much. Even now, as caterers, waiters, and other contractors filter in and out of the castle, its hustle and bustle doesn't feel so overwhelming. Being in these walls, I can finally take a moment to breathe. Standing on the staircase, I look at the place around me, at its ugly carpets, and its questionable wall décor, and for the first time since I left, the persistent throb of fear subsides.

Still feeling as though I have been lifted by my ankles and shaken until empty, I walk slowly through the hallway towards my room. With my eyes fixed on the floor beneath me, I take each step carefully, as though one slip could see me shatter completely.

My depression is like a chip in a window screen. It's always there. You can just see it bugging you from the corner of your eye, and with every bump and pothole, you wonder if this might be the one that will finally send the whole thing bursting into a million shards.

I had thought Atticus would be the final blow, but still I walk, clinging to all of my cracked pieces.

A pair of boots hesitate at the opposite end of the hallway. Slowly they inch closer and closer towards me, but I still can't lift my head to see who wears them. When they are within an arm's length, it is his aftershave that I recognise first. Though subtle and stirred with the cold scent of the earth, it seems to envelop the corridor and pulls my eyes instinctively in his direction.

Fraser Bell steps quietly along the carpet, his eyes fixed in front of him, not diverting from his path. He looks dishevelled, as though only moments ago he was rushing around, but now he nurses each of his steps as though able to spend an age in this hallway. A wayward wisp of hair falls across his forehead and the sight of its amber strands glowing in the late afternoon sun that comes in puddles through the windows sends a shock of heat through me.

I want nothing more than to reach out and snag him by the arm, but my body won't cooperate, and he simply passes me by. I know he sees me, for as the breeze of his body hits me, he nods his head and gives a polite 'my lady' all still without meeting my gaze.

By the time I can summon the strength to speak, metres separate us. 'Fraser . . .' I say, though my voice is painfully quiet. Whether he hears or not, he doesn't stop, and only the soft bump of the door swinging closed behind him answers me.

* * *

159

Sinking down into the bottom of the bath, I allow the spray of the shower to pelt me as I stare numbly at the steaming bathroom. Tiny droplets are swallowed up into mammoth ones as they race down the glass, and for just a moment, as the water trickles down my face in a substitute for tears, I allow myself to feel the hurt. Clutching at my chest, it is physical. Pain ripples through me with an unstoppable force and yet I don't bleed, I'm not broken, there is nothing I can do to fix it, to make it stop, besides sitting here, in this bathtub, trying not to scream.

This pain isn't just Atticus. It isn't just a broken heart. No, I'm sure of it. This is the pain of failure. The pain of turning into my mother despite every one of my efforts to be nothing like her. This is the pain of fate, the pain of feeling like you're losing control only to realise you were never in control to begin with.

Why can't I cry?

I squeeze my eyes tightly, hoping to force out just one tear. It's just like vomiting, isn't it? No one likes to vomit, but after those moments of breathless pain as your stomach cramps and your nostrils sting, equilibrium is restored. If I cry, perhaps the pain will go away. If I cry, maybe I will find peace for a moment.

'Alice?' A voice travels through the steam along with a soft knock at the bathroom door. 'Can I come in?' It's Sophie. Her usually chipper tone is gone, and even through the mahogany door, I can hear her worry.

After I manage a rasping 'yes', the maid enters, a plume of steam released back through the door with her arrival.

Finding me curled up and naked, Sophie gives me a sad

smile and, without a word, grasps the bottle of shampoo from the side and lathers my hair. Taking down the shower head, she gently rinses me off, like I am child, too worn, too ready for bed to care for myself. After repeating it over again with the conditioner she then dampens a flannel and softly scrubs down my back, across my face, lifting each arm gently until all stench of Hamish is gone.

'Now babe . . .' Sophie steps back with a smile '. . . despite you giving me the fear and running off, I love you, I'd do anything for you, but I'm going to draw the line at washing your Mary.'

'My Mary?' I croak and she smiles.

'Aye, your Mary. Fairy? Minnie? Fanny?' She whispers the final word as though her mother would appear from around the corner and tell her off for her brash language, but I only smile weakly back at her. 'You okay if I leave you to finish up? I'll just be waiting outside the door, and I can take you down to the dressing room.'

I offer her a grateful nod, and she leaves the room, satisfied. After finishing off my shower, I slide out of the bathtub and drape myself in the towel Mrs Buchanan had given me and meet Sophie back in my bedroom.

'Ready?' she asks, her familiar smile back on her features.

Before I nod in agreement, I draw her in and hug her tightly in an embrace I think I may have needed for years. 'Thank you,' I breathe. No one has ever been so kind to me before now. I came back here with every expectation to be rebuked, to be mocked, to have them all say 'I told you so', or do as Fraser did and simply act as though I don't exist and yet, I have never in my life experienced such . . . *love*.

'Come on.' Sophie pulls back and pushes the wet hair from my face. 'Forget whatever has happened just for tonight. The Ghillies Ball is the one night a year where anything goes in this place. Be who you want to be. Or don't. Just for one night let it all go, and try a different you on for size.'

Chapter 17

'Now, I have a wee surprise for you.' Sophie smirks, clasping her hands together. 'Close your eyes.' She guides me the last few steps to the door and I hear her push it open. She drags me by the hand across the threshold, and my bare feet sink into the plush carpet. I can already tell that this room is not often frequented.

'Sophie?' My tone is nervous as she releases her hold on me and can be heard shuffling things about the room.

'Okay, okay.' I can hear the smile in her voice. 'Open.' Doing as commanded, I peel open my eyes to see her stood in the centre of the rounded room, arms outstretched as she presents the suitcase that I'd had to leave behind in Braemar all those weeks ago. Propped up on a chaise longue in the middle of the room, Sophie skips around it. 'Ta-da!'

If I was stood here even just a week ago, I think I would have dropped to my knees with joy. But now, the sight of the designer labels, the array of tiny bottles filled with various potions to make me look youthful and beautiful, have no attraction to me anymore. As Sophie rifles through the fabrics, I scan the room, taking it all in for the first time.

From floor to ceiling, fabrics are draped around the entire circumference of the room in every colour imaginable. As though plucked straight from a fairy tale, this dressing room is the stuff of dreams. A cabinet of tiaras and coronets is framed by hanging dresses, gold laced scarves and shoes for every occasion. Floating around the room, I run my fingers along the fabrics, like a piano of silks, linens, and finely tuned appliqué. Every touch feels like history, with every single piece in this collection aged to perfection and ready to tell a story.

'Okay, why was I forced into all of those itchy jumpers when this place has existed all along?' Turning back to Sophie, I smile in awe at the richness of fashion around me.

'Oi, I tried my best with those jumpers. I was scrounging for days,' she says, picking up a short, puffy dress from my suitcase and twirling around with it. 'That right there is the royal collection. Only to be touched on special occasions. I've only ever been in this room twice in my life. The first time was to do the dusting; the second is right now. The contents of those wardrobes and that jewellery cabinet are worth more than my life, tenfold.' Sophie shudders at the thought and sets down another dress she had picked out of my suitcase.

'Mrs Buchanan has said that the king has given you permission to wear any of your own clothes, if you so wish it, but he has personally suggested this one.' She waltzes over to one of the rails and releases a sealed bag. Hanging it on one of the hooks dotted about the room, she unzips it slowly, as though revealing a dress so fragile it may well be made from the wings of a thousand butterflies.

I'm not far off. Beneath the protective layer hangs a dress of ivory satin, embroidered all across the bodice with pearls. I have never seen anything more beautiful in my life. The clothes in that suitcase no longer feel like me, at least not tonight. Tonight, I wish to be the kind of woman who wears dresses like that, who floats about a castle in a satin gown and has her shit together.

'I'm allowed to wear *that*?' Still in disbelief, I stare at the dress in awe.

'You know, for someone born into royalty, you aren't half awkward about fine things. I'd have thought you'd be used to all of this fancy stuff by now.' Sophie chuckles as she begins to deconstruct the dress to help me into it.

'I don't think I could ever get used to anything like this.' I slide the fabric between my fingers, and my fingertips tingle with the caress. I can't wait to feel it flowing over the rest of my body.

'You ready?' Sophie asks, as the opening sound of drums is swiftly followed by bagpipes, signalling that the party has begun. Nodding, I drop my towel and allow Sophie to shimmy the fabric up my body. I feel like a crustacean returning to its shell. The cinched waist and smooth satin feel like home as the dress fits like it was made just for me.

Looking in the mirror, I hardly recognise myself. This

isn't the woman who was reflected back at me in the muddied plastic windows of the train just hours ago. This isn't the girl with no light in her eyes who was staring back at me in the bathroom tiles only moments ago.

'It wouldn't be Balmoral if you didn't also have to wear a tartan sash though.' Sophie hooks the red royal tartan over my shoulder and, for the first time in my life, I feel like I belong. 'Perfect.' She grins, smoothing down the plaid carefully.

'Oh, Sophie, this is amazing. Thank you.'

'What are you thanking me for? I hardly made the thing,' she jokes. 'Now, let's get that hair sorted.'

I think back to the photograph of my mother in the pub. Her blonde hair wild, like a golden halo of curls glowing around her. 'Can we leave it down?' I ask, usually forced to have each and every strand hidden away into an updo that is tight enough to give me a facelift.

'Absolutely.' Diffusing it until it looks positively unrestrained, my friend and maid returns with one final piece to complete the outfit: a tiara. Teardrop pearls hang in arches of diamonds and swing gently with each of my breaths. The burden of it is indescribable. In one breath, it feels weightless, as though designed specifically for each curve of my skull, matched perfectly for my constitution. In the next, I feel as though I can hardly lift my head. My eyes must remain fixed on the floor or my neck will snap and all of this will be over.

'What if it falls off?' I suddenly panic, risking a glance at Sophie.

'If you keep your head up and walk with confidence,

there's no way it would even dare to fall.' She grins, admiring her work.

'What about you, Sophie? Aren't you coming to the ball?' I ask, noticing her not rushing to get dressed, panicking that I will have to do this without her.

'I will be, just a little later. My dress is still in my dormitory.' She looks around longingly at the endless wardrobe.

'Why don't you just dress in something from here?'

Her eyes widen and she shakes her head nervously.

'I could never. Only the king and queen can give people permission to take from this collection. I reckon I'd be done for treason if I rocked up in duchesse satin.' She doesn't cease shaking her head. 'No, I have a dress I wear every year. I'll just go and stick that on.'

'Nothing in there is from the royal collection,' I say, pointing at my suitcase.

'No, no, I couldn't possibly.'

'You absolutely can. You shared your clothes with me, it's only right that I can return the favour. How about this one?' Walking over to the suitcase, I pull out a pale blue silk dress from within.

'I'd never pull off something like that, honestly.' Sophie's eyes are wide as she stares at the way the soft light of the room shimmers with each floating movement of the dress.

'At least try it on?' I push, insistent on helping her as she helps me.

Reluctantly, she takes the dress behind the screen and seconds later returns for me to zip it up.

The fabric is still perfectly pressed, but ebbs and flows over her figure like the soft lapping of water on the shoreline. The colour of a loch in the cool of winter, in every movement there is a reflection, like sunlight tickling the surface. All the beauty of the earth is captured right in those very pools and never before has that dress suited a person so perfectly.

'There is no way I'm having that dress back, whether you choose to wear it tonight or not.' Sophie persists with her deer-in-headlights expression. 'Not once in the whole time I have owned that has it ever looked that good on me. You cow.' I chuckle and she relaxes in the mirror.

'You really think so?'

'It is the only thing I can be certain of right now.'

'My grandmother's tartan was always blue.' Sophie looks at herself in the mirror but I don't think it's herself that she sees. Snapping out of her thoughts, she turns to me. 'I think I still have it somewhere. Would you mind, if we went to fetch it?'

'It would be a pleasure,' I say, heading for the door, my excitement finally blossoming.

'What about your suitcase?' Sophie asks as I slip out of the door.

'You keep it, all of it. I don't need it.' Her shocked expression returns. 'It's not a gift,' I say, hoping to make her less uncomfortable. 'Think of it as payment, for all you have done for me, and the clothes you have shared with me.'

'Alice—'

'I insist. Plus, I don't want it anymore. I've rather taken to itchy woolly jumpers in August and skirts the length that a nun would wear.'

* * *

'The Ghillies Ball, one of our longest traditions,' Mrs Buchanan begins as soon as Sophie and I step into the ballroom. She sways a little with the glass of punch in her hand precariously sloshing against the rim. 'It was begun by Queen Victoria in 1852 as a "thank you" to her staff and has been continued by every monarch since.'

A band sit on the balcony playing their toe-tapping jigs as a sea of kilts and gowns overflow through the room in the various twirls and leaps of the Scottish country dance that everyone just seems to know the steps to. Scanning the room, I know I am only looking for one face in particular, my heart full of both anxiety and anticipation. It sinks, however, when I have no choice but to turn back to the housekeeper once my search proves unsuccessful.

'Every royal in residence and every member of staff is here right now. You know, Ghillie can stand for two things. The first is your shoes.' She points at the little black, ballet-esque shoes that are laced high around both of our ankles. 'Those, my dear, are ghillies. Designed specifically for Scottish country dancing. The second is that its Gaelic for gamekeeper. A ball for the servants, named after the servants. Fandabidozi!' She takes another swig of her drink and I have to repress a chuckle at the sight of her unwinding. Sophie was right; this really is a night where anything goes.

The king sits stoically in the royal dais and, not wishing to strain his voice above the music, he chats closely in the ear of another kilted individual. The monarch cracks a genuine smile and chuckles animatedly as his raconteur returns to his full height. Fraser Bell stands beside the king, his shy, dimpled smile out in full force, giving all of the ladies' tiaras a run for their money for the thing of greatest beauty.

Excusing myself from Mrs Buchanan, and sliding in between Sophie and the partner she has had no trouble in finding from the royal household as they swing around the floor in dance, I make my way over, almost instinctively. I curtsey to the king. He looks me up and down, his familiar impenetrable expression returning.

'Lady Walpole.' He speaks softly. 'It seems I have exceptional taste in ladies' dresses.'

'You do indeed, Your Majesty.'

'Beautiful, is it not, Pipe Major Bell?' The king turns back to Fraser, who stares only at my ghillies, his dimples long gone. I look all across his face, almost willing his eyes to meet mine. When they don't, the cold tingling begins in my toes and despite the way everyone else in this room is slick with sweat, coldness spreads through me.

At the king's command, he finally steals one reluctant glance and visibly swallows. 'Undeniably, sir.' My cheeks flush.

'You know, I have had that dress saved in the collection for decades. I believe it was your grandmother who wore it last, to this very ball.' Still keeping my eyes on Fraser, I can hardly hear what is being said but the king persists. 'Don't be surprised if a few of the more antiquated of us in this room mistake you for old Alex. She was very much revered in Balmoral.'

How many times must a woman be told how exceptional her family are, and how many times must she be reminded how much she doesn't fit in, before she screams? Hopefully not as she is face to face with the king, but boy is she close.

Though it pains me, I politely chuckle.

'Have you ever been to a ceilidh, Lady Alice?'

'No, sir. I must admit that I am rather out of my depth.' I look again about the room as the pace of the song ever increases and the steps get faster and faster until I am surprised the queen is still standing with how she is swung from partner to partner.

'That shall not do,' the king says, and looks to Fraser. 'How about you show my great niece how it is done, young Bell? You have been dancing at this ball for years, have you not?'

'Since I was a bairn, sir.' Fraser still refuses to land his eyes on me and I can almost hear my heartbeat above the music with how it hammers against my chest.

'Perfect.' The king clasps his hands together. 'I would show you myself, Lady Alice, but I'm afraid my knees can't really take the Dashing White Sergeant anymore.'

'It is a terrible shame to miss you dance, sir.' The king pooh-poohs modestly. 'I am afraid I know none of the steps, and I wouldn't wish to dirty the pipe major's shoes.'

'Can you hear her trying to make excuses, Bell?' A smile draws at the corner of his mouth. 'Mrs Buchanan is a terrible dancer and that has never stopped her before.' He nods to the party and Mrs B skips about in the very centre in a spectacle reminiscent of a stag on ice.

'If I may say, my lady?' Fraser speaks and I nod to urge him on. 'Having my toes stepped on is a small price to pay for the privilege of seeing you dance.'

The music stops. Or at least it does for me.

Chapter 18

I have always dreamed of attending a ball, of being wooed on a dance floor that isn't sticky with a spilt 'Blue Lagoon'. The pleasure of savouring each fleeting touch of a hand, a ghostly caress across the small of your back, has been so lost in this age of anti-romance and I yearn for it. The thought of intimacy is always more indulgent when it is forbidden, when a chaste kiss is a scandal.

Is that why Fraser leading me by the hand to the floor feels so hedonistic: knowing that the best friend I have ever had is the one who truly deserves him, and yet my heart taps out a ceilidh jig, and my palms moisten in his hand with every desire for him to hold me closer.

Fraser Bell is silent. His chest rises and falls in his ghillie shirt but still he neither speaks nor so much as looks at me. The pleasure of seeing him again stirs with the pain that the feeling is unrequited and I find myself amidst the whole population of Balmoral, unable to pry my eyes from him.

'Fraser . . .' I begin in a whisper, hoping to force him to look at me, but the music fires up and we are swept away in the tide of 'The Military Two-Step'. With one hand in his, we skip down the line side by side, and the piper guides each of my steps as I am spun, I skip, and my hands are imprisoned by his.

'Talk to me, please,' I beg in a low voice, hurt by his silence. 'At least tell me what I've done.' Before he can answer I am spun out again and forced to chasse beside him for a few beats until I can return to his full hold.

'I have nothing to say to you, my lady,' he says, before the song forces us to part again and I have to fight to keep my legs strong under me.

'Must I order you to speak plainly, Pipe Major Bell?' With each word, I have to force my confidence.

'My lady may do as she wishes. I am at your service, ma'am.' His expression is blank, and despite the fact I have just watched my boyfriend get engaged to another woman, it is Fraser's coldness that is truly biting.

'Don't you dare act as if we aren't f-friends.' My voice wobbles, though still we dance. 'Please.'

Before he can speak again, the music draws to its final cadence, and with a bow he leaves me stranded on the dance floor as he strides through the crowd and out of sight.

Overcome with frustration, with pain, I bustle through the party after him. Bursting through the doors, I walk quickly down the hallway, the wide expanse of his back still in my sights. Even the glimpse of Mrs Buchanan's ghillie shoes behind the curtain with a rather muddied pair of boots doesn't detain me as Fraser leaves the castle, and I hurry after him.

The rain lashes against my face as soon as I step over the threshold. Its cold kiss numbs me for a moment and I almost lose sight of the piper in the downpour.

'Fraser Bell!' I call after him, my desire to speak to him far outweighing my fear of being perceived by others. 'Do I have to beg you to speak to me?' My voice feels broken, I am soaked to the bone, and only when he finally ceases his retreat does the pain subside just a little.

'Go back inside, Alice,' he calls back to me.

'Not until you tell me what I have done.' Shivering, I remain stubborn.

Fraser stops in his tracks, finally, and with his back to me still, calls back, 'Is that what all of this has been? Is that the only reason you wanted me? Get close to the stable boy, make him feel *treasonous* things, just so you can use his horse to piss off back home to a man who could never love you half as much as I—?' He cuts himself off with a frustrated grunt and he rubs his face roughly.

'No, Frase—'

Finally, he turns back, his red hair so dark as it drips down across his face, his white shirt clinging to his skin. 'I wish you all of the happiness in the world, my lady. But know that a life with Atticus Beaumont isn't the life you deserve.'

Turning to leave again, I call out, 'Atticus Beaumont is engaged.' Fraser stops in his tracks. 'Atticus Beaumont proposed to another woman right in front of me and do you know what hurts the most? The fact that it hardly hurts me at all. All I could think to do was run back here, and yet your disdain, as much as I can't blame you for it, somehow breaks my heart more than his betrayal ever could.'

Tearing his jacket from his back, he jogs back towards me and hooks it over my shoulders, pulling it tightly across my chest where his hands remain, clutched to the fabric. He is so close now that the rain runs down his nose and drips from the end to slide down my cheek like a tear. With him so close, I don't feel the cold.

'You shouldn't be out here,' he says softly.

'You shouldn't have run from me,' I retaliate and he scoffs.

'And you shouldn't have run from me . . . from here. At least not without telling—'

Reaching up, I silence him by brushing the rain from his face. Without thinking of anything but him, his damp features, the warm throb of his body so close to mine, I reach up in my muddied ghillies and press my lips to his.

I am kissing Fraser Bell and though that fact should terrify me, nothing has ever come so naturally to me in my life. I don't feel the weight of this tiara as he slides his hand into my hair. I hardly feel the rain hammering against us both as his arm slinks around my waist, drawing me desperately closer. His lips, his tongue, his wandering hands, soothe every single worry, silence every thought in my mind, until I feel more at home in his embrace than I ever have in my life. Being held by Fraser Bell is like slipping into a deep sleep, the weightlessness of floating through the ether and riding off into the sunset of a dreamworld.

When he pulls away, the both of us are breathless and our chests collide with each heaving inhalation. Fraser's lashes are thick with rain as he rakes his eyes over my face as though trying to memorise every single freckle. I have never felt so seen, and yet, I don't shy away from his gaze. His irises are so full of light, swimming with such affection that he doesn't have to say a single word, for every one of his thoughts is projected loud and proud.

Holding me gently by the cheeks, all he can do is smile until he can hold my gaze no longer and is forced to turn away to shake his head. 'What is it?' I ask in a whisper.

'Nothing,' he replies, still shaking his head. 'Just you.' He plants a kiss on my forehead. His smile still persists, and it's infectious.

'Me?' I chuckle.

'You,' is his only reply before he ensnares my lips in his once again.

Grasping the back of my head tenderly, Fraser pulls me closer and closer still until we are stumbling through the deluged flowerbeds. Desperate to have me even nearer, the piper taps me gently against the back of my thighs and I instinctively spring into his arms, wrapping my legs around his waist and submitting to him, his body, his lips, and the incessant rattling of my heart. He rests his wide hands over the curve of my backside, and my body is on fire with every gentle caress, every press of his fingertips. I am electric, I am alive, and I . . . am a *horrible* friend.

Sophie's disappointed glare flashes through my mind and I pull away, as though struck by lightning. I have betrayed her – my one friend who spends her free time taking care of me, who bathed me when I could hardly raise my head, who dressed me when all I wanted to do was rot. What sort of friend would kiss the man she loves, the man I had sworn to set her up with? What is wrong with me? Why do I have to ruin everything?

'Alice?' Fraser says breathlessly, his words hardly audible over the lashing rain. I can't look at him; I am too lost in my thoughts as I worm out of his grip and return my feet to the boggy ground. 'Are you okay?' He tries to reach for my face but I avoid his touch.

'I'm sorry. I can't— I shouldn't be doing this.' The words are painful to deliver and the way Fraser's face freezes over with his professional coldness is the twisting of the knife.

Before he can say anything that will only break me further, I turn from him and flee back across the gardens. Thick mud splashes against the satin of my dress. My hair is plastered to my face, and all of my organs feel fit to explode.

I burst through the door of the kitchen, and a startled member of staff jumps at my swamped appearance. 'Lady Alice? Are you okay?' she asks meekly but I don't stop to answer.

Leaving a muddied trail in my wake, I race through the castle until I reach my bedroom. I scrub the dirt from my hands, feeling just like Lady Macbeth crying 'Out damned spot'. The guilt only seems to mount more relentlessly the more I scrub. Though my hands turn red with the effort, I still feel filthy.

Peeling myself out of my dress, I dump it into the bath, praying a soak will relieve it of its soiling. The taps hiss as they fill the tub to the very top, but the water doesn't stay clear for long. Filth seeps from the fabric and the murky water just serves as a sick reminder that my friendship isn't the only valuable thing I have ruined today. After lifting my tiara carefully from my head, I lay it down on the chest of drawers, praying that its outing in the downpour hasn't caused any lasting damage.

Though the ceilidh still rages on loudly, I crawl, still muddied and wet, into bed, and hope that sleep will favour me and take me away from my mind for a few hours.

With Sunday morning arriving like a period in white trousers, so does the sweet, sweet alarm of screeching bagpipes as Pipe Major Bell uses his day off to stand beneath my window, rattling each of the bones in my body in a call that's impossible to ignore. First, he haunted my dreams, invading the nightmares of Sophie and her anger with his lips and desire, and now he haunts me from my very first waking breath.

After shuffling from beneath my duvet, I make my way over to the window. His uniform is dishevelled, his hair peeks out from beneath his bonnet, and remnants of dirt linger on his shoes. The sight of him makes my legs weak and I have to cling to the curtains just to keep myself standing. As soon as his eyes meet mine, the mouthpiece falls from his lips, and his brows furrow in a pleading expression. Before he can speak, however, before I cave in his presence, I slam the window shut, draw the curtains and climb back into bed. His muffled piping is hesitant, reluctant, until it ceases just moments after beginning.

How can I face him?

Even worse, how can I ever face Sophie?

The summer is almost over. Soon the king and queen will be returning to London. Perhaps the only way I can stop hurting everyone around me is to go with them. Perhaps the only way to make everyone happy again is to leave the only place that has ever felt like home. Perhaps the only way I can make everyone happy is to give up my chances of finding my own joy. I'd sooner live in misery than allow myself to ruin anyone else's lives.

Chapter 19

'What do you mean?' I warble into the receiver as I clutch my phone so tightly that my fingertips begin to throb against the screen.

'Assault Alice, I'm talking about assault.' My mother's voice tears through the telephone waves, the lashing of her tongue just as sharp and painful as it would be in a direct attack. 'Your little stunt at the *Beaumont & Sons* conference has been making waves in society. There is absolutely no way that you can return before Michaelmas and that is being exceptionally optimistic. I shall wager that a quiet return in the winter may be best for all concerned.'

'So I really am banished?' The last few days, I have avoided everyone almost as much as I can. The king and queen were informed of my little escapades in London the day after the ball and I haven't been invited for an intimate dinner with them since. I have been scampering around the castle, hiding behind curtains, rushing off down perpendicular corridors, and hiding in any room with an unlocked door when I hear Sophie humming towards me. Unable to face anyone, I have successfully isolated myself and have not had to talk to another human for days. That was until my phone rang for the first time in months with an unwelcome phone call from Mother.

'Ever the drama with you, isn't it? Even when you were a child you would have thought I was some wicked stepmother locking you in a tower every time you were sent to your room for misbehaving.' I'm surprised she even remembers that I was ever a child. I can hardly remember having a mother.

'I'm not going to apologise if that is what you're after,' I add stubbornly, my hackles up, my fight instinct ready to kick in.

'You're just lucky Mr Beaumont isn't pressing charges, Alice. One day you're going to have to grow up and realise that your recklessness has consequences. I can't keep sending you a thousand miles away to try and keep you out of trouble,' she adds as though Atticus is somehow doing me a favour when he deserved so much more than a pair of bruised plums.

'Mother, what was I meant to do?' I plead.

'Protect your dignity. Be the bigger person, Alice. No one will care that Mr Beaumont is an adulterer, or that he hurt your feelings. That isn't what society concerns itself with.' Her usually cold voice is thick with emotion as she rants into the phone and I can't bring myself to reply.

'Soon you will come to realise that no one cares for truth, or what motivates you, or whether your actions were justified. All they care about is the story. They get off on seeing the regal lady lose her composure. They want you weak, they want you vulnerable so they can feel as though they are better than you. Man is entertained seeing the caged lion squirm at the crack of a whip. Then calls it violent when they prod that lion's wounds and it takes their hand in retaliation. Whether you like it or not, your role in this life is to keep the public sweet, to be that tamed lion, that performs perfectly for their circus. Be angry in private, because they won't be content until they see you buried. Then and only then they might start to appreciate you.'

I have never heard her speak like this. She is always so composed, so emotionless. If she carries on in such a way, I might have to start worrying that she's been possessed, or even worse, that she's actually human.

'She wreaked havoc up at Balmoral just to entertain herself. A true free spirit.' That's how Callum the pub landlord had described my mother and her own time in Balmoral. Was she really once like me, with her own mind, her own feelings? All my life, has she just been that performing feline, too afraid to roll over and show her soft side for fear of being poached?

'Mother?' I ask once she falls silent. She hums, encouraging me to continue. 'You had to learn all of this the hard way, didn't you?' There's a pause before she responds.

'I shall have one of the staff send up some of your winter clothes. Goodbye, Alice,' she says bluntly, hanging up the phone before I can return a farewell.

Staring from the window, I picture her in the scene. Her shock of blonde hair, her carefree smile, running through

182

the gardens, chased by the groundskeeper's dog and the housekeeper as she trails her fine dresses through the mud. I picture the tutting gentlemen, the disapproving shakes of the ladies' heads; I don't have to imagine those at all. They're stuck in my mind clear as day from when I was as young as four, tugging at the ruffles of my dress, skipping down the aisle for a royal wedding when I was told over and over just to walk.

If she has been doing this all along to protect me, couldn't she have just once shown me a glimpse of the love she is capable of? If she wished to harden me to a world that bays for her blood, couldn't she have still loved me in private?

But then, why must everyone love me in private, or in their own messed-up way? Why must I be contented with that being how they show their love, when it does little to soothe me? Why can I not be loved loudly? Why must everyone hide their love for me? Is that why I was so taken in with Atticus? For the first time, someone was unafraid to admit their feelings; for once, loving me wasn't something wrong or a weakness that must be concealed. But even then, his love wasn't true. Does being loved loudly mean being loved insincerely?

I don't realise how long I have been staring blankly out of the window until a soft tap against the glass startles me out of my own mind.

Fraser Bell is tucked behind some of the bushes and shrubs beneath my window, his light eyes wide, his expression nervous as he attempts a smile. Just as I am about to draw the curtains closed to escape him, he tosses another berry from the bush at the window and, before I can turn away, he beckons me to him with a shy hand. I think about his offer for a moment. I should refuse, just close the curtains, sleep the day away again, but my mind is too scrambled, too tired to try to fight against my real desires. Before I can talk myself out of it, I slip on my shoes and rush down to meet him.

'You came?' he whispers. His jaw is speckled with red stubble and he searches my face.

'What can I do for you, Pipe Major Bell?' I plaster on my best performing lion smile, though every one of my instincts screams at me to reach out and stroke the back of my fingers down his rough cheeks.

He straightens himself out, and I notice he isn't in his usual attire but clad in a plaid shirt with his jeans muddied and bloodied at the knees. 'It's Clover, one of the horses, my lady.'

'Is she okay?' A rush of panic washes over me until his rugged face cracks into a glorious smile.

'Come and see for yourself.' Excitedly, he strides off towards the stables, but – hesitating for a moment – I stay, stuck in place. 'If you'd like to, of course,' he adds, folding his rough hands over one another timidly. Warmed by his nerves, I jog to catch up with him. We walk in silence side by side. Fraser steals glances at me every few metres, and I watch him every step in between.

'My lady.' Fraser stops suddenly in his tracks and turns to me. I give him a pointed look and he corrects himself. 'Alice,' he breathes with a smile. 'I just wanted to say, nae, apologise. I shouldn't . . . it's my fault, I—'

I cut him off before my cheeks grow so hot that I begin to sweat. 'Look, Fraser, let us just pretend like nothing has happened. I'd had a bad few days. I wasn't thinking straight. We never have to even mention it again.' I rush out my words. Each one seems to fill me with a sick feeling, but I know it's for the best. Perhaps I kissed him because my heart is broken. Perhaps I kissed him to just feel *something*. If I convince him of that fact, perhaps I can convince myself also. Fraser's face contorts in a display of pain for a moment but he quickly masks it with his professional smoulder.

'Whatever you say, my lady.' He nods, and my heart throbs at the sight of him. Despite all of my efforts to forget it, the only thing running around in my head is that damned kiss. We stand face to face, only just gathering enough sense to carry on breathing.

With only silence between us, Fraser bows his head, our bodies instinctively drawing closer to one another as though pulled, like we are two halves, desperate to be reunited. Only when I can feel his breath on my face, and it sends a shock of goose bumps down my neck, does the piper draw away, cough, and speak without looking at me.

'You aren't squeamish, are you? Not going to boke at the sight of blood?' A nervous blush splashes over his face.

Clearing my throat, I do as he does and pretend that the last few seconds, the last overpowering feelings, never took place. 'Okay, I might need you to spoil whatever this surprise is before I start thinking you're going to show me a dead horse or reveal that you're a murderer.' Folding my arms over my chest, I stare at him down my nose with a laugh.

'No dead things, I promise.' Fraser raises his hands in surrender with a chuckle. 'There is, however, some rather beautiful new life.'

'A baby?' I eagerly ask. Fraser only turns away with a timid smile and continues towards the stables. Skipping up right beside him, I try to force him to look me in the eye as I press and press. 'There's a baby isn't there? A foal? Has she given birth?'

'If you just wait thirty seconds longer, you'll get to see.' The light in his eyes is so bright as his eyes are pinched with his smile.

'Oh my, I'm right, aren't I?' Clapping my hands together, I race ahead of him to the stable and push through the door. Greeting both Hamish and DeeDee as I pass, I draw up to the final stable that belongs to a quiet mare that can't seem to get much attention when DeeDee and Hamish are involved.

The palomino mare stands in the middle of her stable, licking ceaselessly at something out of sight behind the gate. Moving forward cautiously, not wishing to startle the new mother, I see her baby in the flesh. A tiny blonde foal lies folded up in the hay, slick with afterbirth and saliva. With its eyes hardly open, the tiny foal drops its head with each firm lick from its mother as she tries to sleep but is interrupted each time.

Fraser finally catches up and leans through the hatch beside me. 'A little beauty, isn't she? Less than an hour old.'

'I didn't even know Clover was pregnant,' I whisper.

'She has always been a quiet wee thing. No fuss from her at all, at least compared to DeeDee. She's the easiest mare ever.' Fraser fusses at her golden mane, and whispers affirming words against her face with an affectionately rough kiss. 'Now if you had come to me when you wanted to ride, I'd have recommended Clover any day of the week. If she wasn't pregnant of course.'

Clover staggers over towards me and nestles her head in the crook of my neck. Giggling, I return her affection.

'If the summer wasn't almost over, I would have suggested you taking her out for a ride once she's recovered. She suits you.' Fraser looks at the both of us with an air of pride and I have to look away before he sees me blush.

'I'm not leaving,' I say, unable to raise my gaze to meet his.

'Pardon?' he splutters.

'My mother finally called.' I sigh, keeping my eyes fixed on the foal as he nuzzles for his mother. 'I'm afraid you're stuck with me until she sees fit for me to return in the winter.'

Fraser begins to smile, but catches his expression and distorts it into a frown. 'I'm sorry.'

'Don't be. There is nothing for me in London anymore. I haven't heard from any of my friends, and the last time I saw my now ex-boyfriend, I kneed him in the you know—' I flick my eyes down to the crutch of Fraser's jeans and with a mouthed 'oh' he instinctively covers himself with his hands. 'Yeah so, not leaving.' I shrug.

Fraser is silent for a moment and I see in his face he is scrambling for what to say. 'I'm glad,' is what he settles on, and we both stand in a warm, comfortable silence, watching the foal navigate his first minutes on the earth.

Chapter 20

'If I were insecure, I'd think you were avoiding me.' Sophie's voice startles me awake as she stands over my bed, stripping my pillows from their cases one by one.

Still groggy with sleep, I rub my eyes just to make sure that this isn't another of my anxiety-inducing dreams. When Sophie pulls the pillow out from beneath my head and it bounces against the mattress, however, I am firmly awake.

'Are you making my bed whilst I'm still in it?' is the only thing I can think to say as she straightens out the new linens.

Looking down at the bedclothes in her hand, then at me, still bundled up in my duvet, Sophie shrugs. 'Yeah, suppose I am. You don't usually wake up when I do it, though,' she adds casually.

'Hang on.' I sit up against the headboard, feeling my hair standing on end with my movement. 'You've done this more than once?'

'I do it all of the time. You're a really heavy sleeper, you know.' She goes to grab the duvet but I cling to it tightly like a child, refusing to get up for school. I'm not quite ready to leave the perfectly warm nest I have created for myself.

'I'll pretend you never said that, and will put aside my slight concern that I can sleep through someone changing my bedding, whilst I am in the bed, *if* you allow me five more minutes to rot in here.'

'Fine,' she huffs, sliding off her shoes and choosing instead to climb into the bed beside me. After making herself comfortable, she turns to me again. 'You didn't acknowledge what I said.' Sophie looks at me across the pillows, like a wife looking at her husband and dreaming of divorce.

'I'm sorry,' I say softly, like said apologetic husband. 'I was just a little more concerned with the whole watching me sleep thing.'

'Have you been avoiding me?' She snuggles deeper into the blankets, unable to look me in the eye as she asks again.

Guilt curdles in me, and I debate whether or not I should tell her the truth. 'A little,' I admit, ashamed.

'Why?' Her hurt expression cuts through me.

'I think I've been avoiding everything good.'

'But that makes no sense.'

'I know.' Looking at the blank space on the wall, I think of all the ways that I have sabotaged my own life the second anything goes wrong. It used to only be me getting hurt, but now I see Sophie's sad dark eyes and entirely innocent being, I realise that what I thought was just self-destruction has hit my best friend in collateral.

'I could give you ten self-pitying reasons why I've been ignoring you,' I confess. 'That I ruin everything good before I lose it, or I don't believe I deserve to be happy, but my own issues with myself are no excuse to hurt you. You aren't like the people I've had in my life up to now, where they're fine with seeing me disappear from their lives the moment things get tough, or they don't even notice when I'm spiralling. You are everything that is good in my life, Sophie, and you haven't deserved any of this.' Though the truth flows out of me uncontrollably, I still can't bring myself to confess to the kiss. I can't bring myself to break her heart. I pull in a shaking breath and Sophie takes my hand in hers but allows me the room to speak without interruption. 'I thought I was doing the right thing, but honestly, I've been a shitty friend. And now I have no idea how I can even begin to make it up to you. I'm so sorry.'

I've had enough therapy in my life to know where all of these actions and emotions come from, and I can logically see that they're destructive, and yet I'm still not equipped to deal with any of them. I can't seem to escape them, no matter how much I know that it's all just . . . *wrong*.

But how am I meant to tell anyone that? How am I meant to say that expensive therapists and medicines still don't work and at the end of the day, my brain seems to conspire against me so that I end up losing all that I love? How do I explain that I know shouldn't do the things I do but I can't seem to stop?

I can't lose Sophie. I have never had a friend like her, and I don't think I ever shall again. I'm taking back control. I refuse to drive her away too when all she's ever been is good.

'Make it up to me?' Sophie sits up straighter in my bed, a look of confused intrigue crossing her face.

'Well, since I'm going to be staying here for the foreseeable, it's only fair that I repay all of the favours that you have done for me.'

'And how are you thinking of doing that?' Sophie raises an eyebrow and I rack my brains.

'I'll come to work with you, for a week.' Happy with myself, I sit up straighter, folding my arms over my chest with contented pride. After a few seconds to process, Sophie's serious expression cracks into her widest smile yet as she laughs hysterically. She shakes the bed with her laughter, and I watch on, confused, until she finally runs out of breath and talks between giggles.

'You . . . work . . . Oh, Alice.' She resumes her knee-slapping laughter. 'The great Lady Alice changing bedsheets and scrubbing toilets?'

'Are you scared I'm going to steal your job, eh?' Hopping out of bed with a laugh, I continue what Sophie had started and wrestle with the duvet cover. Sweat soon dapples my forehead and I am ever so slightly stuck in the fitted sheet, but still I persist.

'No offence, but I reckon that you would be more of a hinderance than a help.' Sophie frees me from the fabric and then deftly finishes the bed before I even have a chance to stop sweating.

'Okay, okay, maybe your job is safe,' I confess. 'There must be something I can do, and not be completely useless.'

Sophie taps her chin with a hum. 'Well, there has been something I've been wanting to do for a while.'

Knee-deep in dust in the Braemar Village Hall, I begin to regret wearing the pale pink silky slip dress. It turns out my returning favour for Sophie isn't helping her dye her hair, or finally fixing her up with Fraser, it is clearing out the community centre that has seemingly stood derelict for the best part of a decade.

After an hour of transferring most of the contents into a skip, finding a dead mouse inside of an old tea-stained mug is enough for me to tap out for a break.

Sat on the wall on the side of the road, sipping tea from a flask, I watch the sleepy village around me. Every now and again, a car will trundle past slowly, or someone walking a dog crosses the road to simply stop and say hello. Sophie seems to know every single one of them and talks to every person, of every age, as though they are a life-long friend. Not one person who tootles by seems to be in a rush. Every step is almost savoured, as though to rush would be to miss all of the important things. As though getting somewhere quickly is not as important as taking in the scenery of the same streets, the same faces, and the same joy that all of it brings.

I used to love London for its busyness. Life flew by at such a pace that you never had the chance to really stop and think. My mind didn't have the space to self-destruct. I could leave the house and go entirely unnoticed for days and days, as everyone is so caught up in themselves that they simply don't have the time to take an interest in the life of a stranger. I thought that I loved it. I thought I loved the anonymity it brought. I loved what I thought was freedom, when in reality, it was just isolation.

Sophie introduces me to every single new face and there are no awkward curtseys or muffled replies, only warm smiles and welcoming words. She even tosses handfuls of breadcrumbs to seagulls that look big enough to eat a healthy-sized terrier and she chitters away to them as though they too are her neighbours. By the size of them, I'd say they are definitely fed human-sized portions and if you stuck a tie on the fattest one, I'm sure he'd look like he has a thirty-year mortgage on a bungalow around the corner and works for the local council.

'They haven't had a place like this to come for years,' Sophie says after she waves goodbye to a pensioner and her little scruffy dog. 'They used to have coffee mornings, wedding receptions, kids' birthday parties. It was literally the hub for everything social around here. Now there's only the pubs and they're mostly full of tourists wanting to find their Jamie Fraser only to be sorely disappointed that it's only auld Jack, Victor, and all their pals propping up the bar.'

'What happened to it then? How did it get so bad?' I ask, looking at the dilapidated building behind us.

'The upkeep was too expensive. People couldn't afford to volunteer; council cut its funding. A few local neds broke in and were using it as a little hideout for a wee while and trashed it. Then once one big thing needed doing, like the boiler or the roof, there was no money to fix any of it, so it just got left.' Sophie casts a sad reminiscing glance at the boarded-up windows.

'And you've decided to fix it up all by yourself?'

'Nope.' She grins. 'You're helping me now.'

'Why hasn't anyone tried before?' I think out loud, wondering why, if this has been such a staple of the community, it takes a young woman in her twenties to try and repair it all herself.

She shrugs. 'I suppose it isn't much of a priority. People are just trying to feed their families, or earn enough to pay for the heating this winter. I'm lucky. I live where I work; they feed me. I never went to uni or anything like that, so I've been putting my wages aside to do this for a while.'

Watching her now, pride flows from me uncontrollably. Here is a woman who has worked and worked and worked, and the money she has saved, she's gifting to her community, doing something good. Sophie is far more of a woman than I could ever be, and I envy her; I envy the fact that I could never hold such goodness in me. Fraser would be lucky to have her. Both of them have a kindness so rare in this world, both of them would give every last fibre of themselves just to please everyone else around them. They deserve each other. Good deserves good.

'Come on then.' I hop off the wall and dash the dregs of my tea into the weedy garden. Sophie looks at me, confused. 'All this junk isn't going to shift itself now, is it? Make the most of this hunk of pro manual labourer whilst you've got me.'

She laughs, shaking her head as she follows me back inside.

The damp, musky smell is overwhelming. I have no idea where to even resume. But I know that I owe it to Sophie, and people just like her, to do at least something to give back. If that is pulling dead mice out of old doll's houses, so be it.

'Alice . . .' Sophie says as I pick up a nondescript piece of rubbish with my fingertips. 'Here.' She hands me a pair of pink marigold gloves, and I accept them with great fervour.

Without being exactly sure how just yet, I decide I am going to help her. I don't mean helping her find a boyfriend – that's a given – but surely I must have something I can offer her, some way I can be of use. This place, this person, all of it makes me want to change. The world would be a far happier place if we were all just a little more like Sophie.

Chapter 21

'The king and queen have requested your company at the final dinner tonight.' Mrs Buchanan strides into my room and launches open the curtains like a vampire hunter excited to turn their prey to ash.

'Am I allowed to politely decline?' I have become rather accustomed to eating alone and thoughts of having to make small talk for hours, unable to cram more than a morsel in my mouth between conversations, is pretty low on my list of desirable things.

'Nope,' the housekeeper replies, as bluntly as ever.

'You know, as weird as it was, I miss when you were being all nice and mumsy.' I grin, throwing my legs over the side of the bed as she hands me a stack of folded clothes.

'And I miss being twenty-five. That doesn't mean I'm going to wake up in the morning and my hot flushes have miraculously stopped and I can put my legs behind my head again.' Mrs Buchanan rolls her eyes as she busies herself around the room.

'All right, I take it back. I don't think I want to know that much about you.'

'Think how I feel – I have to wash your knickers every day.' The housekeeper gives me a sidelong glance, though a ghost of a smirk dances across her wrinkled lips.

'Are . . . are you actually being . . . *funny?*'

'Hmm, don't push your luck, lass.' She chuckles, sedately. 'Just make sure you're dressed for dinner by six. Don't be late.' She points at me with a warning finger, and I salute her in reply. Giving in to her smile, she slips out of the room with a shake of her head.

Stuffed into a dress and perfectly polished, I am suitably uncomfortable, meaning I am ready for dinner. Fixing a smile to my face, I head down to the dining room and am ushered to my seat. Though entirely on time, I am the last, aside from the king and queen themselves, to arrive at the table. Every eye at the long table tracks me across the room as I am shown to my place beside an older gentleman and an even older lady who sits curled over her placemat and doesn't so much as look up as I sit down.

'Good evening,' I address the table just as I have been taught, and receive varied levels of enthusiasm in response.

Looking about the room, though trying my hardest not to look too eager, I realise that I am the youngest here by far. Recognising only the prime minister and the chancellor, I turn to my neighbour and make an attempt to control the small talk before anyone begins a topic that will fluster me.

'Good evening, sir.' I outstretch my hand, and he looks at it reluctantly. 'I'm Alice. Pleasure to meet you.'

'Lord Punchard,' he says with an entirely straight face, simply placing his hand in mine like he's the Pope and I must kiss his ring.

Releasing his sweaty fingers as quickly as possible, trying not to laugh at his name, I attempt one last time to be the perfect lady. 'How are you finding Scotland, sir?'

'Hate the place. Bloody Jocks, no manners whatsoever, you know. One called me a—' he leans in closer to whisper the next part and his rancid red-wine breath hits me square in the face '—see you next Tuesday, right to my face yesterday.'

I have known this 'Lord Punchard' for less than five minutes and already I wish to track down that brilliant Scot and applaud them. Stifling my laughter, I feign a shocked expression and reply, 'Well I must say you and I must have seen very different Scotlands. You know, it is often used as a term of endearment here.'

Punchard only chunters to himself. I don't listen to exactly what he says, but I can imagine its some sort of outdated xenophobia, and my desire to be here falls below zero.

'Walloper,' the old woman beside me announces, still without looking up from her cutlery.

'Excuse me?' I turn to her, with my brows furrowed, wondering what I could have done wrong.

'That wee dobber there.' Her Aberdonian accent is thick as she points proudly at Lord Punchard, and makes no attempt to lower her voice. 'Walloper,' she reiterates.

The rest of the table hear her – it would be difficult

not to – but the 'walloper' in question and all of the other suited and kilted guests only avoid her eyes. No one says a word, except me. 'I'm Alice. Nice to meet you.'

'Aye, I know. You're Alex's granddaughter. I'm her old pal Baroness Mckay. You won't have heard of me. The moody cow never spoke about her mates. I reckon she didn't want anyone talking to them to find out how much of a wild thing she was.'

For the first time, Baroness Mckay actually looks at me. Scanning me up and down several times, she shrugs before adding, 'You're a lot like her. Though you're much softer around the middle.'

'Thank you,' I reply, deciding to take it as a compliment. For years, my whole existence has been my image. Forced to maintain a perfect figure, a controlled face, tamed hair, for the first time in my life what I look like hasn't been at the forefront of my thoughts. This body isn't just for photographs; it's for racing through glens on rusted bicycles; it's for swimming in ice-cold lochs; it's for sharing good, hearty food with friends. I actually don't care that my bones aren't on display for the world to see.

'Good lass,' is all she replies before the whole room is silenced.

Fraser Bell strides in, bagpipes ablaze, cheeks pinked from the strain. His uniform is perfect, from the neat pleats of his kilt to the spotless tunic; he really is a spectacle of Scottish excellence. Pride flows through me and I find myself wanting to make childish gestures at the miserable codger next to me, just to rub it in his face how wrong he was about such a culture. Instead, I watch Fraser, unable to remove my eyes from him even as the whole congregation stand to welcome the king and queen, who take their seats at the heads of the table.

Once Fraser has finished his piece, his silence invites the king to greet his guests. Still, however, I can't tear my eyes from the piper. My hands grow hot at my sides and I am forced to wipe them on my napkin. Stood right in front of me, when the mouthpiece falls from his lip, his gaze finds my own and we are locked in a stalemate across the table whilst the king continues his speech.

For a moment, I am in the gardens again, my legs wrapped around his waist, his lips on my neck. Suddenly, the room grows very hot and I have to shift my weight back and forth on each foot just to keep stood upright. I have to finally cut the eye contact between us before I end up fleeing the room and dragging him with me. When I look back up from my placemat, the piper has the audacity to wink his pretty little green eyes and I splutter on my own saliva.

'Am I boring you, Lady Walpole?' The sound of my name falling from the king's lips stuns me back down to earth.

My cheeks flame as every eye falls on me, and I have to fight the urge to duck under the tablecloth and sit out of sight. 'My deepest apologies, Your Majesty.' I can't look at the king and his burning glare.

The king finally finishes off his speech as my face shows no sign of letting up on its ever-deepening redness. Finally, we are all allowed to reassume our seats to Fraser's light accompaniment.

For the whole of the first and second courses, I am grateful when no one makes an attempt to speak to me. No one makes any attempt to engage Baroness Mckay either, but she seems as content as me in the silence. As the meal has progressed, various members of the staff have lined the walls, ready to ferry the dirty dishes back to the kitchen as soon as the attention has been turned from them. Amongst the staff is Sophie, and every now and again she gives me a cheeky smile, but it does little to comfort me. Do I really want my new-found friends to see me so out of my depth in what is supposed to be my own world? The more I am ignored, the more that shame floods through my chest and I have to fight back the shadows that threaten to overtake me.

'Alice Walpole, isn't it?' a man with a greasy forehead asks me from across the table, looking down his nose through his half-moon spectacles.

'Lady Alice will do just fine,' I say with a smile. If everyone else in this room can be given the respect of their title, then so can I. 'And you are?'

'Sir Charles Hornby,' he replies, puffing out his chest proudly.

'Pleasure to meet you.' I perform just as I should, and Sir Hornby leans closer towards me over the table.

'I have heard many stories about you, Miss Walpole.' He grins and my stomach turns.

'Lady,' I correct politely, attempting to control my composure.

'Many of them would suggest that you aren't much of a lady.' He pushes his glasses up his nose, but they slide down again almost instantly on the slick sweat making its way down the bridge. I'm clutching my knife and fork so tightly in my hands that my knuckles pale with the force. 'I also hear you're back on the market.'

Instinctively, my eyes flick to Fraser as he stands to attention before me, waiting for his next cue to play. He is already watching me closely, his fists shaking by his sides as he holds his form.

'Punchard,' Sir Hornby calls to the equally repulsive man beside me, who looks up from his potatoes at the sound of his name. 'What have you heard of little Alice Walpole?'

Punchard laughs a spine-tingling laugh and leans in closer to me, his breath on my neck again. 'Ha. What haven't I heard? A little troublemaker for your good great-uncle, aren't you?'

Beneath the table, I feel his rough palm rest against my thigh and I tense at the sensation of it. What do I do? If I get up and make a fuss, I'll only be in trouble. '*Be angry in private*' – that's what Mother said. But the further his hand climbs up my leg, the closer I am to taking his name as an instruction. As he leans closer still, I tremble at his proximity.

Without warning, a deafening screech sounds through the room. Punchard removes his hand with such speed that he fires his hand right into the hard mahogany of the dining table and I use the moment to leap to my feet. Fraser stands opposite me, his bagpipes squeezed tightly in his hand, his eyes burning through me as the party buzzes on in the background.

'Pipe Major?' The king addresses him, massaging his own ear.

About-turning, Fraser bows to the king. 'My deepest apologies, Your Majesty. I believe I was a little too keen with my next piece.'

'Yes, indeed. I think you just about deafened us for a moment there. But, at least it was good timing. Francois here was just telling me what my naughty nephew the Viscount Fairfax has been up to these days and I think we have all heard quite enough.' The party chuckles at their king, and Fraser stays tense.

'Lady Alice, were you hoping to make a speech?' The king directs the attention back to me, as I remain standing.

'Please excuse me, sir. I have come over a little unwell,' I manage to stammer out, before fleeing from the room.

As I burst from the dining room, staff fuss around me, but I can't take any notice. The clinking of cutlery on china, the gabble of pompous voices, the hushed uttering of orders given left, right, and centre grow louder and louder, until I am overcome with the desire to cover my ears to escape it. My head throbs with the sound. My chest feels drawn and strained like skin stretched over the mouth of a drum. I can't catch my breath. I can't breathe.

Rubbing my hands down my legs neurotically, I attempt to keep a grip on myself, and stop myself from sinking completely. Rubbing faster, harder, my hands burn, my dress stretches but still I can't stop.

'I'm okay.' I repeat the words like a mantra over and over, but soon the words mean nothing. Pacing the halls with high ceilings only makes me feel trapped, like the walls themselves are crushing my chest, refusing to allow the breath to reach my lungs.

I need to leave. As I launch myself out of the front door, a footman bows to me. Opening his mouth to bid me farewell as he has been ordered, he quickly slams it shut at the sight of my face and instead calls out my name as I run across the gardens.

My face burns; my neck burns. I fight the urge to throw up all of my starter and main course into Jimmy's flowerbeds. Pulling my heels from my feet, I launch them as far as I can throw them, an animalistic cry ripping its way from my throat with the motion.

Everything is just so loud. The wind cuts through the trees like a chainsaw through a rainforest. The hooting of owls is like the feral screeching of a woodland beast. My hair is pulled too tightly. The seams of my dress are scratching at my waist. I just need to keep running. Ghostly clammy hands run up and down my body and yet I can't decide whether to tear the clothes from my back, or drag on layer upon layer so I can't see any more of myself.

I don't know where I'm running until I get there. I force open the barn door, and the old wood creaks open just enough for me to slip through. My heartbeat still races and the sweat pours from my brow, but the smell of hay, the soft snort of Hamish, and the darkness of the room soothe me. I'm hardly able to see a few feet ahead of me, and the only light is from the moon as it slices through the window above Clover's stable. Moving using muscle memory alone, I wander up to Hamish. I stretch out my palm to him, and he presses his snout against it and allows me to slide my fingers into his coarse mane. The soft stallion nuzzles in against me, and over the gate I rest my head against his, breathing in his wild smell. Soon, the rising and falling of my chest plateaus to a level that doesn't make me feel like I am one missed inhalation away from death.

Once the feeling of numbness overtakes me, I can finally lift my head again. After kissing the horse on the side of his face, I move down the stables to Clover. She doesn't see me at first and I can observe her and her new baby unperceived. They lie in the corner of the stable, foal tucked into the mother as she delivers her warmth and protects her young with every inch of her body. Each time her foal stirs, Clover licks her, and keeps guard for another moment longer before stooping down beside her and slipping back to sleep. They seem so peaceful, so contented. Just a mother and her daughter, sleeping side by side, each one warmed by the other. They're safe here.

As I'm sat in the stable in the puddle of moonlight, the night passes slowly. The horses softly shift against their hay, and all I do is watch the darkness numbly. My body is exhausted but I can't bring myself to sleep.

'Alice?' A warm voice fills the cold barn as a silhouette slides in through the doors. I don't stir, or call out. I know that voice better than I know the one in my own head these days, and he knows I'm here.

Fraser Bell strides through the darkness and kneels before me, the moonlight curling around him, and shrouding him in an ethereal glow. Flooded in moonshine, I see his disordered appearance closely. It is evident that he has torn his bonnet from his head. His hair is dishevelled, as though many a rough hand has been run through it, and his brow is almost permanently furrowed as deep lines score his forehead. Dimples are ironed flat, and his eyes are as dark as the night around us, though as he scans my face back and forth, they soften back to an evergreen and I am home once again.

The piper places my shoes by my side, before untying his own ghillie shoes and, with tender hands, slides my feet into each of them. Barefoot on the stone floor, he doesn't say a word, only places his hands softly against my cheeks and kisses me on the forehead. Thoughts of Sophie linger in the back of my mind and I know I should feel guilty, but I can't stop myself from relaxing against his touch. His presence is the only thing that can warm me now. With him beside me, the draught through the stables doesn't even touch me. Shuffling around to sit beside me, Fraser remains silent as he holds me against his chest like the mare swaddles her foal. For the first time this night, I feel safe.

Chapter 22

The king and queen depart Balmoral as soon as their morning bagpipes have ceased. The staff and I line the driveway to bid them farewell and they pass by each of us to say goodbye. Mrs Buchanan is the very last in the row and for a while, the king and queen stand before her shaking both her hands. For the first time, I see her blush as she looks up from beneath her lashes to take in what is undeniably their praise. Curtseying over and over, she is actually flustered as she waves off the monarchy in their sleek Range Rover.

As soon as the car vanishes into the treeline, an audible sigh is heard across the maids, footmen, cooks, and gardeners alike. Mrs Buchanan's blush is wiped clean, her face drops back to its natural frown, she brushes down her apron, and returns to her regimented posture.

'Right. I'll have no mucking about.' She addresses her troops. 'If you get this place turned around and shut down by noon, you can all take the rest of the afternoon off.'

A hum arises as all of the staff marvel at the Buchanan's unusual kindness but she quickly shushes them. 'That is if, and only if, I am happy with how you leave this great castle. If even just the one of you fails at my inspection, all of your holidays will be delayed by another day.' A groan goes up amongst the crowd and she dismisses them with a flick of her wrist.

Finding Sophie in the crowd, I draw up beside her. 'Holidays?' I ask.

'Yep, two weeks of freedom. Which usually, for me, means spending two weeks doing odd jobs around my mum's house less than ten miles away.' Sophie rubs her hands together with a chuckle.

'So do I just get free rein of the castle for two weeks?' I ask, picturing a few of my own *Home Alone* scenarios, and wondering if I'll be able to jump on the king's bed without being caught.

Sophie laughs. 'You'd be so lucky.' She nods her head towards Mrs Buchanan. 'She doesn't have any family since her husband died. Mrs Buchanan is here all year round. Balmoral is her baby and nothing can seem to take her away from it.'

Pity stirs in my stomach. 'She stays all by herself?'

'I'm sure she loves the peace and quiet. I like to imagine that she just sits and eats biscuits in the anteroom.' Thoughts of Mrs Buchanan wandering the halls in her curlers or eating toast with her feet up on the king's table amuse me and I truly hope that is the reality for her. 'Plus, Jimmy usually stays too. He has his wee cottage and doesn't have another home so it's usually just those two.'

'How have you never told me this before?' I grin, wide-eyed at Sophie, and she furrows her brows in confusion.

'You're not still hung up on them being in love, are you?'

'What would you do if you were left alone inside a castle with your one-night stand from two years ago?' I wiggle my eyebrows. 'That is the plot to a raunchy Mills and Boon if ever I've heard one.'

'God, you need a shag. Now you're picturing the old folks at it, and I think I'm gonna boke.' Sophie pushes against my upper arm playfully.

'Who needs a shag?' Fraser Bell draws up behind us, his voice making me jump, and turning Sophie's cheeks scarlet.

'Alice is scheming about Jimmy and Mrs B again. Making up scenarios of them alone in the castle whilst we're all on holiday,' Sophie explains and Fraser cracks a smile.

'You're off on your holidays too?' I ask him, my gut sinking as my subconscious had clung to the hope that it might be me and the piper left in these great halls alone.

'I am indeed,' he replies. 'Spending a few nights over in Inverness with some of the lads I know from the army who have just gone on leave. Should be fun.'

'Will you be seeing Eilidh at all?' Sophie enquires about his sister.

'I don't think so. She's got this fancy new job in Aberdeen so she's quite busy these days. The lads are thinking about having a party though, so she might pop over and join us for that.' Sophie's eyes glow as she listens to him speak, her gaze refusing to leave his face even when his sentence reaches its end. A bolt of jealousy strikes through me and I curse myself for such a thought.

'You're all forgetting something incredibly important.' I fold my arms over my chest in mock annoyance.

'What?' they say in unison.

'Why, me of course,' I reply with a snigger. 'Please don't tell me I have to stay here and third-wheel all of the repressed sexual tension of the groundskeeper and the housekeeper. I'll be stir-crazy by the time you both return.'

My friends laugh, and Sophie fakes a gag. 'By all means, come home with me. But my mam will put you to work, royal or not. And we don't have much room in the house so you'd probably be in the shed.' She laughs at the mental image she has conjured for herself.

'The work, I don't mind. In fact, I'd love to get stuck into something *not* royal, for once. But the shed doesn't sound too appealing in the Highlands in September – I cannot lie.'

'Fair enough.' She shrugs with a smile. 'You're welcome to visit any time you like though. We could always spend a couple of days down at the Village Hall.'

'Village Hall?' Fraser looks confused as we all gather in the doorway, delaying going our separate ways.

'Sophie's latest project.' I grin, pride in my friend flowing on my words.

Again, she blushes as she looks at him. 'I decided to try and fix up the old Village Hall in Braemar. You know the one that we all used to have our birthday parties in when we were kids? Give something back and all that jazz.'

'That's amazing, Soph,' Fraser says sincerely, and that evil pang of jealousy courses through me again. Reaching up, he takes her by the shoulder and gives her an affectionate squeeze. 'I'm sure I know a few people I can rope in to help if you need it.'

Sophie nods modestly. 'Thanks,' she utters shyly. 'Anyway, must get on unless I want to be the most unpopular person that ever dared walk through this castle. I'll catch up with you both later?' I give her a nod and wave her off. Fraser does the same, his dimpled smile on full show.

No matter what happened last night, Alice, no matter how many kisses we've shared, or how desperate each touch is, your best friend is in love with him. And she is his perfect match.

I need to get back on track. My feelings may be betraying me, betraying Sophie, but my head is strong. I must do all I can to help her win the piper's heart. I shall simply watch them from afar, knowing the better woman got the man she deserves, and I will be content to see the both of them happy.

'What are your tasks today then, Piper to the Sovereign?' I turn to Fraser, trying to push down all of my urges to throw my arms around his neck and leap into his arms.

'For the first time in Lord knows how long, I have none.' He grins, chuffed with himself. 'I just can't wait to get some trousers on.' Fraser leans closer to whisper, 'The old horse-riding legs don't half chafe in this flaming kilt.'

I can't hold my laughter in. Pushing him away playfully by the chest, I shake my head. 'How very enlightening.'

Fraser shrugs with his boyish smile and the sight of it warms me to the core. Every day that passes I feel as though I get to see more of him, as though he isn't afraid of showing me the real person that he hides behind his uniform.

'Are you busy?' he asks me, his face lighting up with an idea.

'In the months you have known me, have I ever once been busy?' I chuckle. He thinks about it for a moment and laughs.

'Aye, fair enough.' Then growing a little nervous, he fiddles with his bonnet in his hand, averting his eyes from me entirely. 'I was just wondering, if you had no plans, well . . .' He trails off, unable to find the words. Then, as though finding the courage, his words tumble out faster than I've ever before heard him speak. 'I have something to show you that I thought you might like.'

'What is it?' I ask, already knowing that he could be asking me to look at a muddy puddle in the road and I'd still say 'yes' a thousand times.

'That would have to be a surprise.' He stands up straighter, his eyes tracking my face to gauge my reaction. As I remain silent, trying to control my excitement and not allow myself to be too pleased at the thought, he falters again. 'Or, I could just tell you – it isn't really much of a surprise. I just thought—'

'I trust you.' I cut him off before his excitement dwindles any more. 'I'd love to.' The piper lets out a sigh of relief and a nervous laugh, before straightening again.

'Amazing. Well, I just need to get changed and then it's only a wee walk, if you're okay with that?' Nodding my head eagerly, I follow him along the garden path. 'I could come back and fetch you if you like? You don't have to come all the way to mine.' His cheeks redden.

Still, I follow him anyway. 'Why, have you just remembered that you've left your underwear on the floor?'

'Well, I wasn't worried about that, but now I am very much doubting myself.' Walking side by side, we head for the treeline.

'It's okay, I've seen it all before,' I say before my brain can register what has just fired past my lips. 'I mean— not yours— I just— I have no idea what I'm saying.' It's my turn to become flustered and, though he laughs at my blunder, Fraser's cheeks stain the colour of the nearby dahlias too.

'I know what you meant,' he says quietly. 'But I have to warn you, I don't usually have visitors, particularly not royal ones, so you will have to excuse the mess.'

After walking for a few minutes, we come to a clearing in the trees and a small wooden cabin sits in the centre of it. Shaded by an abundance of browning leaves, and surrounded by the last of the season's wildflowers, I wonder for a moment if I have stumbled across the home of some sort of magical helper from a fairy tale who is going to set me on my quest to defeat the evil queen.

'Not much, but it's home,' Fraser says, pushing open the door. As he moves into the room, he grabs a few things that he had left lying around and tucks them under his arm before showing me to an armchair in the middle of the lounge. Once I am comfortable in my seat, he wanders off to the adjoining room to change, leaving me precious moments alone to take in my surroundings.

The interior is very basic: one chair, one mug on the mug tree, and I'd half imagine there's just one knife and fork and one plate in the cupboards. In spite of its simplicity, it's homely. A small lamp warms the light of the room in the corner beside the chair, which in itself feels like sitting on a soft bed of moss. Just like Jimmy's wee cottage, there's no television, or even any electricals in sight. The room is instead littered with photographs and various musical instruments. Sheets of music clutter the coffee table but, for a bachelor pad, you can tell this is a home that is well taken care of.

One photograph in particular catches my eye. This one is not fastened to any wall or up high on any shelves or mantels; it is the only one I can grasp from right here in my seat. The frame is filled with dimpled smiles. On the first row are three children, their thick amber hair glowing in the lens flare. Their faces are almost identical too, though the one in the middle has a front tooth missing and shows it off proudly. Behind them stand a couple. The father's genes hardly stood a chance, for the mother seems to have gifted her children almost all of her features. Though, it is the father whose dimples are firmly imprinted on his offspring.

'Fraser,' I call out to him and he replies through the walls. 'Is this your family?'

The piper peeks his head around the doorframe, his bare shoulders just visible, and I avert my eyes to hold up the frame. 'It is indeed,' he says with a breathy laugh. 'I'll give you one guess as to which one is yours truly.'

Smiling at the photo, I look at each of the children again.

It is obvious that the one in the middle with the missing teeth is his sister Eilidh, her red hair braided over the top of her head in a crown of smouldering bark. Even as a child with gaps in her smile, she is as beautiful as Sophie has described. Two boys huddle closely at her sides. The one on the left is clearly the younger of the two. He stands with his legs parted, as though ready to run away as soon as the adults turn their backs. The other stands perfectly upright, hands folded together in front, a serious look on his face, though with a familiar playful glint in his eye.

'Are you the one who looks like a six-year-old butler by any chance?' I tease and Fraser nods proudly, his body still tucked away out of my sight.

'I'd say not much has changed since that photo. Eilidh still smiles like that, Aonghas is still hard to pin down in one spot long enough to snap a picture, and my mum looks almost exactly the same. It's only Dad who's changed. But it's still my favourite photo.'

'You look like him,' I say softly, staring at the photo. Fraser's father, the Piper to the Sovereign who preceded him, wears the same uniform I see his son in each day, with the same serious expression that always seems to be threatening to break into a disarming smile.

Fraser disappears for a moment and then returns in a pair of jeans, though still remains naked above the waist. Unable to tear my eyes from his chest, I swallow. His wide shoulders slope into strong biceps, and a spattering of red hair trails all the way down the softness of his stomach until it disappears into the low line of his trousers. My imagination runs away from me and I have to remind myself where I am before I can wet my lips enough to speak again.

Fraser perches himself on the arm of my chair and leans his arm across the back of it until he is so close that I can smell the faint spritz of aftershave across his neck. Leaning down over my shoulder to take a closer look at the photograph in my hand, he is so close to me now that I can hardly focus on the glossy paper anymore. Swallowing again and again just to try and remedy the overwhelming dryness in my throat, I am grateful when Fraser speaks first.

'I had to be Dad when he died,' Fraser says candidly, and I allow him to continue without interruption. 'Took on his job, provided for the family. Mum was utterly broken so it was down to me to help her, and become a father to my younger siblings. It feels so disgusting to admit it, but I hated them both for a while. I had my own career, my own plans, and suddenly everything was upside down and nothing was in my control.' I grasp his free hand that he has rested on his lap and stroke across his knuckles tenderly. Sighing, Fraser continues, 'I wouldn't have done any of it differently though. I'd do it a thousand times over. They needed me, and I am glad that I could serve my family. It's just nice to be needed by no one every once in a while. I suppose that's why I live in a cabin in the woods: a chance to be alone.'

'I know that I never knew him, but one thing I know for sure is that your father would be so indescribably proud of you, Fraser.' He catches my fingers in his thumb as I take another stroke across his knuckles, and he squeezes them gently.

216

'Anyway, enough of that.' He gets to his feet and grabs a checked shirt from his bedroom and buttons it slowly across his chest. 'I promised you a surprise. Never before have I broken a promise and I certainly won't be starting today.' After pulling on a pair of brown boots, he stands up straight and claps his hands together. 'Ready?'

As I nod, Fraser offers me his hand and helps me slowly down the steps of his home. Reluctantly releasing my fingers, he walks beside me through the castle grounds. With each stride, my heart throbs harder, enthralled by each and every prospect.

Chapter 23

Despite the fact that I have been at Balmoral for over three months now, it seems that I have never trodden the same path twice. It's as though a new path opens up for whatever one may desire, then grows over again at the close of the day, only to be rediscovered when it's truly needed. I think I could live at Balmoral for a century and still have not seen it and its grounds in its entirety.

Fraser and I walk for a mile or two, and the only few living souls we pass are those of the herd of deer that watch us from afar as we cross the fields. Swooping birds of prey circle the skies, their wide wingspans casting shadows across the heather and their screams riding on the breeze. We walk in relative silence. There is no reason to say a word, for we are both taking in our surroundings and the warmth of the company. Fraser only disturbs the paradise to point out a rare flower, or to hold my hand when the terrain gets rough and I lose my footing in a rabbit warren.

Coming to the edge of the forest, Fraser stands before

me, obscuring my view of the path ahead with his winning smile. 'Now can you remember what you said to me after I said that Balmoral wasn't ready for love?'

Nodding, I return his smile. 'That this place was built on love.' The memory steals a fond place in my heart and it warms me to know he remembers too.

'I had a wee think about that. I've been to the place I'm going to show you a hundred times, and yet until you corrected me, I had never *truly* understood its purpose or its importance.' Fraser glances over his shoulder, and I steal a peek too. A stone structure fills the distance, and I am eager to see for myself what he is getting at.

The piper turns around to finish the journey, and I follow at his side. As the trees clear, a stone pyramid fills the landscape. Its magnificence isn't dwarfed by, nor does it dwarf, all of the beauty surrounding it. For a manmade edifice, it slots right into the backdrop as though it had sprouted from the earth in the times of the Celts and Picts. 'For centuries Scots have lain stones in a structure called a cairn as a memorial or to mark a place of significance. The grounds of Balmoral are full of them,' Fraser begins as we draw up to the pyramid.

Running my hands along its weatherworn surface, my fingertips tingle at the touch of the cold stone.

'Most of them were erected at the request of Queen Victoria, and this one is by far the biggest and most beautiful. Now, at first, I had always believed it was more of a symbol of status: The Balmoral Pyramid, the great monument. But, it's only now that I've realised it is a monument to love.'

Walking around the perimeter, I listen intently to Fraser and his story. 'This is the Prince Albert Cairn. It was erected after his death and has stood here since, in this wilderness, a tribute to the loss of the queen's greatest love. Here—' Fraser points to a large engraving on the side of the structure and we both read the words in silence.

To
the Beloved Memory
of
ALBERT,
The Great and Good,
Prince Consort,
Erected by his Broken-hearted Widow,
VICTORIA. R.
21st August
1862

Then beneath it, a smaller inscription reads:

He, being made perfect in a short time,
Fulfilled a long time,
for his soul pleased the Lord.
Therefore hasted he to take
him away from the Wicked.
Wisdom of Solomon
Chap IV, verses 13 and 14

My heart throbs at the sight of it, with both pleasure and pain. This isn't simply a stack of granite in the sticks. This is grief and love objectified. A pyramid, a monumental structure, that persists through the wind and the rain, that stands against the attack of time to personify a widow's love. In this pile of stones, that love, and the grief of losing that love, lasts in this natural world for the rest of time.

In nearly two hundred years, it seems to have hardly crumbled, and I can believe that Queen Victoria's love for her Albert would have still endured too, and her grief in losing him would still stand fast even after all of this time. The queen has made sure that her love for her husband survives her in every acre of this estate, and thus this landscape tells a love story no author, no fairy tale could ever replicate.

'It's beautiful,' I breathe. Fraser looks to me with his bright eyes, and the soft drizzle slides over his dimples. 'Thank you for showing me.'

'It's only fair that I share this place with the woman who finally made me understand it.' Fraser's eyes search my face, and I fight the urge to reach out and rest his cheek in my palm.

'It strikes me how plain it is compared to her memorials for him in London.' I speak in an absentminded babble. 'And yet, this one seems to hold more feeling. It's raw. Unlike the glittering gold of the Albert Memorial at the Royal Albert Hall, this one is personal. I can imagine the grieving wife sat on a fallen tree, looking over this little pocket of the world with her stacked-up love beside her.' This memorial feels like my relationship with my home. London is glitz and glamour, gold-plated and stuck on a pedestal. But here, in Scotland, away from everything, I am honest, unrefined, and more authentically me.

Perhaps love isn't supposed to come bathed in gold, lifted high for all to see and out of reach to touch. Perhaps love is a pile of stones meticulously placed to overlook the happiest part of the world, and left alone to endure the weather.

Perhaps love isn't the heir to some fortune, or the son of a man with a title. Perhaps love is a bagpiper who lives in a cabin in the woods, who remembers all of the times I have smiled when telling a story, and who will protect me from a world that's always threatening to chew me up and spit me out. Love is Fraser Bell, his burnt auburn hair, his deep dimples, and the feeling of calm he brings with his entrance into every room.

Looking at him now, deep in thought as he reads the engraving over and over, I blush. As much as I have tried to repress it, I'm falling for him. I am falling for Fraser Bell, Piper to the Sovereign, when everything in our lives keeps screaming at me to stay away.

'Fraser?' I say his name softly and his eyes snap to mine in an instant. For a moment every single word of confession is on my tongue, and then as soon as his gaze fixes upon me, they are locked back up like sins forbidden to see the light of day.

He waits patiently for a moment for me to speak again. 'Alice?' he asks, encouraging me gently.

If I speak now, I will tell him I love him. It has crept up on me so slowly, in a feeling so perfect and yet entirely foreign, even I can hardly comprehend how I feel.

'I . . . I . . .' I bumble out, my heart so desperate to release the pressure in my chest, but my brain, trained for years and years to constrain my emotions, refuses to allow such a confession past my lips. 'I would like to go home now.' My voice is quiet, and I hardly recognise it as my own as I speak.

Fraser releases a breath as if he had been holding it in and then mildly replies, 'Aye, aye, of course.'

Wandering back the way we came, neither of us say a word until Balmoral is back in our sights. When we are just far enough away from the castle walls that we can see the bustling staff leaving with suitcases and smiles, Fraser clasps me by the hand, preventing me from travelling any further. 'I have been trying to work up the courage to ask, because, well I don't even know if you'd be allowed let alone want to, and it's just that, I would really love it if you could and I reckon it would do you good to get out of here . . .' the piper babbles, his cheeks turning pink, his eyes looking everywhere but into my own.

'Fraser.' I place my hand on his and smile at him softly. 'Just spit it out.' I chuckle and his face cracks into a grin.

'I'm only going for a couple of days. The accommodation isn't the best – it's just my mate's gaff – but I can make sure you at least get a bed. The lads are all right, an acquired taste but they're military so they know how to behave when they have to and they know how to treat a royal lady . . .' He trails on and my lungs seem to struggle in my chest as though with every word it becomes harder and harder to catch my breath.

'Fraser . . .' I breathe, reminding him to get back on track before the both of us end up hyperventilating.

'Would you like to come to Inverness with me?'

He speaks so quickly but I catch every syllable, every inflection, every single movement of his lips.

'I'd be honoured to.' I grin, and Fraser's face lights up. So overcome, he grasps me by the cheeks and leans closer, and closer still—

'Where've you two been all morning? I've been looking for you both everywhere.' Sophie's voice takes us by surprise. I pull away from Fraser frantically and face my friend, still panting.

'Fraser took me to see the pyramid,' I say guiltily, as though that isn't the truth and we have in fact been off making love in the wild on a bed of heather. That thought makes me blush even harder and Sophie gives me a questionable look.

'Oh, nice,' Sophie says, a little distantly, and my stomach sinks. She must know. Surely she must know there is something going on between us. There's no way that she doesn't hate me. Especially not after this. 'I was just going to see if you both had any plans this afternoon? I wondered if you fancied going for lunch somewhere in town? We've just finished here.'

'I still need to start packing for my leave,' Fraser replies to Sophie, though his words are directed at me and a knowing smile slots onto his face. 'Although, I feel as though I can spare enough time for a picnic?' he suggests, finally removing his gaze from me, and his words light Sophie's eyes.

'Oh my gosh, yes, that would be perfect. I can lift a load of stuff from the kitchens. No one will miss it; it will only go off whilst everyone's away anyway.' She turns to me, buzzing with excitement. 'How're you fixed?'

'Sounds like a plan to me.' And so, the three of us wander back up the garden path and head towards the kitchen. Sneaking in the back door, each of us takes a corner of the room to scour for leftovers. With our arms suitably stacked, and us only having to hide from Mrs Buchanan behind a couple of suits of armour once, we run back through the grounds until we reach the clearing of Fraser's cabin. We leave our bounty on his little patio table, and Fraser nips inside to retrieve a blanket and soon enough we are sat around, feeling the fallen twigs beneath our bottoms, laughing into the king's leftover finger sandwiches and little glasses of jelly.

'Have you thought any more of what you're going to do for the couple of weeks we're away, Alice?' Sophie turns to ask me after we have fully feasted and the three of us lie side by side with bloated bellies.

I shouldn't lie to her. She deserves better than that. 'I'm going to head to Inverness for a couple of days,' I say a little vaguely.

'It is lovely down that way. Have you got some friends there? Or family?' Sophie clearly hasn't put two and two together to realise I'm leaving with the piper and my face betrays that fact as I steal a glance at his pink-dusted face. Sitting up straighter, Sophie looks between us, back and forth, piecing everything together. 'Are you two . . .' she waggles a finger between us '. . .shagging?'

'Yes,' I answer at the same time Sophie finishes her sentence.

The three of us stare at each other open-mouthed as I realise what I have just inadvertently said. 'No, no. God's no.' I overcompensate with a laugh. 'I thought you were asking if we were going together.'

Fraser stays silent, his cheeks hot.

'Oh God, am I third-wheeling? Did I interrupt a date?' Sophie rushes, her eyes ablaze with worry, and her cheeks flushed.

The sick feeling rises in my throat. 'It's nothing like that, really. I think Fraser just felt sorry for me here alone.' I look to him for backup.

'Aye, it's nothing,' he mutters, refusing to return my gaze.

'Could there be room for another?' I ask Fraser, my guilt and feeling of betrayal outweighing my politeness. Perhaps if Sophie came too, I wouldn't be in danger of being so in love with him. Perhaps with them both away from work, they can finally explore their relationship more. And I can simply be their travelling wing woman.

'Aye, room for the whole castle population. If they don't mind sleeping on a sofa.'

'Well?' I ask Sophie, trying to look excited. 'Why don't you come too?'

'I don't want to get in the way, or force myself onto you both.'

'Oh hush,' I reply.

'You're always welcome, Soph,' Fraser says, sincerely this time. 'Plus, it's nothing like you think it is. My mates and my sister will be there, hardly a romantic rendezvous.'

Sophie's face lights up. Her wide dark eyes are full of her excitement as she accepts the invite, and the three of us part ways to pack.

Chapter 24

'Come on, hurry up.' Sophie rushes into my bedroom, finding me bent over the desk scrawling a note. 'Fraser is waiting downstairs.'

As if on cue, a little beep sounds just outside the window. Looking out, I find Fraser Bell in his usual spot, though this time, his kilt and bagpipes are not in sight. Instead, he is leaning against the side of a classic red Mini Cooper, his arms folded across his chest, grinning up at me.

Scribbling down the last of my note, I grasp my bags from the bottom of the bed, and Sophie and I rush along the empty hallways with the same enthusiasm as children leaving school on the last day before summer.

We cram our bags into Fraser's boot, and the piper has to give it a last shove with his heel before the lock clicks into place and we can set off on the journey. Despite it being his car, Fraser's head touches the cushioned roof and his hair splays out above him in a nest of amber. I can't help but let out a silent giggle as we hit a rather rough patch of the driveway and he bumps against the roof with a repressed 'oof'.

Sophie slides forward from the back seat so her face is firmly wedged between the two of us. 'What were you writing, Al?'

'Oh nothing, just a little note for Mrs B,' I reply casually, and the both of them take their eyes from the road ahead to stare at me, open-mouthed.

'You mean just a little "see ya later" note, right?' Sophie sees my sheepish expression and sighs. 'Right?'

'Sort of . . .' I suddenly feel as though I have been sent before my parents with a terrible school report, with the expressions that currently face me.

'Sort of?' Fraser parrots back.

'Well, just letting her know where I was going and stuff. Just so she wasn't worried,' I admit guiltily.

Fraser brakes suddenly. 'I thought you had asked permission. That it had all been formally approved?' He breathes heavily and looks at Sophie with an expression of horror.

'Yeah . . . About that . . .' Looking in the rear-view mirror I catch a glimpse of a figure in the distance, a thin frame rushing from the castle. 'We should probably get going.'

Sophie and Fraser follow my gaze as they too notice the housekeeper in the distance. 'We're all dead after this,' Sophie whispers.

'I'll take the blame, I promise,' I plead with them both. 'I just knew I'd never be allowed to do anything like this. Everything has to be approved, risk-assessed, made utterly boring. I just want to live. I just want to be a regular girl in her twenties for one weekend, whose mistakes don't make the front page.'

Fraser looks at me for a moment, then at Mrs Buchanan, then back to me before pressing down the accelerator and ejecting his tiny car from the driveway and into the winding country tracks of the Highlands.

'Just grab one of those tapes out of there, Alice.' Fraser points to the glove compartment and a stack of tapes leap out at me as I click open the drawer.

'You know, you're really living up to all of those Hollywood stereotypes of Scotland right now. Woollen skirts and tape decks? What's next – we're going to hunt a stag for our dinner? Or sing the Proclaimers on repeat for the whole journey?' I joke as I slide through his collection that ranges from ABBA to Judas Priest.

'This was my dad's car,' Fraser says with a smile. 'He didn't believe in getting rid of something that still performs just fine, so we've had this trusty thing for near on thirty years. It has yet to let me down.' Fraser pats the dashboard and one of the nobs on the stereo pings off and hits Sophie square in the forehead. He apologises with a blush.

Settling on the tape labelled '*erasure*', based mostly on the stained-glass cover art of the album, I slide it out of its case and hand it to Fraser. 'I may be old enough to know what a tape is, but I'm not old enough to remember how a tape deck works.' I laugh as Fraser slots it into the deck and after a whir, a song crackles through the speakers.

A synthesiser cuts through the silence of the country and Fraser grins, shaking his head as he hears the song begin. As though he can't help himself, he sings along to 'A

Little Respect', quietly at first, until both he and Sophie are belting the words of the first chorus. I accompany them with my laughter. Cranking open the window, I lay my head out of it, my hair taken in the breeze as I feel the cool country air hit my face. I am alive. All of my senses are filled to the brim with joy and I wonder why no fairy tale has ever included a scene of driving through the wilderness as the person that makes your heart race and your mind calm belts out Eighties synth pop.

By the time we have listened to the end of two tapes, and have snaked our way through the Cairngorms, we finally hum through the streets of Inverness. Sophie has been asleep across the back seats for the last three-quarters of an hour as Fraser has sung every song emanating from the speakers word perfectly, as though these are the same tapes that he has listened to over and over and they still haven't gotten old. His voice is soft, not pretty, but melodious. As he murmurs along to the acoustic ballad in the background, I could almost fall asleep.

Never in my life have I done anything like this. Yes, I've snuck out to parties in grand houses, but I've always been taught that adventures such as this are too dangerous to fathom; that cars with non-tinted windows and friends without titles are a recipe for a publicity nightmare. Yet, I have never felt safer. Fraser's rusty old car; his silly, slightly out of tune singing; Sophie's soft snores – all of it seems to wrap around me like an embrace, and for once I can switch off my brain and place my trust in these people, in their lives, because in their presence I am unafraid of the world.

'Now, is there anything I should know before we get there?' I ask, worrying that my finishing-school education hasn't quite prepared me for a Scottish house party.

Fraser hums in thought for a moment. 'They like to think they're funny so they will more than likely take the piss out of you. Don't take it personally, it's actually a sign of affection.'

'Noted: the more names I get called, the better I am liked.' I chuckle.

'Exactly. But don't worry, I won't leave you alone with them if you don't wish me to, so I'll always be here for backup.' Taking his eyes off the road for just enough time to smile at me, he suddenly becomes serious again. 'Oh, and if anyone offers you a Dragon Soop, don't accept it. Those things could be used to sanitise a nuclear power plant.'

'What about Buckfast?' I ask, using my very limited Scots pop culture knowledge to make him laugh again.

'What about it?'

'Will there be any at this party for me to try?'

'Alice, love, that's like asking will there be dogs at Crufts, or will there be a microwave in a Wetherspoons kitchen.' He chuckles, and I furrow my eyebrows. 'Aye, probably not the best simile to use on a lady – can't imagine you've ever been treated to Purple Rain and fish and chips served on a plate with the same pattern as your granny's carpet.'

'Can't say I have.' I try and picture it in my head and fail with a laugh.

He fakes a gasp. 'You haven't lived.' Fraser shakes his head. 'It's a date. Royal or not, everyone must experience a Wetherspoons at least once in their life.'

'Would it give my mother a heart attack to know I have been?' The thought excites me.

'Oh, without a shadow of a doubt.' He grins.

'Then I'm in.'

Fraser's eyes comb over the road, and he doesn't notice me as I gaze at his side profile. I'm not sure what the me from three months ago would say if she could see me now, excited at the thought of going to a budget chain pub to have my supper microwaved. Although, I don't think that me from three months ago would recognise the woman I am in this car now. My cheeks are hurting from smiling, my hair is a mess from the breeze from the window, and my chest full of hope for the future. For the first time in as long as I can remember, I can say I am happy. And I actually mean it.

Sophie stirs in the back seat as we slow to a stop in a small car park. 'Now,' Fraser begins a little sheepishly, 'it's no castle or London palace, but it also has no nosy housekeepers or many rules, so I hope you'll find it at least a little comfortable.'

Sliding out of Fraser's Mini, I lean back down to speak to him through the open door. 'I have been to after-dark parties in the Louvre, and smoked a cigarette in the most expensive house in Mayfair.' Fraser blushes, and fiddles shyly with his fingers. 'And I can quite honestly say that this is the most excited I've ever been for a party.'

Looking up at the short block of flats, there isn't much to see. There aren't window boxes filled with flowers, or ivy and wisteria climbing the walls. In fact, the whole thing looks as though it could use a good power wash as its Victorian grime has turned the stone a patchy shade of black. Shrouded by an overcast sky, it's hardly inviting in the traditional sense, but there's something homely about it. Unsure of whether that is down to the company, or the idea of escaping into a warm building to avoid the attack of the Scottish autumnal elements, I simply allow myself to feel excited.

I drag my bags out of the boot and take Sophie's under my arm too. Fraser reaches out to relieve me of my load. 'As much as I appreciate you being a gentleman, and as stupid as it sounds, I'd quite like to carry my own bags for a change.'

Smiling softly, he takes his own bag from the car. 'Okay, but as soon as you see the stairs in that place, you might just change your mind.' Winking, he walks away as the three of us clear the boot and head for the flat.

As we reach the door, Fraser presses the buzzer and a muffled voice calls through the speaker. If the tinny voice wasn't hard enough to hear, the thick accent that is emitted is even more impenetrable and it seems that even Fraser's usually mild dulcet tones have been laced with an accent I have never heard fall so heavy from his lips.

Sophie shivers with excitement beside me. 'I can't believe we're going to be partying with the Bells,' she whispers in my ear and I have to laugh. Only a few weeks ago all three of us were at a ball with the heads of the British monarchy and a whole host of famous faces and she hardly seemed fazed. And yet, the prospect of a house party in an Inverness flat with a family she has known since childhood sends her jittering in her boots. I suppose that is exactly why she is the best friend I've ever had.

The buzzer on the door sounds and Fraser pulls it open to reveal a cold stone reception. 'I'm afraid they're on the top floor and the lift in this place hasn't worked until 2003.' He looks down at my arms as they droop to hold on to my bags. 'Are you sure I can't take at least one of them?'

Pushing past them, I take the first flight of stairs two at a time and stop at the first landing. 'I'm determined,' I reply with a grin, my voice echoing around the brutalist interior. Fraser and Sophie share a look before following me.

My pacing becomes an issue by the time I reach the first floor. Setting out rather too sprightly, I am already sweating by the second floor and my fingers slip on the handle of my case. Still, I refuse to allow anyone to carry my bags. From the corner of my eye, every now and again I notice Fraser watching me with an amused smirk but he doesn't say a word.

By the time we reach the fifth floor, my hair is stuck to my face and I have to lean against the wall to stop my legs from collapsing beneath me. 'You good, aye?' Fraser skirts past me, that mocking grin still firmly stuck on his face as he knocks on the right door.

'Aye,' I manage to squeeze out breathlessly. Sophie only shakes her head with a chuckle.

Before anyone can say anything about the map of the world forming across my back in sweat, the door swings open and Fraser is dragged into a tight embrace by the figure on the other side. 'Bell End!' the voice cries, and slaps the piper on the back roughly.

'Aright, Cammy.' Fraser returns the pat and his friend draws away to take a look at Sophie and I.

'Get your ugly grid out the way.' He jokingly shoves Fraser on the chest to get a better look. 'Now who are these two beauties you've brought to this shithole? I'd have scrubbed up a bit better if I'd known.' Cammy scruffs at the light dusting of dark stubble on his chin with a wink.

'Put your tongue away, or I have no doubt that one of them will put it away for you,' Fraser says, rather proudly, though still in jest. 'This is Sophie Chorley, and *this*,' he says, pointing to me and pausing, 'is Allie,' Fraser finishes and I raise my eyebrow at the nickname.

'Just Allie? You like Madonna or something?' Cammy asks, shaking my hand softly.

'Hmm, I was thinking more Cher, or Prince.' I give Sophie and Fraser a teasing sidelong glance. 'But sure.'

'Well, Prince, it's a pleasure to meet you.' He bends down to kiss my hand and I blush before turning to Sophie with a similar flirty smile. 'And you too, Chorley.' Stepping aside, Cammy invites us into his flat and grabs both mine and Sophie's bags from us before we can protest.

'Can't believe that wee cretin has made you two ladies carry your own bags.' Fraser shakes his head at his friend's words. 'Aren't you meant to be the gentleman?'

'I was just doing as I was told.' Fraser holds his hands up in surrender.

'Whenever we'd go out when we lived down in London, this bloke only ever left the club with a girl to escort her to a taxi. Never once saw him get a goodnight kiss.' The piper blushes as we move through the cramped flat. 'He once carried one lass's handbag for the whole night because she handed it to him so she could go to the toilet and forgot to ask for it back because she was busy getting off with one of our pals.'

'All right, all right, no one wants to know any of this,' Fraser murmurs as Cammy pushes open another door into a box room.

'Now, when our Fraz said he was bringing a lass, I was under the impression it was his missus. Now he's brought two, I'm a little confused, if not impressed. So, I'm afraid the room is only really big enough for two.' The small double bed is shoved right into the corner, with just a small walkway in between that and an overflowing wardrobe.

Fraser looks at me nervously, his blush still not evaporated from his complexion. 'I can sleep on the sofa – it's no trouble,' he offers.

'No can do. I've got Mo and Riley from the Grenadier Guards staying on there for the weekend.' Cammy shrugs. 'I have got a bivvy bag you can have down there though?' He points to the thin strip of carpet.

'Aye, nae bother,' he says, before looking at Sophie and I. 'As long as you both don't mind?'

'Doesn't bother me,' Sophie says. 'I once visited my mate at Edinburgh uni and had to sleep upright on a two-seater sofa with her cousin and her cousin's boyfriend.' She turns to me. 'I don't snore, I promise.'

'I'm fine with that,' I reply, honestly.

Once we have left our bags on the end of the bed, Cammy gives us a tiny tour of his even tinier flat and introduces us to his friends who are both slung over one another on the sofa, seemingly wrestling for a games controller.

'You couldn't tell just from looking at them, but these

236

are a couple of His Majesty's Grenadier Guards,' Cammy says, with the same air as someone commentating on a nature programme. 'In their day to day they are trained soldiers, the King's Guard . . .' Still they roll about, the sofa cushions pushed across the room in collateral. 'On leave, hardly even toilet-trained animals.'

I look at Fraser and raise an amused eyebrow, and still that look of shame crosses his expression. Taking matters into his own hands, Fraser crosses the living room and slaps the smaller, and more aggressive of the two across the head, stunning them both to attention. The smaller one sits back on the sofa, legs folded neatly, palms resting sedately on his knees. Only his tousled blond hair and slight sweaty sheen would imply he has been doing anything other than sitting smartly for the last few minutes. His opponent, however, is much more laid-back. Built like a body builder, he lounges with his arms across the back of the cushions, completely unfazed.

'All right, Bell End.' He addresses Fraser with a thick Fijian accent and a casual nod of his head. Both of the men have a messy splattering of stubble, as though when finally freed from the confines of uniform for a couple of weeks, their shaving routines are the first things to slip. Whereas the blond looks as though his few ginger strands have been grown in an evening and could be taken in a twilight breeze, the other's dark hair is so thick that the only thing that would imply he hasn't been growing it for years is the way its wearer constantly scratches at it as though it's been strapped to his face overnight.

'Allie, Sophie, this is Jamie Riley.' Fraser points to the

blond who salutes almost sarcastically. 'And this is Mo Lomani.' The other winks and all of the other men in the room seemingly roll their eyes in sync.

'Mo here is a shameless flirt,' Cammy says with a sigh. 'I reckon he'd try and chat up a lamp if he was given ample time.'

'You're only jealous.' Mo gets to his feet and shakes mine and Sophie's hands tenderly and kisses them one by one until the both of us blush. 'The only thing you ever turn on is a lamp.' He gives Cammy a sloppy smooch on his cheek and then plonks himself back down on the sofa, very much pleased with himself.

Chapter 25

'Ring of Fire!' Mo calls out and slaps down a pack of cards on the coffee table.

'No, truth or dare!' Riley whines.

'Truth or dare? Are you twelve?'

'Okay, okay, never have I ever.' Jamie Riley grins. 'I want to see who has drunk piss through a sock. My bets are on Allie.' He shoots me a wink.

'You're literally the only greebo who would do something like that,' Mo fires back with a cringe.

By the time night falls, Mo and Jamie have bickered over one thing or another at least four times, three other people have arrived including Fraser's sister, and the piper is now sat less than two inches from me as the new arrivals have also crammed themselves onto the singular couch.

'You regretting your choice to come yet?' Fraser bends down close to whisper in my ear. Whisky stirs with his aftershave and the scent is intoxicating. It doesn't help that I too am on my third rather strong drink of the night, and

I know that as soon as I manage to pull myself out of this sofa, the drunkenness will hit me.

So far, I have done little but observe everyone around me. Giggled along as the Grenadiers argue, watch as Sophie talks the ear off Eilidh Bell in the corner, and savour the feeling of Fraser's arm pressing its heat against mine throughout the night.

'I'd say I'm rather content.'

'Aren't you used to balls and banquets and all of those fancy things? Surely this is horrendous compared to all of that.'

'You'd be surprised how much, much worse the "posh" parties I've been to are.' I chuckle. 'Wealth very rarely equals class.'

'Do you fancy heading outside?' Fraser seems to take himself by surprise with his words. 'I mean, I heard there was supposed to be a meteor shower or something tonight, and these two are driving me mad.' He gestures to the bickering guards and I clamber to my feet to follow him out without a second thought.

Out on the streets of Inverness, the September winds are biting. 'Stay there,' Fraser says, noticing me shiver. He runs off into the darkened end of the car park, and I hear the door of a car open and close before he returns under the orange glow of the streetlight.

Handing me the jumper that I had woken up in what feels like months ago, I smile at the memory. Dragging my head through the wool, I savour the smell of hay and cologne. 'Thank you,' I breathe and Fraser reaches up, smooths down my hair and untucks a few strands that are snagged in the collar.

'There's a little river just down here where the lights aren't so bright,' the piper says, looking up at the stars, his whole face seeming to smile in the moonlight.

I trust him, blindly. I could follow him to the ends of the earth and it would be no more effort than falling asleep at night. Being with him, walking beside him, existing in his vicinity is like breathing: like my heart, my lungs, the very blood in my body is made for this exact purpose.

'I should be getting déjà vu, but somehow everything I do with you feels like the first time,' I say, thinking out loud, remembering the smoggy night in London when Atticus took me out to dance under the stars that were hidden from sight. That perhaps should have been the first sign thinking back.

'So, you've left a house party full of bickering guardsmen to look at shooting stars with a man who wears a skirt for a living before?' Fraser teases.

'Something like that,' I jest, and follow him deeper and deeper into the night, until the only light around us is that of the still, sleeping water of the river that glows silver in the moonlight.

A flat bridge crosses it, joining together two gardens of wildflowers shrouded in darkness. Fraser walks to the middle and then sits down on the mossy walkway, beckoning me over. Forgetting all of myself, all of my upbringing, I follow him, and sit down beside him on the cold dewy ground. With a smile only just visible in the soft shine of the moon, he lies down facing the stars.

'You're lying on the ground?' I ask, a little of my snobbery seeping through. 'Isn't it dirty?'

241

'Aye, course it is – that's why it's fun,' Fraser replies, propping himself up on his elbows, his red hair already ornamented with little flakes of moss.

Lying down, I hardly notice Fraser move until my head hits something soft and I realise it is his bicep under my skull. Fraser Bell has his arm outstretched beneath me, both protecting me from the hard floor, and drawing me into an intimate embrace that has never warmed a woman so quickly.

Resting my hand instinctively on his chest, I snuggle deeper into his arm and shoulder, until his once-tense arm relaxes to snake around me and we lie, cuddled together in the middle of a footpath, watching for the stars to shoot across the sky.

'There!' he gasps, pointing into the abyss of the night. I miss the one he gestures to, too invested in the look on his face, too enamoured by his presence to care about the once-in-a-lifetime event.

'What did you wish for?' I ask in a whisper.

'This . . .' he says, taking my cheek in his hand and pressing his lips to mine. The kiss is only fleeting, and leaves my whole face tingling in the desire for more, and yet everything about it is perfect.

So contented, so at peace, I turn my face back to the sky, allowing the nightly breeze to cool the heat of my complexion. The meteor shower bathes the sky in a sea of shooting stars but for the first time in my life, my wish isn't to find true love, or love like a fairy tale. My wish is for this moment, this night, to last just a little longer.

* * *

242

I don't realise that I have fallen asleep until Fraser gently wakes me by stroking my hair from my face. 'Am I that boring?'

'No, no,' I hum sleepily. 'It's just so peaceful.'

'We should probably be heading back before someone starts to worry.' Fraser's words don't match his expression, as though he fights with his own self to do what he knows is the right thing, though I know full well the two of us would rather stay here. 'Plus, I can't let you go catching a cold now, can I?'

That seems to spur him on and he clambers to his feet, offering me his hand to help me up.

'Alice,' he says as we walk hand in hand back towards Cammy's flat. The piper stops to look at me, his wide, bright eyes filled with doubt. Watching him closely, I wait for him to continue. 'Is this all a rebellion?'

His question takes me by surprise.

'What makes you say that?'

'It's just you and I are from very, very different worlds. I have almost nothing to offer you except what I am in front of you right now. And I can't help but feel like a lass like you could only want a guy like me to prove something to your parents.'

'I can't deny that the thought of making my mother positively choke in shock isn't appealing, but no,' I admit truthfully. 'I never set out for any of this to happen; in fact, I've been trying everything I possibly can to repress how I feel and yet I am always drawn back to you.'

'And how do you feel?' His eyes are wide, searching across my face. Though everything in me is screaming to

243

tell him what he wants to hear, I can't allow myself. Not when my best friend is only feet away probably wondering where we've slipped off to and surmising that I have once again betrayed her, and I have.

'I don't know,' I whisper, almost guiltily.

'You don't know?' Fraser's face cracks with the pain of rejection and his dimples flatline. 'Now I never expected you to give up your family and run away with me if I asked, but I thought at least you might feel a fraction for me what I feel for you.'

Stumbling over my words, I can only bumble some syllables in reply. Fraser doesn't say what it is he feels, but I know that whatever he may feel for me, I feel for him tenfold in return.

I love him. Like Darcy loves Elizabeth. Like Heathcliff loves Cathy. Like the sun loves the moon. Against all better judgement. Against the wishes and expectations of all those who don't matter to me. Messily, violently, and yet as easily as breathing.

'I stayed for you this summer, Alice,' he says softly, sadly.

'For me?' I can only parrot his own words back to him.

'I had heard all of the stories of the spoilt lady banished to Balmoral, wild and out of control. Yet when you arrived, I heard you call someone every morning when you thought the house was yet to rise and reach his answerphone each and every time. I saw you every day, even when you didn't want to be seen, and I knew straight away that you weren't the person they'd all been talking about, the person I could read about. I could see you were sad, so sad.' He stops for a breath, and I can't seem to catch mine. I stand stupefied, absorbing his words until they sit heavy in my stomach and I have no idea how to digest them.

'A week after you arrived,' he continues, a man on a mission to finally say what he has clearly been holding back for so long, 'I was offered a post at Edinburgh Castle. I'd been recommended by the king and I was to start imminently. But I couldn't bring myself to take it. I needed to get to know the real you. And most of all, I didn't want to leave, knowing that I was the only one who was listening, for when you needed to cry, for when you needed to talk to someone who would find it an honour to hear your voice. You deserved to be heard. You deserved to be seen exactly as you are, and that's how I wished to spend my summer. So, I delayed the start date, until next week.'

'Fraser,' I whisper, guilt clawing through me. He smiles, an urgent smile, but all I can see is that smart little child in the photo on his coffee table. That child who gave up his life to make sure everyone else around him was happy. The child who never got his dream because he took on responsibilities no young lad should have to shoulder.

'Tell me now, tell me now that it was all worth it. Tell me that you . . . you *love* me just half as much as I love you, and I'll delay it, indefinitely.' His words, *that* word, seems to stun me back to some sense and instinctively my feet move, closer and closer to the house. My mind swirls. Both pleasure and pain overtake me until I positively tremble at the reality of it all.

'Alice,' he calls. 'Alice, please.'

I love him. It's obvious. But I can't let the man I love give up his life for the sad little royal, to take care of her, only ever from a distance. Fraser Bell deserves someone happy who can make him equally so. A life with me is only filled with misery; my relationships are as cursed as my mother, father, and all the loveless marriages before them. Even so, he could never fit into my life. Who would allow it? No matter how I tried, he'd never be welcomed, and I couldn't bring him into a life that would only break him as it has me.

So, I do the only thing this life has fully equipped me for: I lie. 'The world isn't wrong, Fraser; you are,' I say, feigning strength though my voice warbles. 'I am not the person you think I am, nor can I be the person you want me to be.' Pain pinballs through me with every lie, and every crack that forms in his usually cheery disposition.

'What do you mean?' he breathes, leaning forward to take my hand, but falling short as I draw it away.

'You have me all wrong.' The words sting us both. 'The only reason I gave you the time of day was to try and set you up with Sophie. I saw she liked you, and that was my way of entertaining myself – to see you both together and in love. Buchanan and Jimmy were just the subplot. It was you two that were my real target.'

'Sophie?' His brow furrows, and his tone grows more burning, more agitated.

'I had intended you for Sophie. Never myself. How could we ever be together, Fraser? The piper and the lady. None of it could make sense.'

'I don't understand.' He rubs his face roughly. 'But tonight? The kisses? The ball?' None of it makes sense; I know it too. The only thing that does make sense is how I feel for him, how I would move heaven and earth to make him happy. But I can only do that by first breaking both our hearts.

'It was just a bit of fun, Fraser.' I can almost hear my own heart crack, and his even louder still.

'Who do you think you are?' Fraser stares at me in disbelief and the sight of it makes me turn away to shield myself from its attack. 'You think that you can play around with people's lives as though we're all just props in your doll's house. Our lives are simply your entertainment.'

'Fraser? Alice?' The raised voices have caught the attention of Sophie and Eilidh who emerge from a dark corner of the apartment's gardens, and Sophie's brows are furrowed with concern. 'What's going on?'

'Did you know, Sophie?' Fraser's anger rises in his words.

'Know what?'

'That we have just been the pawns in Lady Alice's little game?' Fraser can't bear to look at me.

'Fraz, calm down, just tell us what's going on.' His sister talks to him softly, and he relaxes a little as she touches his forearm gently.

'Alice?' Sophie turns to me. 'What is he talking about?'

'I knew you loved him, Sophie. I could see it. And I'm so sorry.'

'Loved who?' Her confusion only mounts.

'Fraser,' I say quietly. 'I never meant to take him from you, or make him love me. All I wanted was for you to be happy.'

Sophie looks at Fraser and scoffs.

'She has spent these last months trying to play Cupid,

forcing us together. All the while, toying with the love of both of us.' Fraser laughs bitterly, and Sophie's face contorts with pain.

'I don't love Fraser, Alice.' Her pain shifts to disappointment. 'If you'd only spoken to me about it, you'd have known that.' She shakes her head and disappears inside.

Eilidh stands beside her brother, urging him to follow Sophie.

'You really had us all fooled, Alice.' A lone tear streaks down his face and I resist the urge to brush it away. Fraser Bell turns from me without another word, follows his sister and my best friend inside and I am left alone in the garden, wrapped in his jumper, sobbing into his sleeves.

Chapter 26

Alone in Inverness, I stand at an empty, graffitied bus stop, clutching my phone in my hand, not knowing who to call. The only family I have would never answer – no matter my desperation – and the only friends I have, I have hurt and left behind. Just the thought of them renews my tears all over again.

Sliding aimlessly through the device, void of any notifications other than spam, I can hardly see the screen for crying. There is only one number, from an unsaved contact, that has attempted to reach me in the past few weeks and, with barely a shred of hope, I call it.

'Lady Alice? Are you all right, lass? Where are you? Tell me and I shall fetch you at once.' Mrs Buchanan's voice answers first ring and I can only respond in choked sobs.

A muffled voice comes in the background that I can't quite make out and Mrs Buchanan turns away from the speaker to respond though I still hear her. 'She's crying, Jim. Go and fetch the car.'

'Why do I mess everything up?' are the only words I can squeeze past my tears.

Mrs Buchanan sighs softly. 'There is nothing we can't fix, my child.' Her words caress me. 'Now you just tell me where we can fetch you from and I promise, I promise you, we will make everything okay.'

Breathing through my tears as though each tiny droplet is another stab of hurt, I finally manage to draw together some semblance of a direction. 'You just sit tight okay, and you stay on this phone whilst we come and get you.' I do exactly as I'm told. Though I can't bring myself to speak, I sit clutching the phone to my ear for an hour and a half, listening to the housekeeper's reassuring words that break the silence every so often as she listens to my broken breathing in response.

Time melts into the night and all I can do is watch the quiet street around me. The usually unobserved pockets of life come out to play and soon the empty streets of Inverness are teeming with stories that I make up to try and distract myself from the tragedy of my own.

As the stars cloud over with the threat of rain, Mrs Buchanan's car finally arrives. With Jimmy in the driver's seat, the housekeeper sits beside him, still holding her phone to her ear, as she offers me a sad smile. Sliding out of the car, she first stops off to collect something from the boot. Unfolding a tartan picnic blanket, she lays it over my shoulders before sitting down beside me, clutching my cold hands in her bony pair.

In silence, I wait for her anger, for her to say 'I told you so'. I prepare to be scolded. In silence we stay, only the soft hum of the running car filling the space in between us as she presses my hands in hers until they grow clammy with the heat and I rest my head on her shoulder.

'Shall we go home?' Mrs Buchanan's voice is soft, as though speaking to me through a dream.

'Yes please,' I answer in a whisper, and she gets to her feet, my hands still in hers as she walks me to the car and closes the door behind me.

Jimmy doesn't say a word. He only turns up the heater until I can feel the puff of warm air hit me in the back seat. When Mrs Buchanan gets in beside him, he murmurs to her, 'I've let him know we've got her. Poor boy is beside himself with worry.'

Unable to muster desire for anything, let alone being nosy at a time like this, I don't bother to ask who this mysterious 'him' may be. Instead, I sink down in my seat and rest my head against the window, clinging to the sleeves of Fraser's jumper, wishing I had never bothered to come at all.

'You're safe with us, child. Now try and get some sleep. Give your brain a wee break and we can sort everything with a clearer mind.' Mrs Buchanan leans through the front seats and taps me affectionately on the knee as Jimmy pulls away from the kerb and we set off on the road back to Balmoral.

Sleep takes me without a fight. It constantly claws away at me anyway, pulling me back to bed, and refusing to release me.

My sadness isn't a black dog, it's a black hole.

We reach Balmoral as morning begins to break.

Wordlessly disembarking, the three of us walk into the sleeping castle, and follow Mrs Buchanan to her office. When the door is opened, I see that a large mahogany captain's desk takes up most of the room with two green leather Chesterfield chairs facing one another on either side. Mrs Buchanan sits in one, and I take the seat opposite.

Her desk is neat. Nothing clutters the top aside from the scrunched-up wrapper of a Werther's Original that she brushes off into the waste paper bin. Jimmy joins us a few moments later, though I hadn't noticed his absence. In his fists he clutches two mugs, one of them dribbling with whipped cream down the sides. Placing them down in front of both me and Mrs B, he squeezes my shoulder and plants a warming kiss on the crown of my head.

It's only now, in the light of the desk lamp, that I notice the both of them are bundled into their dressing gowns and Mrs Buchanan still has one stray curler in her hair as though she had forgotten it in her urgency.

'Sit up with us for ten minutes to drink your hot chocolate and then get up to bed, lass.' Her face is unchanged from the day I met her. Her expression is still firm, her words still authoritative, but this time, I understand her. Mrs Buchanan cares. She cares more than a mother, or a friend. In her company, with her stern love, I believe her when she tells me it's going to be okay.

'I'm so sorry.' I can't stop the tears as they come. I have done nothing but ruin everything since I got here. So caught up in myself, in rebelling, in being angry, in having my head in the clouds, I never saw any of these people for who they truly are. I saw them as characters in a story, as people existing as a plot around me, and it's only now, when they stay good, when they stay true, when I have shown my true colours, that I realise just how awful I have been. Using my own sadness, my hatred of myself and my life as an excuse to sabotage the happiness of everyone else, I didn't stop once to realise just what I do have. I have been loved this whole time, and not once did I allow myself to see it.

'It's okay. Shhh, you're okay, lass.' Mrs Buchanan walks around the desk to hold me to her chest. She embraces me, comforts me, allows me to cry and cry and cry until her dressing gown is positively soaked through.

I have been so sad for so long that I have refused to allow myself the privilege of feeling happy. Perhaps I had forgotten what it was like, not noticed what such a feeling was. Or perhaps I believed that staying stuck in this pit is easier than the strain of trying to clamber out. It has been the safer option to bask in the melancholy, than risk the pain of losing every happiness. By pushing away Fraser, I have renewed my misery, on the off chance that one day the heartbreak of losing him in another way would be even more painful to bear.

'You just let it out, lass.' Mrs Buchanan strokes my hair. 'We have all day, and an empty castle. Cry as loud as you want.'

'I love him,' I choke through my sobs.

'We know you do, hen.' Jimmy speaks, and neither of them ask who I refer to.

'No, not Atticus. Fraser,' I say, looking between them both, but neither of their faces change expression.

'You think us old crones haven't noticed?' Mrs Buchanan laughs.

'We may be crabbit auld bastards now, but we know what love looks like.' Jimmy places a hand on both mine and the housekeeper's shoulders. 'And I know for certain that that boy thinks the world of you.'

'I wish I wasn't me.'

'And who else would you be?' Mrs Buchanan says sternly. 'Do you think that if tomorrow you woke up in a whole different body, with a new name and in a different part of the world, that you'd suddenly know what you're doing? That all of the things that you have suffered through will all of a sudden be easier to deal with?'

I blink up at her.

'None of us have a clue what we're doing, Alice. Certainly not in love. Life isn't a fairy tale. There isn't one conflict to overcome; there isn't a singular bad guy to defeat before you're allowed your happily ever after. Life is a series of battles, and you can't give up after the first. So what? You lose your shoe at a ball and when no one comes to find you just carry on living a life that's slowly driving you insane? No. You need to go out there, be your own hero, be your own fairy godmother and chase whatever it is that will make you happy. Stop counting down the minutes to midnight and enjoy the moment as though time has stopped altogether.'

Her words, though delivered like a telling-off, are so impassioned, so emotive, that I can only sit in a stunned silence as she pants with fatigue.

'There is no such thing as the perfect time, or the perfect

circumstance,' she says after catching her breath. 'If you want something, you make room for it, you make it work, and every struggle to get there will be the most rewarding thing you've ever done.'

'What if it all goes wrong?' I breathe, my tears slowing to a silent trickle down my cheeks.

'Then at least you can say you've tried.' She wipes my face with her calloused hands and tucks my hair behind my ears. 'Right, now get your arse to bed. I'll wake you up for breakfast so make sure you're wearing pyjamas.'

'Thank you, Mrs B,' I say, earnestly.

'Call me Mary, lass.' She smiles, and I nod. 'And Alice . . .' her voice halts me as I reach the door to leave '. . . above all, the love of a man isn't the key to happiness. Falling in love isn't going to miraculously fix everything. Take your time, to heal, to get to know yourself, your own mind. If your love is meant to be, it will wait.' She casts a quick side glance at Jimmy who blushes softly in the corner of the room.

'Goodnight.'

Chapter 27

So long as I remain here as a burden to my friends, and all those I love, there will be no way for me to prove my sincerity. There won't be enough room for me to change. The one clear thought that has plagued my waking moments and my restless sleep is that I must leave Balmoral.

Stuck here for so long, waiting for my parents to approve my return, I have simply accepted my own lack of agency, convinced that being allowed to make my own decisions will only bring great humiliation to my name. And yet, all that has been done to prevent me making a mistake has caused the greatest of all. In yearning for control over myself, I looked for it in others instead. If I had no choice in my own life, at least I could make choices for others, play the author, play fairy godmother.

If I want to truly be a person worthy of Sophie's friendship, of Fraser's love, I have to take the reins of my own life. So far, my identity has been one long, censored, pre-written speech, which has had me thirsting to go off script. I must take responsibility. I must stop trying to rebel against the prescriptive tracks, and just rewire them completely. I must write my own story.

'Are you sure about this? Isn't it a wee bit hasty?' Mrs Buchanan stands at the door of the castle, holding my last bag as I load up Jimmy's car. 'Why don't you come back in and let me make us breakfast? Give yourself another half an hour to think about it. You can't make a good decision on an empty stomach.'

Smiling sadly, I lean down to kiss her on her soft cheek and she wafts me away with a blush. 'If I don't make this decision now, I never will.'

She places my bag down and takes me by the hands.

I need to prove myself. No, not just for a boy. I need to prove to myself that I am more than what everyone else has told me I am, or should be.

'You're a good girl, Alice. Even if you can be a little madam.' She pinches my cheek like a grandmother and I smile against her touch. 'You're welcome back any time – you know that.'

'I'll be back for the wedding,' I reply with a cheeky grin, looking between her and the groundskeeper as he fusses about the car. Mrs Buchanan hushes me with another deepening blush and waves me off into the car.

'Can I ask one more favour?' Buckling my seatbelt, I turn to her, with all playfulness stripped from my countenance. The housekeeper nods. 'Make sure he takes that job in Edinburgh.'

'Of course, lass.' She looks at the castle, then to me

again. Her usually stern façade has melted away for soft, sloped brows and eyes brimming with affection. 'You just look after yourself. You deserve to be happy.' Before I can leap from the car to embrace her, she closes the door and returns to the castle without looking back.

'Ready, ma'am?' Jimmy says, getting into the driver's seat and striking up the ignition. Unable to tear my gaze from the ivy-covered stone, and the worn-out patch of gravel beneath my window that the piper stood to attention upon each day, I nod wordlessly, knowing if I had to speak, I'd only change my mind.

'He'll forgive you, you know?' Jimmy says after we trundle through the countryside in mostly silence. He doesn't look at me, nor I him.

'I know. That's why I need to leave.' Everyone knows that Fraser Bell is a person better than the rest of us. Not for one second have I doubted his love for me. But he needs to start being selfish. If I stay, so will he. If I stay, he will resent me for all of the opportunities he missed out on because of me. If I leave, he has a shot at a happier life, and how could I say I love him if I didn't let him try?

I only allow Jimmy to drive me as far as Inverness train station, and he leaves a departing kiss on my forehead and wishes me luck. Waving him off, I know there really is no turning back. Marching through the station, I decide that the change starts right now. I walk into the little platform shop, pick up a notebook with the words 'I <3 Edinburgh' on the front, and, after panicking I'm in the wrong city for a few moments, I take it to the checkout.

* * *

When my train eventually arrives after a few delays and one sneaky platform change, I squeeze down the carriage and find a spare seat on a table of businessmen, clearly on their way back to London from some meeting or other. They look me up and down as I take a seat, but I quickly force my headphones into my ears and block out their narcissism with a little classical music. Okay, it might be the *Bridgerton* soundtrack cover of that one Pitbull song but it's mostly piano so I'm saying that counts. Small steps, small steps.

Opening the notebook to the first page, I scrawl in rushed handwriting:

> *How I can become a better person.*
> *How to be more Sophie.*
> *Step 1:*

Staring at the already messy paper occupies my mind for much of the journey. By the time the train pulls into London, I have crossed out most ideas, torn out most pages, but I keep coming back to one in particular: the community centre.

If I can somehow use this position that I'm in to help Sophie with the community centre – and all of the people in places just like Bracmar who need a place to go for a coffee and a chat – surely that's a step in the right direction? If people of all ages, all backgrounds, have a place to meet, a place to be comfortable, warm, and safe with their neighbours, then perhaps a few of us wouldn't be so lonely.

'Lady Alice.' My father meets me personally from King's Cross Station. He stands, leaning up against the sleek car, which of course he didn't drive here himself, with his arms folded like some mob boss coming to pick up his new hit.

'Father.' I nod to him, opening the car boot and tossing in my bags by myself. 'You really didn't have to go to such effort for me. I could have made my own way to the house'

'Your mother wanted me to make sure you didn't stop off anywhere on the way.' He grimaces at the thought of what I could possibly get up to if left to get a taxi alone. 'Plus, I was over at the British Library for some ambassadors' event so was in the area.'

'Lucky me,' I grumble under my breath.

'Now,' he starts as we settle into the drive, stopping and starting every two feet in London traffic, 'if you are coming home, we must set some ground rules, Alice. We can't be having any repeats from the last few months . . .'

Zoning out almost as soon as he begins, I watch the population from the tinted windows and formulate my strategy in my head. How can I make this work? How will I get the funding? Would Father approve this as a business venture? Even then does it really matter? Thinking back to Sophie, how she set aside her own money to rebuild the hall, I realise don't have to use someone else's cash to get what I want. All of my inheritance from my grandmother is sat corroding in a bank vault somewhere ready to pay for my grand royal wedding . . .

'Are you listening, Alice?' Father's voice pierces through my thoughts and I nod absently. 'Make haste, your mother is waiting.' He opens the door and strides out of the car and I realise for the first time that we are outside of the house, with its cold brick, its overly manicured garden, its clinical atmosphere, and my mother stood on the steps in full glam like a mistress turning up at a funeral. Dread surrounds this house. It is no home.

'Mother,' I acknowledge her as I take my bags from the car.

'We never sent for you,' is her welcome.

'Funny that. I realised that I have my own legs, and own mind, and decided to come of my own accord. I have work to do,' I reply, standing up to her.

'Work?' Mother only scoffs. 'I hope you don't mean the same "work" you were doing before you went away that just about gave your father a heart attack?'

'You'll be pleased to know it is not.' My desire to remove myself from her only mounts and mounts the more she snipes.

'Did you learn your lesson in Balmoral?' She follows me inside.

'I learnt many lessons, Mother. I learnt a lot about you too. That was rather illuminating.'

Her face matches the shade of her lipstick. 'Such as?'

'That you weren't always like this. That I could almost pity you.'

She gabbles, trying to regain control of her composure.

'Oh,' I add, 'and that once upon a time, you knew how to smile. And it was beautiful.'

She doesn't follow me up the stairs, she doesn't find me in my room to call me down for dinner, and I am left in isolation to flesh out my plans.

* * *

By the time the house wakes for breakfast, they find me already sprawled out on the dining table, with papers and plans scattered about the place. With one glance at the 'mad lady' they each decide to take their tea and toast in one of the reception rooms instead.

Just after lunchtime passes, Kitty sashays into the room without knocking. I haven't seen her since I left, nor have I heard from her since I was publicly humiliated by Atticus Beaumont. Such a turn of events can't be good for the image, I suppose.

'Alice, Alice, Alice!' she croons and, placing both of her hands on my shoulders, leans over to kiss me on the cheek.

'Hi, Kitty,' I reply absentmindedly, still furiously scribbling away at my notepad.

'*The fairy-tale community?*' she reads from the page. '*Increase funding to community centres across deprived areas and start a reading initiative, led by both elderly members of society and young people.*' Kitty lets out a forced giggle. 'Community centres?'

'Aye,' is all I reply, still writing away.

'Eye? What's wrong with my eye?' She whips a spoolie out of her handbag and combs through her eyelash extensions somewhat neurotically.

'No, *aye*, as in yes.' Covering the bored tone in my voice is becoming such a struggle that I hardly even try.

'Oh, he he.' Kitty pops her little eyelash wand away. 'How very . . . *quaint*.'

'I'm a little busy at the moment, Kitty. Is there something I can do for you?'

'A few of us are off to Hugo's mummy's estate in the

Cotswolds for a little knees-up. We were wondering if you'd like to come and regale us with your tales from that lovely mythical place you've been roughing it these few weeks.' She fiddles with the things on my desk, and fingers the collar of my woollen cardigan. 'My, my, how you've gotten into character. Such fun.'

'I have a lot of work to do. I hope you can manage to find some alternative entertainment so last minute.' Scribbling down another list of things to do, I smile as I imagine Sophie running rings around Kitty and her ignorance.

'Oh dear.' She sits down beside me at the dining table and places her hand over mine, ceasing my writing. 'This is worse than I thought.'

'What now?' I turn to her, already annoyed at what she's about to say.

'I have seen women driven to crazy things after being cheated on. My auntie pissed in my uncle's mistress's contact lens case once, and Beatrice Button's grandmother killed her grandfather – though that was after *he* caught *her* cheating so who knows.'

'Kitty, what are you going on about?' I roll my eyes.

'I have never seen a woman lose herself as much as you in her heartbreak. Cardigans? Messy hair? Work?' The latter word almost dribbles from her tongue like something foreign that she fears is poisonous.

'You have no idea what you're talking about.'

'Of course I do. Your beau.' She winks. 'Get it, beau, Beaumont? Anyway, your beau broke your heart in a horrendous fashion. I was so embarrassed for you that I couldn't bear to even think of you for at least a week. And now you're trying to be someone you're not because you're too humiliated to be you.'

She strokes my hair out of my face and I slap her hand away.

Biting my lip to prevent myself from saying what I truly want to, I slam my pen onto the table and she jumps back with a gasp. 'Look, Kitty, thanks for the invite and everything but I'm too busy to continue this conversation.' Getting to my feet, I shepherd her to the door as politely as I can. 'So unless there's anything else . . .' I gesture for her to leave and she lets out a series of mumbled vocalisations before stepping out of the door, still wide-eyed.

'What about next week? Party at yours? Or Barty's? He's still single and could be convinced to forgive you.' She keeps talking even as I close the door, and looks back and forth between myself and the mahogany as its slow drawing to casts a shadow over her face. The insolence of the action alone is just enough that I don't have to go on some long and malicious rant to prove that I am over her arrogance and I would rather swallow every sword displayed in this house than attend another of the parties she so desperately desires.

Perhaps the old me, the one who left Atticus Beaumont crying for his mother, or the one who rudely called out of windows to tell certain pipers to shut up, would have thrived on this confrontation. But I'm not the old me.

Balmoral has changed me. Sophie, Mrs B, Fraser, have changed me. For the better.

I don't need to humiliate Kitty in the way she so desires to humiliate me. My first step to being more Sophie is almost complete: just walk away with your head held high. Be the bigger person.

Just before I click the door shut, I push my head between the small gap. 'I shall be busy for the foreseeable, so it's probably best to just not bother inviting me to any of your *shindigs* in the future. Goodbye, Kitty.' Fastening the door before she can think of any sort of response, I hear a squeal-like humph from the other side before moving back to the table, sinking back into the chair and resting my head against my open notebook.

What am I doing? I left behind the only people who have ever made me happy, and now I have just cut myself off from the only other part of society that ever welcomed me (whether it was mendacious or not). If I felt alone before, I am certainly alone now.

The buzzing of my phone against the wood of the table stirs me once again. Rushing to check it, my heart hoping to see one name in particular, I am sorely disappointed when it's Kitty's number that flashes up with a message.

You think that you're so much better than us just because you got a bit too cosy with the staff over the summer? What you forget, Alice, is that you're just like me. You're one of us. And no matter how high and mighty you think you are, you always will be. You're just a sad little rich girl, and spoilt just as much as I am. No amount of guilt about your own privilege will ever change that. Don't expect to be welcomed back into society after this. You're finished.

I read it once, then twice, and again a few more times. Maybe I am destined to end up like all of them. Maybe I can't change. Maybe there's not even any point in trying.

But I would rather lose everything trying to become a better person and be perpetually lonely than spend one more minute pretending that people like Kitty, or Hugo, or Atticus, improve my life in any way.

After reading the message one final time, I delete it from my inbox, slide my phone to the opposite end of the table and take a moment to reread the plans scrawled in front of me with the sort of pride that one gets when one finally feels like they're heading in the right direction.

Though the urge to cross the border again, rush to the stables and stand in *his* company, persists. And though I know that such an interaction would motivate me to carry on for at least another century, I can't. I can't see him again. I won't see him again.

I have made my bed, now I must lie in it. It isn't a pea under my mattress that makes my sleep so restless; it is the great planet-sized ball of regret that forces me to toss and turn and wake more tired than when I fell in the first place.

Forcing myself to miss him is my penance. Penance for so many years of being too much like Kitty. For breaking a heart so pure, so good, I don't deserve my happily ever after. Not yet at least.

Scribbling on the front cover of my notebook, I put my main goals into black and white: *Make it up to Sophie. Work to help other people. Live a life where I can be with Fraser Bell.*

Chapter 28

Eleven months later

'Tell us, Lady Alice, what do you find so important about community centres?' A few cameras capture my dirtied trousers and paint-stained jumper as I stand outside the newly refurbished Skegness Community Centre, personally adding the finishing touches.

'Though I have spent my life being photographed at busy parties, surrounded by people, I'm not afraid to admit that I was horribly lonely. For young people like myself, our main forms of socialising have become void of intimacy. Either we socialise behind a screen, or in a pub, club, or at a party where no one has a chance or space to truly talk about how they feel. Community centres are a space to socialise with your neighbours, of all ages, to sit and have a chat, to share a cup of tea and a plate of biscuits and form relationships that we have neglected for years whilst we've allowed these places to become derelict.'

I have no script. My only preparation for all of these press events has been my genuine passion for the work I have devoted the best part of a year to.

Though not a lot in my life has drastically changed – my image still belongs to the public; I am still forced to mingle in circles of people whose philosophies I despise; and I still have this cursed title – at least my words are now my own. My voice belongs to me for the first time in a very long time, and now all of those other things don't feel so oppressive. I have chosen this specific role, I have chosen these specific words, and I am finally in control. I finally feel like myself.

'It's not just young people who need more spaces like this. Every generation will benefit. If we as a society interact more, if we get to know our neighbours, we learn more about ourselves, become less selfish, and find more purpose in our lives. At least, that has been my experience,' I continue, standing strong in front of the crowds as I deliver some of my own intimate truths, unable to allow last summer to escape from anything I do.

Not a day has passed that I haven't thought of Balmoral. Mrs Buchanan calls to check in every now and again. But now the summer has come back around, she's far too busy to waste time on giving me all of the castle gossip, though she still makes sure to tell me that Sophie is well and her usual self, and for that I am grateful. One piece of gossip I have clung to all this time, however, is the fact that Fraser Bell took the job in Edinburgh. That knowledge alone is enough to fend off the pain of having to leave him behind during the day, though it still keeps me awake at night.

'You have been rather open when talking about your

mental health struggles over these past few months. Do you have anything you'd like to say to those people who have criticised you, saying that you are far better off than 99.9 per cent of the population?' This statement has been haunting me these past months. What could you possibly have to be sad about? How can someone like you be so depressed? Don't you have everything you could ever want?

'Mental illness doesn't discriminate. In talking about my battle with depression, not once did I want or expect to gain any sympathy. I am not depressed because I have lost a ruby from my tiara or got my Gucci shoes muddy, I am depressed because I have an illness. In speaking about my illness, I wanted to show all of those people who are struggling that they are not alone. That on the outside, so many of us are pretending, just putting on a show. For once, I wanted to tell the truth, to show all of myself so that all of the people sitting at home wondering why their lives don't look like mine, or his, or hers, realise that even mine doesn't look like it.

'For many years, I struggled to make sense of it all, asking myself what could possibly be wrong. I did the therapy, took the pills. I knew I felt the way I did. I knew how I was told to cope with it, and yet I couldn't. It was like I didn't have control over my own mind, my own brain, and I was constantly trying to justify how I felt. I am very aware that I am an incredibly privileged individual and I most of all am privileged to have access to the support and health care I need for my condition. But people can experience this illness in many forms, for many different reasons.

'No one should feel guilty for suffering. You shouldn't have to prove or justify your mental illness, and if I can help to change any of the prejudice surrounding it, then I am glad to have shared my deeply personal story.'

'Thank you for your time, Lady Alice.'

Releasing a tense breath, I move back inside. The smell of wet paint is overwhelming but the soft chattering that begins to spread through the room, as bodies begin to fill the space, fills me with a pride I've never felt before.

'Where to next?' I turn to my assistant as she follows by my side. Lainey's job these last months has been to sort the logistics of my schedule, and mostly keep me company whilst I travel up and down the country alone. If there is one thing that I can't deny about her it's that she really does try her best, but many times we have found ourselves in places such as Leicestershire instead of Lancashire. And though her timings are usually impeccable, her capacity for remembering dates not so much. She is, however, rather good company, and with a love of yapping away about nothing much, she has been a much-needed companion.

She shuffles a few papers on her clipboard and then grins. 'Well actually, something a bit exciting has happened. Your mother called earlier to say that the whole family has been invited by the king to Balmoral Castle in Scotland for something called the Ghillies Ball? I'm not too sure what exactly it involves, but I thought it sounded fun and it matches up quite nicely with some of your Highland projects so I accepted on your behalf.'

The Ghillies Ball. The night where all social order is flipped on its head. The night where ladies disappear into the night with pipers and return with swollen lips and permanently altered heart rhythms.

I know that this is one date she hasn't gotten wrong. The slight chill in the air reminds me that summer is almost over, and that only means one thing in Balmoral. But how has it already been a year?

How much must have happened in his life? He'll have moved on. He'll have found his happiness.

He won't even be there. And what is Balmoral without him?

'We do need to hurry if we're going to make it in time, my lady.' My assistant looks at her watch nervously.

Going back at some point was inevitable, but now? Right now? At the Ghillies Ball no less? With Fraser settled in Edinburgh, at least a chance meeting with him is off the cards. But will Sophie be happy to see me? Or will she still resent me? Would she have missed me like I have her?

'Ma'am?'

I have to find out. I need to see her. I need to prove that I have changed, for the better. I owe it to her to apologise. Properly.

'Yes, yes, let's go.' We make our way to the car, and I turn to look back at the modest little building we have just left behind. I'm proud. I am genuinely proud of what I have helped to create, all inspired by Sophie. This is all for her, because of her, and I need to be able to tell her in person, no matter how much my chest tightens and my heart aches.

'I sent for some more of your things from London this morning, ma'am. Hopefully a little more weather-appropriate,' my assistant says as we set out for Scotland. She hands me a duffel bag containing a few more clothes.

'Thank you, Lainey.' Unzipping the bag, I see that an

271

unwashed woollen jumper sits on the top and I burst into tears at the sight of it.

'Ma'am?' Lainey turns around from the front seat with a look of concern and spots the sweater gripped between my fingers. 'Well, I saw it when it arrived and did think it was a bit ugly. Then I just assumed it was one of those chic grandpa sweaters that are supposed to be ugly in, like, a sexy way. I'm sorry, ma'am, I can bin it if you'd like?' She stretches out her hand to take it and I instinctively snatch it to my chest.

'No, no, it's okay.' Swiping my tears, I clear my throat and try to regain some face. 'I just thought I had lost this, is all.' I didn't. I knew exactly where it was: tucked in the back of the drawer of my dresser where the tips of my fingers can just reach it when I need something to keep me going. Something to remind me exactly why I am doing all I have done since leaving Balmoral.

Folding up Fraser's jumper, I place it on the window, and rest my head against it. It still smells faintly of him, though with a year since he last wore it already been and gone, there is only a ghost of him in it now: the slight holes in the sleeves where he's tugged on it with nerves; the pulled thread on the left shoulder from Hamish taking a playful bite of him; the stretched-out collar where he's pulled it over his head again and again. It is the only thing I have of him to remind me that it was all real. With the same thoughts of him running through my mind like on a perpetual playlist, I fall asleep to memories of him and the hum of the car on the motorway.

* * *

We drive through the night and I sleep just enough for my mind to descend into lucid dreams of him but not enough for the ending to be satisfying or for me to be properly rested. By the time the car pulls to a halt, the sun is beginning to wake the birds in the trees and their soft song draws me out of my stupor.

The Balmoral Arms stands before us and on its doorstep, Callum and Rose, landlord and his dog, come to greet us. I give him a knowing smile from the distance, remembering our journey to Aberdeen together, where I pretended to be someone else, and he pretended not to already know. Neither of us knew then that I'd return, humiliated, believing I'd lost the love of my life, only to actually lose him a couple of months later.

'We shall rest in the rooms here for a few hours and head into the village by lunch to have a little look at their community centre. I shall bring your clothes through once you've managed to have a sleep.' Lainey fusses in the way she knows best and shuffles a load of bags over to Callum and attempts to shake his hand.

Approaching cautiously, as to not disturb, it is Callum who disrupts the conversation to bow to me. 'Lady Allie.' A wink follows his words and Lainey's horror is evident on her face as she looks between us both, trying to decipher if she should correct his breech of protocol.

'All right, Callum. How've you been?' I shake his hand with genuine appreciation and he pulls me into the warmth of the pub.

'No' bad, no' bad. Haven't found any royals on my doorstep for a wee while so it's all been pretty uneventful.'

He pours myself, Lainey, and our driver a tea from the pot on the bar and encourages us to take a seat at the hearth. 'Not on horseback today then, lass?'

'Thankfully not. I did think about it, but we're on a bit of a tight schedule.' He chuckles and I take a much-needed swig of tea.

'Mary Buchanan from up at the castle has been telling me what you've been up to.' My cheeks flush as he places his hand firmly on my shoulder and gives it a squeeze. 'I'm proud of you, lass.' Unable to hold myself together enough for a PR-trained response, I draw him into an embrace and he returns it. Hardly able to think of the last time I heard those words, I squeeze him tighter.

'Thank you,' I whisper in his ear before drawing away and brushing myself down, as if trying to shake some sense back into myself. 'Don't tell anyone about that.' I point a warning finger at him, though my glassy eyes tell a far softer story.

Callum puts his hands up in surrender, then taps the side of his nose as if to say my secrets are safe with him. 'You get up to your room,' he says, handing me a key. 'Make sure you have a good rest before your big day. I hear a lot of the folk in the village are very excited to see you.'

'See me?' I say, confused.

'Aye.' He scruffs Rose's head and disappears with Lainey and leaves me to climb the rickety stairs to bed.

Chapter 29

'Ready?' Lainey says behind me as I survey myself in the mirror.

Every single strand of hair seems to be out of place; nothing I wear seems to look, fit, or feel right; and I know if I leave this chair right now my stomach will feel like it's dropped from under me and I'll end up with sick on my blouse anyway.

I've done this upwards of fifteen times: stood outside community centres up and down the country, shaken a few hands, taken a few photos. But this one, in this tiny village in a tiny corner of Scotland, is more daunting than standing in the House of Lords, asking for their backing.

'Lainey, I can't do it.' My hands are too clammy to hold on to my hairbrush as I rake it through my sleek hair for the hundredth time, and it clatters against the wooden floor. My assistant looks at me with widened eyes as my stomach begins to cramp and sweat rolls down the crease of my spine like damp fingertips groping at my skin.

What if Sophie is here? Surely she will be. This is *her* project. This is the thing she devoted herself to. What would I say to her? Would she even want to speak to me? Even worse, what if she isn't here? What if she feels as though I have usurped her, in donating the money, in setting up these reading schemes? What if she feels as though I have stolen her ideas, her passion?

My heartbeat throbs in my ears. I can't hear Lainey as she paces about the room on the phone. I can hardly hold on to a breath as each one leaves me more and more breathless each time I try and suck in another. I'm clinging to the dressing table, and the whole thing shakes as I tremble against it.

'Bottling it, aye?' A voice so familiar manages to slice its way through my ruminations. 'After all this time and effort, you're just gonna let those folk down out there who have come to see your wee blonde arse?'

Sophie smiles in the doorway, a teasing kink in her brow. In a year she has hardly changed, except there's something more grown up about her. As though she has surpassed girlhood and she isn't quite so new and naïve.

'Sophie?' I say, still trying to catch my breath.

'Course it's me, eejit. You forgotten me already?' She laughs, though there's a shyness to it, as though she too is unsure what she's supposed to say.

Rushing to her, just as I did Callum, I have somehow, overnight, become a hugger. I pull her in tightly, and she wheezes in my ear, 'Bloody hell, woman, you trying to kill me?'

I ease up my grip slightly, and she is able to chuckle and

return my embrace. Drawing back, I still cling to her as I survey her face, double-checking it is her, and trying to catch up on all that has changed in her mien.

'Sophie, I'm so sorry,' I manage to squeeze out along with a collection of tears. How is it that I didn't cry for many, many years, and now I can't bloody stop?

Sophie only looks at me and sighs. 'You really hurt me – you know that?' Her tone is serious and I can feel my heart splinter within me.

'I shouldn't have done it. I know that. It was my messed-up way of trying to make you happy, without stopping once to think about what you might actually want.' The tears flow freely and she shakes her head.

'No, not that. I forgave you as soon as I walked away about the whole Fraser thingy.' She fakes a gag and then returns to her sober tone. 'No, Alice, you hurt me by leaving without saying goodbye. You hurt me when you went a whole year without checking in. You hurt me when you made my dream come true, and you weren't here for us to do it together or for me to even thank you.' I'm stunned to silence. My throat is so thick with emotion that if I try to speak now, I'm not even sure anything will come out. 'You're a bloody good person, Alice, but by God do you make some horrendous decisions.'

Just about able to stomach a laugh, it comes out gargled through my tears and I furiously swipe away the snot leaking from my nose. 'That's why I had to leave,' I say once Sophie hands me a tissue and I regain a little of my dignity. 'I wanted, no, needed to be better, to make better choices, to be a better person before I could truly be a good friend to you.'

'You know that you're allowed to make mistakes, right?' Shaking her head, Sophie holds my hand, then grimaces a little at the slickness of it. 'I wasn't your friend because I thought you were some sort of perfect princess. I *am* your friend because you needed me, and as much as you think I am some girl with my shit together, I need you too. You might not exactly know how, or always do it in the right way, but you care. Christ, you care enough that you spent the last year pumping cash into a shitty little village hall in the arse end of nowhere just because I told you what it meant to me. You and that community centre have changed my life. Not many people can say that their best friend is their flaming fairy godmother who has made their dreams come true. The best thing of all, Alice, is that you didn't even have to do it. You don't realise it, but you have always been a good friend. Even good friends fuck it up sometimes. They just don't run off and Mr Darcy the shit out of their pal's lives instead of having a normal-people argument and then making up the next day.'

Shaking my head, I can't control the grin on my face and the budding laugh. 'Sorry, that's a lovely monologue, beautiful. And I'm just going to push down the fact that I am going to cry again and also my overwhelming feeling of guilt that I should be the one saying such nice stuff to you to just circle back to the phrase "Mr Darcy the shit out of their pal's lives" for one second.'

Sophie finally cracks up and her familiar cackle fills the room. Infectious beyond measure, soon my tears are from my laughter.

'My lady?' Lainey's anxious voice draws us both back

down to earth as she watches on, concerned. 'I can't stall much longer.'

Sophie glances at me and she soon shares Lainey's look of panic. 'You're looking like shite,' she says, as honest as ever.

'Thanks, Soph.' I chuckle and turn back to the mirror on the vanity and immediately her reaction is justified. My face is smeared with makeup, my eyes are puffy, a little snot has dried across my cheek and I think I'd probably look better if I just walked out of a car crash.

'Look.' Sophie rushes around the room, collecting a flannel and a few other bits. 'You just need to be you. The new you, the old you, whatever. You don't have to look perfect, or act perfect. What the public want most from their royals is humanity, the sense that you're just like us. Sometimes you have a bad day too, and they want to see it.'

'Yeah, so they can sell the photos to the press? You should have seen some of the stuff that came out about my cousin Theo when he had a few bad nights out.' Shivering at the thought of it, I scrub the flannel against my face.

'No, no. I don't mean letting the world see you at rock bottom. I mean letting them see you just as you are. No fancy frills, no perfectly worded speeches, just you, as you come. Sit and read with us. Be one of us for the afternoon.'

Resisting the urge to tell her that I wish it could be more than just the afternoon, I do as she says. Removing all of my makeup and swapping the blouse and suit pants for jeans and a T-shirt, I feel more at home than I have for months.

'Here, stick this on.' Sophie hands me Fraser's jumper and I look at her, unsure. 'For old times' sake?'

'I don't think—' Clamming up, thoughts of Fraser return at full pelt and it's as though the reminder has pushed me off-kilter for just a moment. She hasn't mentioned him before now. Perhaps even she hasn't heard from him. Would she tell me if he'd moved on? Is it even any of my business?

'Come on, it's not like anyone will notice. And there must be a reason you packed it.' She winks, and pushes it against me so I have no choice but to take it.

'Fine, but I want it known that it was packed for me. I'm not a creep.' Reluctantly, I pull it over my head.

'Whatever you say.'

As we walk the short distance to the Braemar Community Centre, the streets are hushed, lethargic yet tense, as though calm in preparation for a storm. Holding Sophie tightly by the hand, I try and think over and over of what to say, what to do, how to smile, but none of that matters as soon as I see it.

The overgrown gardens are pruned back to make room for a bed of wildflowers, and a lawn broad enough for a little stall to be set up in the summer sun, stacked with cakes and a steaming tea urn. The old stone schoolhouse building seems brighter. The sign has been repainted, the slate of the roof replaced, and best of all, it is teeming with life. Men and women – old, young and everything in between – bustle through the gates to steal a glance at the newly refurbished building.

'It's all right, ladies and gents, she's here. We havnae scared her off just yet.' Sophie announces my presence in a way I can't compare to anything else I've experienced so far on my regional tour of community centres. All of the faces turn towards us at the sound of her voice and she bows to the attention, owning her part in making this whole thing happen and helping to fight off my imminent panic attack.

Waving shyly, I grow nervous under the many eager eyes, and even more so under the gaze of those who still appear to remain apprehensive. When a short, slightly hairy man barges forward to take a photo directly in my face, I tense again, my mind blank. All of the others meant something to me. They were an achievement; they meant something better for people who deserve it. But this time, this one matters the most. If I need to get one thing right in this new role of mine, it is opening the one place that started it all.

'Thank you all so much for coming,' I say a little too quietly for the chattering crowd and the second row from the front begin to ask those in front what I've just said.

'Oi,' Sophie calls out. 'If you'd all just whisht you might be able to hear the poor lass.' After an offended buzz, the noise from the crowd simmers out and Sophie throws the attention back to me with a smile.

'Thank you all for coming out today for the grand opening of the newly refurbished Braemar Community Centre.' Given a second chance to start again, I persist this time with a little more confidence. 'Some of you may know that it was actually right here in Braemar that I decided to begin this initiative to save our community centres and village halls up and down the country. But I would be lying if I said the idea was my own.' I cast a long glance at

Sophie. 'I have no doubt that almost all of you here know my best friend, Sophie Chorley.' A soft cheer goes up in the crowd. 'But what most of you may not know is that Sophie put aside her own wages, her own scarce free time to begin the process of returning this building to the people of her hometown. It was Sophie who made me truly understand the value of the people around you, the beauty of a family that doesn't have to be blood.'

As I address the crowd, two faces catch my eye in that very moment: my parents. Mother and Father stand a little away from the gathering, the former looking me up and down, the latter surveying all those around him. Not once have they been to one of these events; in fact, since I returned to London all those months ago, we have hardly interacted. For better or worse, I'm not too sure. Trying not to choke under their scrutiny, I return my attention back to giving my friend the credit she deserves, the credit she is owed.

'Sophie is one of the most selfless people I know, and in setting up this scheme, my main goal was to always be more like her.' Clearing my throat, I try and hold it together. 'When I first came to Scotland, I was self-absorbed, bored, and so, so lonely. Sophie and all of those who cared for me at Balmoral picked me up and shook me. They spoke to me like old friends, they held my hand through things I had always had to shoulder alone, and they taught me things about myself and the world around me that I had never once stopped to think about. All I had to offer in return was funding for a project that Sophie had already altruistically begun. This is my "thank you", to all of you, and to you, Sophie, for taking me in and showing me what a family is and what a community can be. If this community centre can do even just a fraction for someone in this village that you did for me, then I know it is all more than worth it.'

Searching again for my parents in the crowd, hoping to see just a little pride in their faces, I am unsurprised when the space they once occupied is empty and they're nowhere to be seen. Scanning desperately for another moment, hoping they've just slipped behind another party or have inched closer, another face comes into focus and I have to blink several times to make sure this isn't some kind of sick mirage.

Fraser Bell is tucked within the masses. His thick red hair is covered by a tweed flat cap and his dimples are perfectly ironed flat, but no matter how much time has passed, or how much he may have changed, there will never be a day where I don't recognise those eyes. As though I have conjured him myself, Fraser stands there, so still, so beautiful, that I must be delirious from lack of sleep.

He's supposed to be in Edinburgh.

'Who, Lady Alice?' So occupied with the thoughts of him, the rest of the population melts away from my sight and mind and it is only the sound of Sophie's voice that draws me back from my dream and I realise I have said the words aloud.

When I look again, he's gone. Vanished into thin air like a phantom that never wished to be seen.

Staring wide-eyed at Sophie, my mouth moving and yet no words forming, my heartbeat fills my senses. It is all I can hear, all I can feel.

'Now, enough about me,' I announce to the muster of bodies before me, my mind absent and filled only now with him. 'I wish to hand this over to Sophie Chorley, the one person who should have the honour of opening this community centre today. Sophie Chorley, everyone.' Stepping aside, I gesture for Sophie to come forward and she does so with a blush.

Rushing through the crowd, I squeeze past so many people with an apology to reach the place I saw him, the place I know he stood. Why is it only now that I am desperately searching for a man in a flat cap that it seems as though I've stumbled onto the set of *Peaky Blinders* if it starred a bunch of elderly Scottish men? Tapping on shoulders, following strangers, I search and search for him.

But Fraser Bell has gone.

Chapter 30

'You all right?' Sophie finds me once all of the formalities have been completed and the gathering has moved inside to explore the hall in all its glory. Stood in the garden, staring out at the hills and glens in the distance, I have been replaying the moment I saw him over and over in my head, trying to cling to my sanity.

'Yeah,' I reply, unable to confess that I've been hallucinating visions of the piper in the crowd. 'You've done a really beautiful job here, Soph.' Looking out across the gardens, the reams of smiling faces, I am sincere in my words.

'I'd say we make a good team.' She places her arm over my shoulder and draws me into an embrace from the side.

Smiling in reply, I rest my head on her shoulder and savour a moment of peace. 'You're coming tonight, right? To the Ghillies Ball, I mean?' she says after a moment, as though suddenly remembering.

'Do you think the king would notice if I just didn't turn up?'

'Probably not.' She shrugs. 'But I would, so you're coming. I have someone I'd like to introduce you to.' Her playful brows wiggle with the secret and the sight warms me.

'Yeah?' I say, intrigued. 'Then maybe I'll make the effort, just for you.'

'I'm serious.' Sophie folds her arms over her chest. 'I know everyone in this town. If you try and hide from me, I will find you.'

'I don't doubt you for a second.' I chuckle, though also feeling slightly unnerved. 'Anyway, how have you managed to escape Buchanan's clutches on Ghillies day? Isn't she running around like a blue-arsed fly right about now?'

'I don't quite know what happened when we all went on holiday last autumn, but we came back and it was like she had been replaced, Alice. I was terrified.' With eyes like saucers, she looks genuinely scared for a moment.

'What are you on about?' I can't help my laughter.

'She smiled at me, Alice,' she says, almost trembling. 'And she wouldn't stop.'

'That's a good thing is it not?' Using my confusion to cover up the fact I know exactly why she is so happy these days, I try everything in my power to not let her secret slip, even to my best friend.

'Well . . . yeah. But don't you think it's a just a wee bit freaky? It's like the real Mrs B has been abducted by aliens and now I'm just waiting for her replacement to probe me.' Sophie shudders then checks her watch. 'Oh bawbag. She let me have the afternoon off with the promise that I'd be back by four to help with the finishing touches.'

Sophie begins running frantically down the street before turning back to shout her goodbyes. 'You better be there, Alice!' she finishes before disappearing down the street and out of view.

'Can't have had too much of a personality transplant then,' I utter to myself, amused at how quickly Sophie's mood shifted at the thought of being tardy in Mrs B's presence.

The chill that comes with the end of the summer is thick in the air and the leaves rustle in the trees more loudly than usual, as though they too are clinging to the dregs of the season and refusing to let go. In the Balmoral Arms, my windows are thrown wide open so I feel the breeze on my made-up face. My naked arms prickle with goose bumps as though I have allowed a spirit in from the cold and now it whips around me, and beneath the folds of my dress. With a tight-corseted bodice, my dress fans out from the waist to give way to a skirt so wide I'm afraid it might swallow me if this wind gains any more strength. No one can come within a metre of me thanks to all of the ivory fabric and it is clear that such a choice in attire was entirely purposeful since it was my mother who sent it.

'Put your shoulders back, Alice,' Mother fusses as I descend the stairs and they meet me at the bottom to ferry me to the ball.

Callum stands at the bar, newspaper covering his face, but at the sound of my name, he lowers it. Smiling, he salutes me discreetly and I thank him with my eyes.

Mother and Father seem itchy in this part of the world, as though they have to try doubly hard to keep up appearances. Thinking back to the photos Callum has of the two of them, the joy they once possessed, I pity them both as we all walk in silence to the car.

'Have you been looking forward to seeing Balmoral again, Mother?' I ask her in one last-ditch attempt to engage with her, to find some common ground.

'I have never much cared for it,' she replies sharply.

'Did you ever get to see much of it?' I persist, trying not to let the rejection settle too harshly in my chest as I never expected anything different. 'The pyramid perhaps? Oh, or Loch Muick?'

Only glancing at my father, my mother wears an unreadable expression on her face, and I wonder if she ever understood the love that is infused in all of those places. Did she ever experience what it is to walk there and truly understand their meaning? Did she ever understand the pain, longing, desire of so many before us in history? If not, her misery makes sense, for in the year that has passed, I too feel as though I have left my heart scattered across the grounds of Balmoral and nothing I have experienced since has come close to seeing me regain it.

'I've always thought the place is built on love,' I say quietly into the silence of the car.

Mother sighs and Father speaks for the first time in a while. 'I thought you'd gotten over all of that fairy-tale stuff, Alice.'

Those sad, sad words answer all of my questions. My parents see love as something of a fantasy, something only in stories, made up for the entertainment of delusional little girls.

Perhaps that's the true family curse. Perhaps love is like fairies, or magic. If one doesn't believe, one will never see nor feel. I believe in fairies, I believe in magic, and most of all, I believe in love. As I watch the castle come into view, I hold on to that belief so tightly. Love is in the trees, it's in the gravel paths, it's in the birds, the squirrels, the stags, it's in the ivy, in the stone, in the vast sky all around it.

Though my love may not be here physically, I feel him in every stretch of the place. As I cross the boundaries into the grounds, my heart feels just a little more at ease. Fraser Bell is haunting me and I am glad of it. At least I possessed his heart once; at least this place is filled with him.

Drawing up the driveway, my father turns to me. 'Alice,' he begins in his serious voice, 'we have noticed a marked change in you recently. Your work has been interesting, and we have been glad to see you out of trouble. Do not let your mother and I down tonight.' Other parents would simply say they were proud, but this is close enough to praise so I'll take it.

Before I can respond, the door is opened from the outside and the footmen usher us out. Our names are announced and a head of perfectly neat grey hair emerges from within the cloakroom. Mrs Buchanan, trying to maintain her usual composure, wanders up as close as protocol will allow and stands rigidly, watching us from afar. In a gown of green and gold, her skin glows against the light of the castle. Her eyes, too, seem brimming with life, in such a way that before seemed almost impossible.

Now I understand Sophie's fears; she really does seem like a new woman, despite the ways she tries to maintain her image of old.

'Your Grace.' She bows to my mother and offers to take her shawl. Mother does a double take, her recognition evident, her feathers suitably ruffled at this stark reminder of the past. Regaining her composure, Mother hands over her shawl and disappears into the crowd behind my father, leaving Mrs Buchanan behind.

Unable to embrace me in front of an audience, she catches me by the hand and squeezes it inconspicuously. 'I am so glad to see you, lass.'

'You look beautiful, Mrs B.' She thanks me with rosy cheeks.

'I see the old witch is still as jolly as ever.' She gestures to my mother with an eyeroll and I have to cover my mouth to stifle my laughter. 'I'm so glad you're more like your granny.'

'Is Sophie here yet?' I ask, scanning the room, though I know subconsciously hers isn't the only face I'm searching for. Every man seems to morph into him the more desperately I look and I have to force myself to blink and return my attention to the housekeeper.

'I believe she's already in the ballroom. But wait a second lass.' She pulls off her tartan sash and lays it across my shoulder. 'You can't go in without one; I'll go and find a spare.' She pinches me on the cheek and struts back across the floor, calling out orders to her staff who stand to attention at her approach.

Navigating the castle as though I have never been away,

I quickly find the great hall – made all the easier by the call of the bagpipes that flows from the grand doors. Something stirs in my chest at the sound and as I enter the room, I can't bring myself to look up to the balcony where he stood not so long ago. What if it's him there now? What if I did see him earlier, and he has come home to play for the king? Stealing a glance at the pulpit-like stand, I see that a piper, of course, fills its space. The Balmoral tartan, the bonnet, the perfectly pristine uniform. All of it is the same, all of it unchanged, except the man within. My heart sinks.

'You actually came?' Sophie clings to my shoulders as she shakes me with excitement.

'You did threaten me if I didn't,' I remind her.

'Sounds about right,' replies a voice I had never once expected to hear.

Eilidh Bell stands at Sophie's side, the famous Bell dimpled smile fixed on her face. Her striking red hair curled and pinned so beautifully she could be Alba herself in her corset of sky-blue tartan. Looking again to the piper at the head of the hall, I furiously look for Fraser's face, hoping I had managed to miss him before, only for my disappointment to be renewed.

'Eilidh!' Turning back to his sister, I give her the greeting she deserves. 'I'm sorry, you have taken me by surprise a little.' I hold a gloved hand to my chest to try and steady my heartbeat. She gives me a sympathetic look and I am grateful, above all, that she doesn't seem to hold any hatred for me. Even after everything I said to her brother.

'This may take you even more by surprise.' Sophie leans

in close to whisper then takes Eilidh by the hand and stands proudly beside her, their fingers entwined. 'If you'd only have asked.' Sophie winks and I can't help myself; I pull them both into a tight embrace and kiss them on their respective cheeks.

'Congratulations,' I say with a tear, still clutching them both tightly. Then releasing them to straighten out their gowns, I hold Sophie by the hands. 'I can't tell you how happy I am for you, Sophie. Truly.'

After all of the time I spent trying to make Sophie happy by setting her up with the piper, it turns out it was actually his sister she was in love with the whole time. Sweeping a tear from under my lashes, my goal seems complete, though I had nothing to do with it. Sophie is in love, she is happy, and she well and truly deserves to be.

'Lady Alice Walpole.' The king's voice calls and silences the voices of many around us. Sophie and Eilidh mouth that they shall catch up with me later as I acknowledge my name.

'Your Majesty.' I curtsey before him.

'Which tartan is that one? I assumed your family would be wearing the royal Stuart,' he says, gesturing to his own.

'I believe this is the Buchanan tartan, sir.' Answering honestly, I look out of the corner of my eye to see if I can spot Mrs B and, much to my pleasure, I find her already in the midst of a dance with none other than Groundskeeper Jimmy.

'I see your little Scottish sabbatical worked a treat for you. Found your passion in . . .' he looks at a note handed to him by an aide '. . . community centres. I have heard from my friends in Braemar of course that you have done a rather good job. Who would have thought?'

'Thank you, sir.' I accept the compliment, though it feels a little backhanded.

'Oh, Alice, whilst I have you here, can you remember Pipe Major Bell who played for us here last year?' The question stuns me. I wasn't expecting one so direct and certainly not from the king himself.

'I believe I do, sir,' I manage to croak.

'Well, I have sorely missed him this summer. I allowed him to take a post at Edinburgh Castle and as soon as I heard this fellow play—' he gestures to the replacement piper '—I realised I had made a rather big mistake. Alas, the chap loves Edinburgh, but I have managed to take a loan of him just for the evening, under the promise that I wouldn't force him to play.' My heart stops and I have to fight to stay on my feet. 'Bell, Bell, over here,' he calls into the crowd.

'No, sir, it's oka—' It's too late to protest, and too late to brace myself. He was no ghost. He was no figment of my imagination. Fraser Bell comes before the king as flesh and bone.

Chapter 31

Bowing, Fraser addresses the monarch as is required of him. Unable to do anything but watch, I observe every inch of him, convincing myself that he really is here. He is real. Fraser's broad frame is tense, his hair is just slightly too long and curls over his ears, and a path of stubble lies forgotten, missed on a patch of his jaw. So close, I could reach out and touch him, and even then, I'd fear that he'd disappear into a puff of smoke.

Then he turns to me. The music falls silent across the room, as if every other body has fled, until the only things taking up space, the only atoms that still float through this void are those that make up him and I. 'Lady Alice.' He bows before me like an almost forgotten acquaintance and I resist the urge to hold him by the face and force him to look me in the eye.

'Fraser,' I breathe but he refuses to meet my gaze.

'Must I petition you to return to me, Pipe Major Bell? My wife has decided that it is only your playing that she can stomach so early in the morning.' The king speaks, and with the sound of his voice, the music and chattering floods back into the ballroom with overpowering intensity. Cringing away from the noise, I try and recollect myself. I can't cry here. I won't.

'You shall have to ask those who employ me, Your Majesty. Though I am sure they will not refuse you,' Fraser replies, delighting the king and making him release a guttural chuckle.

'If I remember rightly, Bell, you danced with my great-niece at the last ball, did you not?' Fraser's face flames, and I am sure mine is not much different.

'Yes, indeed, Your Majesty.' Still unable to look at me, Fraser continues to fulfil his duties to the king, though his body language would imply he wishes nothing more than to run away at the first possible moment.

'Why then, you must do so again.' He flings his arms out wide and grins like a jolly king of old. 'Unless she has scarred you from the last time?'

Fraser forces a chuckle. 'I am afraid, sir, that I am needed elsewhere at present. And I have always been a better piper than a dancer.'

'How you tease us so. What a shame. Well, you had better get on then, Bell, and do whatever it is that is more important than taking the hand of my beautiful niece.' I wish for nothing more than the ground to swallow me up and to plunge a thousand feet to a painful death. Fraser simply nods, bows to myself and the king, then departs across the dance floor, and out of the door.

Curtseying again, I excuse myself, and just like this time a year ago, I follow Fraser Bell into the night.

Catching him retreating across the gardens in a way so familiar, I can't stop myself from calling out his name. Not stopping to acknowledge me, he continues at pace, with steps so heavy I can see the prints of his ghillie shoes in the dewy grass.

'Please,' I call into the darkness, the muted sound of music only just reaching us from so far away. 'Talk to me Fraser, please.'

Turning sharply on his heel, he says, 'You can't have anything to say to me, Alice. You said it all just fine enough a year ago when you told me that everything was a lie.' His face is flushed and damp with sweat as he finally looks at me. 'I can't do this. I can't see you.'

'Then why did you come earlier?' Adrenaline takes over and I can't stop the words that fall from me.

'To support Sophie,' he bites, and I have to take a step back. This all played out so differently in my head. He hates me, or at least he no longer loves me.

What now do I have to lose? The man I love is stood before me and I let him go without telling him the truth one too many times before.

'I wasn't good enough for you, Fraser.'

He had begun to walk away when my words halt him once more.

'What?' He looks at me with an expression so pained I can feel the jolt of it run through my body.

'I couldn't tell you I loved you back then, because I didn't deserve you,' I confess.

'That makes no sense.'

'You were going to give up your career for me. I couldn't

allow you to do that. I wanted to set you up with Sophie because I knew she was far better for you than me. What could I offer you? What could I give you aside from a promise that I'm not all of the things I had been up until that point?'

He stays stock still as I take a step forward and I use that as encouragement to step again.

'Alice, I would have given up my entire life to have spent this last year with you.' A tear drops over his waterline and drags the reflection of the moon down his flushed cheeks.

'And what would have happened when you inevitably regretted it? You would resent me. You shouldn't have to give anything up for me. All I have ever wanted is to see you happy, and I knew that as the person I was last year, I couldn't be the one to make you happy.'

Fraser shakes his head and sucks in a shaking breath before he speaks. 'Every day you walked the halls of Balmoral, or swore at me from your window, or I held you in my arms, you made me happier than anything I could have ever dreamed of. It was a feeling written only in the books, and even if this was all a dream, I'd have chosen to sleep forever just to live in it a little longer.' Tears flow freely down my face and I am desperate to hold him. 'You broke my heart, Alice.'

'I know,' I sob. 'Before I met you, Fraser, I was sad beyond all measure. I'm not sure that I ever wanted to die. I just didn't expect to live. It's not like I was actively seeking a way to end my life. I just couldn't imagine growing old; I couldn't imagine having a family, or hitting milestones, or ever being happy. People always asked me what I wanted to be, what were my dreams, but I never had any. I never knew I'd live long enough to fulfil them, so there was no point having them. I have never thought far enough ahead. But, with you, Fraser, it's like I am excited. It was like being woken from a sleep sure to one day kill me. I am excited to go to a supermarket and do a weekly shop, I'm excited to sit down in front of the telly in my pyjamas and fall asleep at 9 p.m. on a Saturday. You made me want to live that beautifully normal life. You make me want to *live*. I'm excited to see you grow old, and myself beside you,' I confess. 'I love you. But I had to figure out how to make myself happy first, so I could give you everything you deserve.'

'And are you?' He reaches forward and grasps me by the face. 'Happy?'

'Happier.' I nod against his touch. 'It's taking time, but I'll get there.'

'You love me?' Fraser sobs as he buries his face into the crease of my neck.

'I do, and I have. All this time.'

In the space we shared our first kiss, he presses his lips to mine once again in a way so electric, yet so calming, I realise that it is right here, in his arms, that is my home. Sliding my hands through his hair, I hold him as close as I can, afraid of letting him go.

Fraser pulls away after a few beats of silence where even the owls and trees have nothing left to say. 'Can we ever be together?' Though they shine in the moonlight, his eyes are sad, troubled, and I don't have an answer for him. 'You say you don't want me to give up anything for you, but surely you'll have to give up everything to be with me.' Stroking the hair from my face, he kisses me on the forehead and holds me there.

'I don't think I can keep you a secret forever,' he mumbles against my skin.

Embracing him tightly, I feel his heart thumping against my cheek. Though the music carries across the gardens, and though voices can be heard for miles around, that throb in his chest is the only thing I can focus on. With his pipes, his foals, his dimpled smiles, Fraser Bell has shown me what a happy life can be. He has proven that not all has to be as is prescribed. I don't have to hide everything I love just to protect the feelings of those who don't matter to me.

Giving up tiaras, gowns, and posh banquets is nothing. They never held me when I cried. They never made me laugh in a loch and warmed me with their affection. They never kissed me as though I am the only thing in the world worth having so close. Fraser Bell did. Being with him wouldn't be giving anything up, being with him would be finally choosing to be happy.

And I'm not afraid of happiness anymore.

Leaning up, I press a long passionate kiss to his lips, before pulling away and dragging him by the hand back towards the ball.

'Where are we going?' he asks as he paces beside me, furiously wiping the tears from his face.

'To meet my parents.' Pride flows through me as I grin and Fraser only returns a nervous gaze.

'Alice . . .' he begins.

'Fraser, I've never been more sure of anything in my life.' Stopping for a moment outside the door, I reassure him with a tender caress of his cheek. 'Everyone I love is standing in this castle at present and I don't think I'll lose any of them by having you by my side. Nothing aside from the select few people in that room matter to me – no titles, no money, no reputation. It wouldn't be giving it up for you, it would be being liberated.'

Bursting through the door, I spot my mother and father before the king, their miserable faces contorted into false smiles for their superior's benefit.

'Mother, Father,' I interrupt their conversation. 'Meet Fraser Bell, the love of my life.'

'Alice, not now,' my mother spits through gritted teeth, looking back at the king with an apologetic smile.

'Yes, now.' I grasp the king's glass from the table beside him and clash against it with the ring on my forefinger. Soon the whole room bends their gaze to me, the band cease their playing, and not once does my confidence waver.

'Good evening, ladies and gentlemen. My name is Alice Walpole and I am unashamedly, indubitably, and *happily* in love with Fraser Bell. I hope you enjoy the rest of your evening.'

Epilogue

The wedding bells of Crathie Kirk can be heard for miles around Balmoral. Melodious chimes filter into the landscape as though it is as natural of a sound as the breeze in the leaves, or the bees in the heather.

The king ordered that none of the staff may remain in the castle whilst the nuptials are being held and consequently the whole of Balmoral, including the king and queen themselves, have gathered with rice and confetti. It's a humble parish church of stone and steeples, tucked away in a pocket of pine trees, and there really is no scene more perfect for a wedding. With a ceiling made of the trees that surround it, the whole thing bows over the pews with its warm grain.

Walking down the aisle with Sophie by my side, I see him for the first time all day. Fraser Bell, my love, my piper, stands at the altar tall and proud, like an idol carved in marble, with a beauty so divine that he would be impossible not to worship. Every step towards him seems to draw more light into the room, as though it is him emitting it. Though I have spent almost every day with him for the past year, I still never tire of the sight of him. I certainly couldn't tire of the sight of him, in his ceremonial kilt, stood so magnificently before the congregation with a tear welling in his eye.

Watching me from the moment I set foot through the door, his eyes have not left me as he observes each of my steps with such a gaze of love, I could combust beneath this stained-glass window and still feel like the most beautiful object within reach. When Sophie and I slide into the pew closest to the front, he finally steals a breath from his bagpipes and with it, offers me a wink that makes me blush just as much as it did the very first time.

When all of the guests have filtered in, including Eilidh who slots in beside Sophie with a kiss, Fraser's playing diminuendos to welcome the groom. Jimmy walks the aisle by himself, stopping at each row to say his hellos and chat with each of his guests just a little too long so that the minister has to retrieve him at halfway to tell him the bride has almost arrived. Placing his pipes in their box, Fraser takes his place on the shoulder of the groundskeeper, where they exchange a few words I can't hear, and Fraser plucks what looks to be straw from Jimmy's wisping hair.

Then, after a short announcement, we all get to our feet and it is the organ that declares the bride is here. With the wooden doors thrown open, we all turn to look as she takes her first steps over the threshold. Mary Buchanan, shrouded in white, smiles her own way down the aisle, towards the man she is to love for the rest of her life. She doesn't need anyone to give her away, nor does she need to maintain her usually stern façade. Right here, before all those who love her, she is exactly herself, and there is no doubting how Jimmy managed to fall for her. By the time she reaches him, the both of them cry silently over their smiles and Jimmy's first order of service is to take his handkerchief from his pocket and dab her cheeks.

The ceremony ends with a kiss, and not a dry eye in the church, and the bells play us out. Following behind the bride and groom, Fraser stops at my pew to offer me his hand. We walk arm in arm, and he strokes his thumb over my knuckles in an absentminded gesture as Eilidh and Sophie filter in behind us.

When all of us gather for a photo, I finally say the words I have been holding in since the very first time I saw the way the housekeeper and groundskeeper looked at one another. 'Would you prefer me to say "I told you so" now, or at the reception?' Sophie shoves me playfully and Fraser kisses my hair as he shakes his head with a grin.

'I don't think Cupid is quite trembling at the thought of losing his job just yet.' Sophie chuckles. 'But I am glad it was this one you got right.'

'I hope you both haven't forgotten about our bet?' I look between my boyfriend and best friend with a mischievous glint in my eye. Sophie's face contorts in confusion, whereas Fraser, clearly knowing what I'm referring to, widens his eyes and scratches the back of his neck with a cough.

'Bet?' Sophie says innocently.

'That *was* just a joke, right?' Fraser tries to laugh, though when I wiggle my eyebrows with intent, his voice cracks a little. '*Right?*'

'Remember many moons ago when I swore blind that we'd see old Jimmy and Mrs B married and you two Debbie Downers thought I was insane?' My grin only tightens.

'Of course. How could anyone forget?' Sophie rolls her eyes.

'Well don't you remember that we made the bet that if they married within two years you two would streak through the maze?'

Fraser pales and Sophie's mouth drops open with the recollection.

'Incredible.' Eilidh bursts into laughter as the other two share a look of fear.

'I shall be cashing in my bet before the week is out,' I say, winking.

Before they can protest, someone clears their throat to make an announcement to the crowd.

'Ladies and gentlemen, the bride and groom invite you to continue the celebrations at Braemar Community Centre. Please make way for your transport.' The minister steps aside as Hamish and DeeDee canter up the country track, manes sleek, ribbons braided into their tails, and hauling a wagon filled with bales of hay.

I shake my head with a laugh. 'Of course,' I whisper to myself.

Sneaking away from her photographer, the bride –

Mrs Mary Campbell – grabs something from the trailer and makes her way towards us. After exchanging congratulations and kisses, she hands me a pair of gloves and an umbrella with an amused grin.

'Got these just for you, hen . . . since Jim told me off the last time.' The memories of my first day in Balmoral come flooding back: the damp hack on Hamish's back, my frozen fingers, my angst against the world, and my cluelessness as to what was to come. Squeezing Fraser's hand at my side, I know that even if the heavens open and our dresses and suits get soaked, the real storm passed long ago, and anything by his side is no more than a drizzle.

When all of the guests begin to pile into the wagon, I spot a familiar face amongst them. 'Viscount Theo Fairfax?' I call to my cousin as he helps a redhead onto a bale. 'Taken to crashing country weddings now?'

'Cousin, cousin, cousin.' He leaps down and embraces me. 'Do you really think you were the first pain in the arse our family had banished to Balmoral in hopes Mrs B and the wilderness could straighten you out?'

'I hear it didn't work for you. Wasn't it the Tower of London they sent you to after that?' I chuckle, remembering the papers from two years ago when he disappeared from the face of the earth after being caught playing dress-up in some muddy field.

Flashing his ring finger, adorned with a gold engraved wedding band, he smiles a soft, genuine smile. 'Worked out just perfectly if one may say so.'

'Good,' I reply, taking another look at his redhead, then at mine as he mingles with his sister and my best friend. If one rogue royal can get his happily ever after, then perhaps there is hope for the rest of us.

With cousin Theo restless to get back to his wife, I take this moment alone to watch Fraser from a distance. With my work in the community centres still expanding and taking me up and down the country, there is nothing greater than coming home to Scotland, home to him. It didn't take the king long to request for him to transfer back to Balmoral, especially after my particularly public declaration (of which he was rather proud and insisted that it was his influence that had made it so).

But things aren't quite what they used to be. With Jimmy finally taking some time for himself and his new bride, he realised he needed a little more help in the grounds. And so, Fraser Bell became Balmoral's latest stable master, with a promise to the king that he would continue his Piper to the Sovereign duties during the summer months when the family holiday in Scotland. I like to think that both of our dreams came true in Balmoral. After a long day, there is no greater comfort than heading home to our little cabin in the woods, and lying down on the rug together before the log burner where we can say anything we want, or nothing at all.

Life with Fraser Bell is peaceful. There is no need for flashy parties, or great displays of wealth. I am the richest woman in the world knowing that I get to wake up next to him every day in our little pinch of paradise.

My parents haven't bothered to trouble me since I 'humiliated them' at the Ghillies Ball last year. Though I invite them to visit my home in the Highlands, I know they won't ever come. And I'm almost glad. I have found my own family in Balmoral. Mrs Buchanan – sorry, Mrs Campbell – is more of a mother than I could have ever asked for, and she still scolds me for asking her to do my washing every now and again. I have found sisters in Sophie and Eilidh who make sure to stop by every weekend for a Sunday roast and a hand with planning their own wedding. Jimmy is the father/grandfather figure anyone could dream of. And my heart is too full to be troubled by the empty space left behind by my mother and father.

I hardly think of Kitty. The last I heard of her, she had begun an affair with Atticus Beaumont and the scandal of it all sent his fiancée packing back to Liechtenstein along with his chances at finally getting his royal title. Feeling nothing for him, or Kitty in fact, I am only glad that no innocent woman has been handed the sentence of having to spend her life with Atticus.

Wandering up to the group again, I wrap my arms around Fraser's waist and look up at him with a grin of admiration.

'What are you so happy about?' He chuckles, brushing a strand of hair from my brow.

'Just you.' I kiss his cheek, and the piper blushes under my touch.

It turns out fairy tales don't actually come close to an accurate representation of love. My love for Fraser Bell is far more than any sonnet or speech or love story could ever contain. Love can't be bundled up into words or song. My love for him is the trees; it is the ground beneath my feet; it is Scotland, the pearl of the world, and a pocket of the universe too beautiful to be retold.

Bad days will still happen. Just because I am loved, it doesn't mean my sadness is suddenly eradicated like a villain defeated once and for all. The villain will return, for a sequel, a trilogy, maybe even a franchise. But each time that villain is weaker. Each time, I am better equipped for battle. And each time, I have faith in the knowledge that happy always comes after.

Acknowledgement

As always, publishing a book is no one woman task.

First of all, I must thank you, the reader. Whether you have been here since *Falling Hard for the Royal Guard* or this is just a random book you've picked up from a dusty shelf in a café, I couldn't do this job (my dream job) without you. Thank you for sharing in my story, thank you for taking these characters with you, and thank you for supporting me.

Rebecca Ritchie and Florence Rees, my two brilliant agents, thank you for always being there whenever I need you both (even when I have gotten myself in a right royal tizz over nothing much) and thank you for keeping me sane!

Amy Mae Baxter, the most patient editor I could ask for, thank you for all of your help in unscrambling my brain and transforming my manuscripts into something I can be proud of.

I must say a special thank you to the talented Sarah Foster for another beautiful cover.

Dad, thank you for always believing in me infinitely more

than I believe in myself and always being around to read chapters and offer ideas even when you're half way through a set in the gym or procrastinating over your own work. Mum, thank you for always being there to let me cry, to keep me on track, and supporting me through every idea and venture.

Lucie, thank you for all of those Friday night karaoke nights, for all of your gossip, and all of the giggles.

Thomas Kilmore, thank you for finally helping me to understand the love I've been writing about all these years. Loving you and being loved by you feels like fiction and I'm sure you'll recognise a lot of yourself within the happiness of these pages.

Thank you to the whole team at Avon and HarperCollins who work unbelievably hard and continue to believe in me and my work. Thank you to Helen Huthwaite, Jess Zahra, Helena Newton, Rachel Rowlands, Emily Hall, Jessie Whitehead, Emily Scorer, Katie Buckley, Molly Robinson, Molly Lo Re, Hannah Lismore, Angela Thomson, Jean-Marie Kelly, Sophia Wilhelm, Emily Gerbner, Melissa Okusanya, Hannah Stamp, Francesca Tuzzeo, Aisling Smyth, Zoe Shine, Anda Podaru, Ashton Mucha, and Helena Font Brillas.

Last of all, thank you to my trusty pals, fluoxetine and propranolol. I always thought that taking medication to help with my anxiety and depression was admitting defeat, but they have allowed me to do so many of the things I never knew I'd be able to do. I finally feel a bit more like me, and I am so confident now in the fact that there is no shame whatsoever in accepting the help you need that I wrote this book for everyone who just needs to see that it is never a weakness.

Don't miss this royally good rom-com . . .

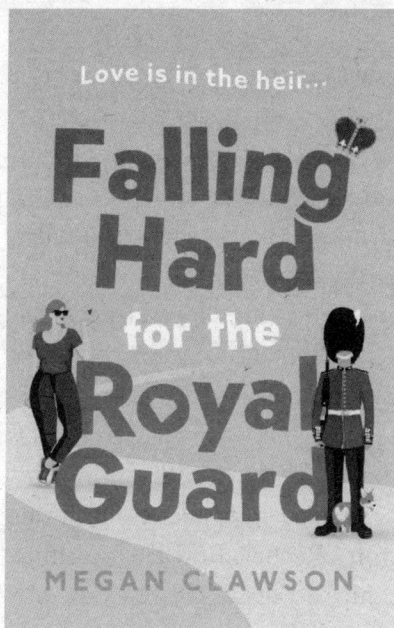

Love is in the heir...

Falling Hard for the Royal Guard

MEGAN CLAWSON

From her bedroom in the Tower of London, twenty-six-year-old
Maggie has always dreamed of her own fairy-tale ending.

Yet this is twenty-first century London, so instead of knights
on white horses, she has catfish on Tinder. And with her last
relationship ending in spectacular fashion, she swears
off men for good.

And then a chance encounter with Royal Guard Freddie
forces Maggie to admit that she isn't ready to give up on love just
yet... But how do you catch the attention of someone
who is trained to ignore all distractions?

Can she snare that true love's first kiss... or is
she royally screwed?

**She's no damsel in distress, and he's certainly not
wearing shining armour.
But one knight can change everything . . .**

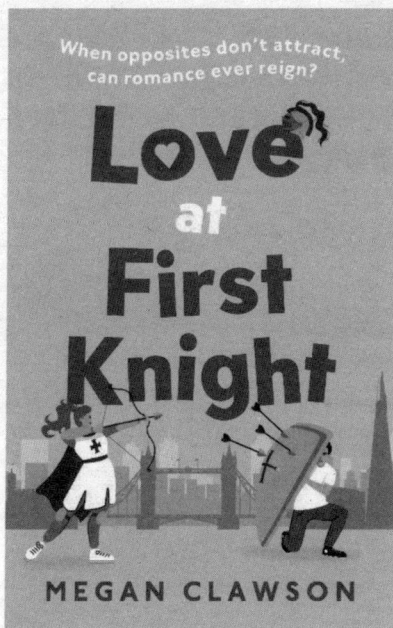

Daisy Hastings has always thought she was born in the wrong
era. So when she bags a summer job at the
Tower of London helping to run their Knight school,
it feels like a step in the right direction.

Theodore 'Teddy' Fairfax is a loose cannon. A disgraced distant
relative of the royal family, he's tall, dark and now (begrudgingly)
helping with the Tower of London's summer programme – and
there's nowhere he'd like to be less.

When Teddy's oath to be an obstruction almost gets Daisy
fired, she declares war. But as the two cross swords, they start to
discover they both need a little rescuing...

And that maybe, just maybe, love can bloom,
even on a battlefield...